CHURCH IN THE WILDWOOD

A Church Stands as a Landmark of Love for Four Generations

PAIGE WINSHIP DOOLY
KRISTY DYKES
PAMELA GRIFFIN
DEBBY MAYNE

BARBOUR
PUBLISHING

Leap of Faith ©2003 by Pamela Griffin
Shirley, Goodness, and Mercy ©2003 by Kristy Dykes
Only a Name ©2003 by Debby Mayne
Cornerstone ©2003 by Paige Winship Dooly

ISBN 1-58660-966-1

Cover image © Ross Jones

Published by Barbour Publishing, Inc., P.O. Box 719, Uhrichsville, Ohio 44683,
www.barbourbooks.com

> *Our mission is to publish and distribute inspirational products offering
> exceptional value and biblical encouragement to the masses.*

 Member of the
Evangelical Christian
Publishers Association

Printed in the United States of America.
5 4 3 2 1

INTRODUCTION

Leap of Faith by Pamela Griffin: Preacher's daughter, Amanda Hodges, is drawn to mysterious newcomer, Matt Campbell, despite everyone's assumption that she will one day marry Zeke Randall. Amanda finds every excuse to visit quiet Matt as he helps her father build a much-needed church. A jealous Zeke tells Amanda that Matt fits the description of one of the notorious James Gang, but rather than be repelled, she seeks the truth by following him. Matt loves the spirited Amanda, though he's tried hard not to. He made a grave mistake years ago, and now he hopes to rectify it by searching out his brother. Will learning Matt's past put hate in Amanda's heart? Even put her in danger?

Shirley, Goodness, and Mercy by Kristy Dykes: Church, church, church. That's all Shirley Campbell has ever known. Her grandfather Hodges is a preacher, and she and her entire family are staunch members of his little church in the wildwood. She wants more out of life than marrying, raising a passel of children like her mother did, and teaching Sunday school. Then she meets Forrest Townsend, the new preacher. His gentle ways and tender love win her heart, and he asks for her hand in marriage. But she doesn't want what she thinks is a drab future as a preacher's wife. Her heart is his, she admits to herself, but her will is her own. What will it take for her to resolve her dilemma? Will she find the love she's ultimately seeking?

Only a Name by Debby Mayne: Eva Hargrove meets Associate Pastor Robert Campbell when she visits his church in Hickory Hollow after moving to a tract home in the nearby Paradise Acres subdivision. Her father has been trying to persuade her to marry James Randall, his business partner, but she has ideas of her own. When a fire breaks out at the church, there are signs that James was the arsonist, and Robert is uncertain what to believe. Can the almost one-hundred-year-old feud between the Randalls and Campbells be put to an end through one act of faith, and can Robert and Eva find happiness?

Cornerstone by Paige Winship Dooly: Resort owner April Russell loves her quiet life in Hickory Hollow, near the church she holds dear. According to local history, some of her ancestors, the Randalls, once had a long-standing feud with the Campbells, but April is thrilled when wealthy Matthew Campbell comes home to Hickory Hollow. She hopes he will revive the dying church his namesake started over one hundred years ago. Instead, Matthew sees dollar signs and the resort potential the property offers. April is furious, as she will lose not only her beloved church but her small rustic resort, too. Will the old family feud flare up again before love has a chance to grow?

CHURCH IN
THE WILDWOOD

Leap of Faith

by Pamela Griffin

Dedication

A heartfelt thanks to all my crit buds and especially to Mom, who helped teach me how to take a leap of faith—one I've chosen many times and have never regretted. Most of all, with loving gratitude to my Lord Jesus, the foundation for the faith by which I stand.

For therein is the righteousness of God revealed from faith to faith: as it is written, The just shall live by faith.
ROMANS 1:17

For by thee I have run through a troop: by my God have I leaped over a wall. As for God, his way is perfect; the word of the LORD is tried: he is a buckler to all them that trust in him.
2 SAMUEL 22: 30–31

Chapter 1

Missouri Ozarks, 1869

An eye-pleasing blend of cedar, pine, and hardwood trees just beginning to bud after a long winter blanketed the gently rolling hills that surrounded Amanda's valley home. Here and there, pink-blossomed redbuds mingled with white-blossomed dogwoods, providing splashes of color. The morning sun cut a golden swathe between two tall hickory trees, casting light into an area often in shadows, and highlighted the few workers building the church for Hickory Hollow.

Amanda watched one man in particular as he helped lift a heavy stone block to place it on another. Rays of sunlight outlined his muscles through his shirt as he toiled alongside the others.

"Amanda Hodges, you stop ogling that man," Ivy Randall stage-whispered to Amanda, loud enough so the other two girls in their company could hear. "Zeke wouldn't like it."

Amanda's eyes slid shut in exasperation. Sometimes the blue-eyed woman with the fair hair was her tormenter, sometimes her bosom friend. Today she'd proven to be a little of both. "Ivy, I told you, I'm not interested in your brother."

One of the workers called out to another, reclaiming Amanda's attention. She looked at the growing rock wall of what would be their new church building. The little timber schoolhouse was fast on its way to becoming unable to hold the growing congregation.

Heavy *chinks* of hammers striking iron stakes, boring holes into rocks that would support the roof's wooden beams, echoed throughout the otherwise peaceful valley. A chill wind had arisen minutes ago, but the change in weather wasn't fierce enough to send Amanda seeking shelter.

The Wilson boys—ten months apart but as alike as two pecan halves in a nutshell—busily worked, slapping and spreading mortar, then together lifting the next block of rock and setting it into place. Zeke Randall worked with them, though he didn't appear as busy as the others. Amanda's father also worked alongside the few townsmen who'd turned out to help. Though he was well into his forties, his body was strong, and he easily kept up with the younger men. Amanda's attention again settled on one dark-haired man in particular, and a wistful smile lifted her lips.

Matt Campbell was relatively new to their mountain valley town, but already he'd proven to be a help to any in need. When a strong set of shoulders was required, he was the first in line to offer his services. And what a nice, strong and broad set of shoulders he had. . . .

"Your mother's coming round the bend," Ivy said into Amanda's ear a little too loudly. "And I'll tell you again, it sure doesn't look proper for the preacher's daughter to eyeball all the workers."

"I'm not eyeballing all the workers," Amanda muttered, then clenched her teeth and lifted her fingers to the offended ear to rub it. Her statement was true. She had no interest in any of the men, with the exception of one.

She moved toward her mother. "Need some help, Ma?"

Huggably stout after bearing seven children, three of whom had died at birth, Clara Hodges gratefully handed a basket of freshly laundered linens to her daughter. "Do see to this, would you, Dear? I must run over to Sally John's and check on her and the baby. She wants your pa to come, but he's so busy I hate to bother him. Would you ask him for me later?" She swiped a damp lock of graying brown hair from her eyes. "And please start supper."

"I'll see right to it, Ma."

Being a preacher's wife and seeing to a host of needs, not to mention also acting as midwife in their town, her mother carried more than her fair share of duties to Amanda's way of thinking. Amanda walked past several of many hickories clustered in bunches throughout the area and quickly approached their three-room log cabin, with its cedar shakes for a roof and the gray stone chimney along one side. The other girls followed like a flock of cackling hens.

"I surely don't understand what you see in Mr. Campbell

when you kin have Zeke Randall," Selena Mills stated. "Mr. Campbell wears his hair too long, his nose is bent—and why ever set your cap for a man who limps when you kin have someone with two strong legs?"

"A pair of shears would fix Matt Campbell's hair right nicely, though it does look smart when it's combed sleek and shiny and brushes his shoulders." Amanda dropped the basket onto the table and gave the redhead a sideways glance. "As to the other, there's a lot more to life than dancing, Selena. I think Matt's limp adds character. As does his not-quite-straight nose, his lean jaw, and that fine dark stubble on his face he always seems to have." She giggled. "He's quite a handsome fellow if you want my opinion."

"We're all well aware of your opinion, Amanda, but you best not let your pa hear you talk like that," Ivy put in. "And calling Mr. Campbell by his Christian name. . .Honestly! You sound almost brazen. Nothing at all like a preacher's daughter should be."

In truth, Amanda felt little like a preacher's daughter. She often spoke her mind and was anything but meek and humble, much to her parents' consternation. Yet she couldn't help the way she was—nor the way she wasn't.

Her hand stilled from laying folded dish towels on a high shelf, her gaze going dreamy as she looked toward the windowpane. "Tell me truthfully, girls, did you ever see such lovely blue-gray eyes as Matt has? They look like the sky after a storm's swept it clean, all sparkling and clear—but sort of misty, too."

"Land's sakes!" Mayflower Starnes replied in mock dismay, her brown eyes wide in her freckled face. "Now she's gone poetic on us. Ladies, we best leave afore she starts recitin' 'An Ode to Love.'"

"Humph." Amanda resumed her chore. "I'm not the romantic in this bunch, Mayflower. That would be you." Though lately Amanda had thought more about love and marriage, especially now that she was seventeen—and now that Matt Campbell was a resident of Hickory Hollow.

"Well," Ivy intoned, "all I have to say is your pa will never let a stranger court you. No one in the hollow knows anything about him. He talks about as much as a turtle, and his snap is likely as vicious. When he gets that brooding look, he almost scares me."

"Oh, fiddle-faddle," Amanda said. "At least he doesn't run off at the mouth like some folks I know."

"Meaning Zeke, I suppose?" Ivy asked in an affronted tone.

Amanda sighed. "It's not that I have anything against your brother, Ivy. I just don't care to have him as my beau."

"You're gonna wind up breaking his heart. I just know it. He's liked you since we were in school together."

Break Zeke's heart? Hardly. That is, if he had a heart to break. Amanda kept quiet, realizing nothing she said would matter. Many in the hollow had already paired her and Zeke as a couple.

Forgetting the three other women, she gazed out the window toward the rock wall a short distance away and watched

13

the tall man who limped in the opposite direction.

Matthew Campbell straightened to a stand, letting the mortar-covered spade drop to the ground. With his sleeve, he wiped the moisture from his brow, then put his hands to the back of his sweat-sodden shirt and tried to massage the kinks out. Damp weather often made his back and hip ache, though he was just twenty years old. Yet after what he'd been through these past few years, he felt like he'd lived a coon's age three times over.

To the west, above the thick forest of oaks and hickories, Matt noticed a swollen storm cloud creeping in their direction. The sun had disappeared more than an hour ago, leaving behind skies of pale gray. An irritated grunt escaped his throat, and he put his work-worn hand to the partially built wall of cold stone, still damp from the last downpour.

"We best get busy and try to finish up before the sky unleashes on us," he told the group of three men who crouched nearby for a breather.

A fair-haired man with a well-groomed mustache straightened, still holding the dipper from the barrel of collected rainwater. His pants, shirt, and vest were neatly pressed, and his lightly sunburned face wasn't one bit shiny from exertion. Probably because Zeke Randall did the least amount of work possible, though he gave the appearance of being busy at his task. Matt knew better. He'd been watching the dapper son of the lumber company owner all afternoon and noticed how he lollygagged behind the others.

And why come dressed for a hard day's work all gussied up as if he were attending his own wedding?

A belligerent expression crossed Zeke's face. "I don't recall anyone dying and making you boss, Campbell." His voice was low but loud enough to issue a challenge.

Matt decided not to take the lure. He'd dealt with a lot worse than Zeke but wasn't interested in a fight. He'd encountered enough violence in one lifetime for ten men.

Bob and Pete Wilson rose from their hunched positions with goofy smiles, their dark gazes focused beyond Matt's shoulder. Matt turned to see what had caught their interest so.

Zeke's sister Ivy stood nearby, staring at both brothers and giggling. Yet it wasn't on Ivy that Matt focused his attention, but rather on the woman next to her—with thick hair the shade of rich coffee containing a dollop of cream. Slightly plump, her skin like pale pink roses after a frost, Amanda Hodges looked his way. Her eyes were as spring-a-green as the buds on the trees, able to rivet a man where he stood—and they did so to Matt now. He felt as if lightning had raced out of the approaching storm clouds and struck him dumb.

Matt swallowed hard when she continued to stare. Some might think petite Ivy with her angel-like features was the only beauty of Hickory Hollow, but Matt would disagree. Amanda's nose might be just a tad too tilted and her lips a mite wide, but her face and eyes shone with the vibrancy of her personality.

Zeke stepped forward. "Ivy, this is no place for you—nor you, Amanda. I'm quite busy with helping your pa. Run along home. We'll talk later." He moved to take hold of Amanda's elbow, but she jerked it from his reach the moment he touched her sleeve.

"I didn't come to talk to you, Zeke." Amanda turned her fascinating eyes away from Matt and to the north end of the church wall. "Pa! I need to speak with you if you have a minute."

A short, sinewy man with tufts of silver hair sprinkled among the dark strands turned from his task. "Trouble?" He pushed his hat farther back on his head and approached his daughter, the hammer still in his hand. His gaze swerved to Matt, then returned to Amanda. His lined brow clouded.

"No, Pa. Leastways I don't think so. Ma said that Sally John Adcock asked you to drop by—you know how nervous she's been about the new baby, it being her first and all."

"Amanda, if there's no emergency, then tell your mother I'll visit later," Pastor Hodges said, "after I get a good day's work in."

As if his words were a signal, the sky unleashed a smattering of raindrops on their heads. Ivy squealed and raised both hands above her piled-up braids. Seemingly bent on being stubborn, the drops abruptly turned into sheets of hard rain.

"Get on back to your homes," Pastor Hodges yelled above the loud sound of water spraying on stone. "We'll try again next Saturday." A deep bellow of thunder underscored his statement.

Matt anchored his hat more firmly on his head and

stared through the veil of silver rain at what little progress they'd made. He knew Pastor Hodges was itching to get the church built, but it seemed one delay after another prevented them from doing so, and the fact that so few men turned out each Saturday didn't help matters one bit.

Before heading to his cabin farther up the mountain, he chanced a look in Amanda's direction and watched her hurry through the door of her home. Matt forced his gaze away. He had no business thinking about a preacher's daughter. Not after the shameful life he'd led before coming to Hickory Hollow.

Chapter 2

Smiling, Amanda inhaled the spicy-sweet scent of warm cinnamon bread. She finished wrapping a second loaf with a towel and stuck it in her basket. If she hurried, she could beat the rain. These past two months their little mountain valley had gotten more than its fair share of that type of weather.

Her mother bustled into the kitchen. "Are you taking the bread to Gloramae?"

"Yes, Ma."

"Let her know I'll be by later. Her ankle seems to be mending, but oh, won't it be nice when young Dirk comes home from medical school and takes up a practice in the hollow? I'm still not certain that Gloramae's ankle isn't broken, with the way she squeals when she puts weight on it. If only we had a doctor to see to things here—that is, if the hill people will let go of their silly superstitions and accept a doc's help. Imagine Sally John putting a knife under the bed to cut the pain during childbirth! Whoever heard such nonsense?

Hopefully, with Dirk being a native to the hills and not an outsider, they might listen to him."

Amanda agreed with her ma, then said a hasty good-bye and slipped outside before her tongue could get the better of her. She would wager a cupboard full of cinnamon bread that the miller's daughter was pretending the injury was much worse than it was so she could get out of doing housework in her widower father's home. She and Zeke would make a lovely pair. Amanda grinned at the thought.

A cool mist caressed her face while she strolled over the lush valley and alongside the narrow river. What used to be Rockford Jones's homestead sat nestled at the edge of the thick wood. The old prospector had traveled farther west years ago in his search of gold. Now the one-room log cabin belonged to another.

Amanda ran the edge of her teeth along her lips to bring out more color, nervously cleared her throat, and rapped on the door. After what seemed an eternity, she knocked again—harder this time. Disappointed when no one appeared, she stepped away. The door swung inward with a protesting creak, and with a smile she pivoted back around. The pleased expression froze on her face.

Matt weakly leaned against the doorjamb, jaw unshaven, blue-gray eyes bleary. From beneath the filthy blanket he clutched around his shoulders, she could see the faded red legs of his long underwear. "Miss Hodges," he rasped in surprise. "What brings you here?"

"Matt Campbell. You're ill!" she softly cried in dismay.

"No wonder we didn't see you at the church meeting. Well, this will never do. It's a good thing I decided to bring you some cinnamon bread." She bustled past him—and gaped in horror.

Dirty tins and remnants of food cluttered a pine table that bowed in the middle. Mud caked the wooden floor, and the odors of sweat and vomit permeated the stale air. Her stomach lurched, but she set her basket down on the arthritic-looking table, determined to stay the course.

"Miss Hodges," Matt said from where he'd taken up residence on a chair that didn't look any better off than he was. "You shouldn't be here. Your ma and pa. . .they wouldn't like it. . . ." His words trailed off into raspy breathing.

Suspecting the worst, Amanda moved toward him and pushed up her sleeve. She placed her forearm against his forehead. "Why, you're burning up! How long have you been like this? Never mind. It's a good thing I came by when I did. You just sit right there 'til I can clean up some."

Before he could argue with her again, she pushed up her other sleeve, prepared to get to work, and moved to the tangled bedding. "Ma has so much to do today—every day, really—and probably won't have time to come now and take care of you. She's taught me well, so don't you worry."

When he didn't answer, she looked at him. His head was propped against the log wall as though he'd been unable to hold it up any longer. His eyes were closed, and a fine sheen of sweat beaded his face. Her heart skipped a fearful beat. Just how sick was he?

His bedding needed a thorough washing, but there wasn't much she could do about that since she saw only the one blanket. A set of ivory-handled revolvers in a gun belt on the floor caught her attention, making her wonder. Every man in the hollow owned a shotgun, but she'd never seen such fancy handguns as Matt had. She looked at them a moment longer, then set to work.

What she could do to clean things, she did, hurrying so she could get Matt back into bed. He didn't seem to notice when she nudged him awake, then helped him to the narrow cot. Supporting him with one arm, she slowly walked with him while he leaned heavily on her, his limp pronounced. He sank onto the straw mattress with a crisp rustle, wincing when he put his weight on his left hip.

Hurriedly, her face warming, Amanda covered him to the chin with the blanket, keeping her eyes averted from the tall form clothed in long underwear. She then laid a fire in the small fireplace and set about putting the room to rights. Once the dishes were washed and the room swept clean, she furrowed her brow. Matt needed something besides cinnamon bread, but she'd found nothing but an inch of wheat left in its sack, a modicum of sugar, and a jar of strawberry preserves.

She frowned. Just who would have brought him strawberry preserves?

Her gaze darted Matt's way again, and her miffed little frown changed to one of concern. Maybe she should drop off the other loaf of bread at Gloramae's right away, then seek out Ma. Matt really didn't look good.

Grabbing her basket, Amanda hurried through the cabin's open door, shutting it firmly behind her.

*

"Is it the cholera?" Amanda whispered fearfully from the foot of Matt's bedside.

At the terror-inflicting words, Matt cracked one eyelid open. Mrs. Hodges stood next to her daughter and poured some foul-looking blackish brown liquid from a bottle into a tin cup. "Nothing so tragic, Dear. By the looks of things, he has a case of stomach complaints and stuffiness in his chest, such as Roscoe Fulton had two weeks past. Enough to make him miserable, but that's about it. A dose of this Hostetter's Celebrated Stomach Bitters, which I bought from that peddler last summer, ought to cure him well and good."

Matt weakly pondered the woman's reassurances to Amanda. He was sure he was dying and they were coddling his senses by not telling him so. Only a dying man could feel this awful.

Steps creaked on the boards, coming closer. A plump, cool hand slipped under his sweaty neck. "Open up, Mr. Campbell," Amanda's mother said in a no-nonsense tone. "I know you're awake. I saw you open your eye."

A foul stench drifted up to assault Matt as the lip of the cup was placed near his mouth. He'd heard somewhere that these potions contained a good deal of alcohol, and while he wasn't a drinking man any longer, he was sure that the brew must contain something even more foul. Like slime from the river bottom.

With what little strength he had left, he pulled his head back in retreat. Regardless, the woman tipped the container, scalding his mouth and tongue with a fiery, bitter brew. He coughed, choked—then gagged, reaching for the pot.

Once he weakly settled back onto the mattress, Amanda gave him a sympathetic stare. For the first time since she'd arrived at his cabin and found him in this condition, then brought back her ma, Matt wished she'd just go. It was bad enough for any woman to see him in such sad shape, fit for nothing, ready for the casket. Yet for that woman to be Amanda was about as bitter to swallow as the devil's brew forced down his gullet—and hard on a man's pride.

"You go on home, Amanda," Mrs. Hodges said as if reading Matt's thoughts. "I need to apply a mustard plaster to his chest. And be sure to put on your go-to-meeting dress. I invited Zeke Randall and his cousin for dinner tonight."

"Oh, Ma," Amanda protested, clearly disgruntled. "Zeke Randall? Why'd you have to go and invite him?"

"Amanda, to hear you talk! Zeke is a nice young man, and his cousin is only visiting this week. Don't you deem it right for the pastor's family to exhibit a little Christian charity during his stay in the hollow?"

"I suppose."

Matt forced both eyelids open. He was startled when he saw Amanda staring at him. A wistful look filled her eyes, and a becoming flush settled over her cheeks. He wondered what she was thinking.

It didn't sit well with him that Mrs. Hodges evidently

considered Zeke Randall a fitting suitor for her daughter. But even if Matt weren't dying, he could do little about it. He certainly couldn't call on Amanda, even if he were hale and hearty. Closing his eyes, he wondered if she would mourn his passing and put flowers on his grave.

ᎦᏃ

Amanda wandered home, in no hurry to dress for supper. Hearing someone humming a tune, she peered toward the swiftly flowing river.

Jeb Hunter sat under one of the willows alongside the water. Clutched between both his hands, which rested between propped-up knees, a long branch extended over the water, a string tied to one end. The thirteen year old reclined his back against the tree trunk, a piece of straw sticking from his mouth. His dirty bare feet tapped a rhythm on the damp, mossy ground.

"Jeb!" Amanda shouted, affecting a stern expression, though her spirit identified with the boy and she wished she could sit beside him. She hadn't been fishing since she was a girl in calf-length dresses and pigtails. "Shouldn't you be in school?"

When his name was called, Jeb dropped the pole and unbent his tall form, scrambling to his feet. Seeing it was only Amanda, he relaxed. A twisted grin stretched across his freckled face, revealing crooked teeth. Lazily, he scratched his stomach, which was covered with a thin undershirt, its sleeves pushed up to the elbows. The color of the material had probably once been white but now was a shade of indeterminate gray. A pair of suspenders held up his trousers, one brown pant leg sporting a hole in the knee.

"Well now, Miz Amanda. I reckon it'd be all right to miss teacher's jawin' jis' this once. The fish are bitin' somethin' fierce. Reckon it be 'cuzza all the rain we got last week? I caught me four already, and I ain't been here but an hour."

Unable to resist his contagious smile, Amanda smiled back. "Well, I guess this once is all right, Jeb. Class will be letting out soon. But just between us, I wouldn't refer to Mr. Pragmeyer's teaching as 'jawin' ' again—especially to his face. I'm certain your ma will be happy to get the fish for supper."

Happy was an understatement, Amanda knew. Many families in the area, including the Hunters, were poor. Years ago, not long after her family moved to Hickory Hollow when Amanda was eleven, she had been dismayed to learn from a seven-year-old Jeb that the Hunter children had eaten nothing but sorghum, corn bread, and wild berries for three days. Wanting to help, Amanda rode up the mountain with her pa to take the Hunters some rabbit stew. They stopped their horses in front of the Hunter cabin, staying mounted, and her pa cautiously yelled out, "Hello! Any Hunters about?"—the universal greeting if you didn't want to get your head shot off.

Mr. Hunter came to the door, shotgun cradled in one arm, though he didn't aim it their way. Matter-of-factly, he refused the food, telling them, "Thank ya kindly, Preacher, but we Hunters don't hold to no charity." Amanda returned home that day with a full pot and an empty heart. The spicy stew hadn't tasted at all good that night, not with the image of the Hunter children's thin faces branding her memory. The Hunters weren't the only ones to refuse charity, Amanda soon discovered. Every well-meaning overture had been politely but firmly refused. Yet since Jeb's father had an accident last fall, he wasn't able to go hunting as much anymore.

A plan crystallized in her mind. Excited, Amanda said a hasty good-bye to Jeb and hurried home, hoping to talk to her pa.

～

"That was a fine meal, Mrs. Hodges," Zeke said, pulling out the napkin tucked in his starched collar. "I do believe I've never tasted chicken quite so tender. When I went back East last summer, I visited a number of restaurants of high caliber, as my grandmother is quite wealthy," he pompously added. "You could easily open your own eating establishment and compete with the best of them."

"Why, thank you, Zeke." Amanda's mother gave him a flustered smile.

"I agree with everything my cousin said," Ned Randall added. "I haven't had a meal this fine since I left my ma's doorstep in Liberty."

"I'm so glad you both enjoyed it."

"Amanda, I understand you made the dessert." Zeke turned his probing gaze her way. "Peach cobbler always has been a favorite of mine."

"That's nice," Amanda dutifully responded. She turned to her mother. "Should we save the broth for Mr. Campbell?

It would probably do him a world of good."

Everyone looked at her. Her pa and Ned appeared surprised, her ma exasperated, and Zeke seemed annoyed. Even her younger siblings—Rosalie, Edmund, and Charmaine—stared at her.

Flustered, Amanda rose from the table and began gathering dishes. "I'll just take these to the sideboard."

An uneasy silence elapsed. "We should be heading home," Zeke finally said. "Again, thank you for the meal, Mrs. Hodges."

"Do you really need to be hurrying off so soon?" Amanda's mother protested. "I'm sure Anson would enjoy a game of checkers with you while we women take care of the cleaning."

Zeke looked Amanda's way. Hurriedly, she focused her attention on scraping three-year-old Charmaine's discarded potato skins onto a plate.

"No," Zeke said a little gruffly. "We best be going."

"Amanda." Ma's voice sounded stern. "Rosalie can do that. Please see our guests to the door. And while you're at it, take the rest of the scraps to the hogs. I do believe everyone is finished. Yes?"

Pa set down his half-eaten honeyed biscuit and looked at his wife in bewilderment. Ma's blatant attempts to push Amanda into Zeke's company made Amanda clench her teeth, but she replied with a dutiful, "Yes, Ma."

"I hope to visit with your mother soon, Zeke," Ma said in a pleasant voice. "I miss news of what's happening back East."

"I'll tell her. I'm sure she'd enjoy a visit; she does enjoy talking to anyone who'll listen."

Amanda dumped the scraps into a pail by the stove, picked up the container, and stiffly moved to the door. Zeke and his cousin hurried to follow.

"Will you be attending Tom and Mayflower's wedding, Amanda?" Zeke didn't waste any time once they were outside and away from her family's hearing. His cousin trailed behind.

"I suppose," she said, never breaking stride as she moved toward the pen out back. Why was he asking her such a thing now? The wedding was weeks away, sometime after Tom completed work on the new cabin.

"It's about time we had a wedding in the hollow," Zeke said.

Amanda came to a stop at the pen. The hogs' grunts turned to ear-piercing squeals as the animals trotted toward them on stubby legs. Amanda upended the bucket over the fence. The scraps fell in lumps, some landing on a gray-and-white-splotched head, but the hog didn't seem to mind.

"You ought to think about getting married soon, too," he continued. "I mean, you are seventeen. And I'm nineteen."

Amanda blew out a little breath and faced him. "Honestly, Zeke. When the time comes for me to marry up, it'll come, I suppose. But I have too much going on to think about it now."

He frowned. "I hear you've been playing Good Samaritan today."

At the accusation in his tone, she narrowed her eyes and

28

crossed her arms, the pail still dangling from one hand. "So?"

"So I'd stay away from Matt Campbell if I were you. He's bad news."

Amanda laughed shortly. "If being selfless, considerate of others, and always ready to lend a helping hand is 'bad,' then my pa's been preaching the wrong sermon of a Sunday morning."

Zeke scowled, evidently not finding her retort the least bit amusing, but then Amanda didn't expect he would. He'd been a trial ever since they were children. Now that he was following in the footsteps of his wealthy father, Zeke had become downright intolerable, thinking he owned everybody. Including Amanda.

She glanced at Ned, who stood several feet away, hands clasped behind him, evidently uneasy with the conversation since he intently focused on a nearby mountain and his face was flushed pink.

"Well, I'd best be getting inside. It was a pleasure to meet you, Mr. Randall. Good evening, Zeke." With a short nod, Amanda headed back to the cabin.

Trying to ignore Ned Randall's outright stare, Matt took a seat on a pile of rocks and balanced his plate on his knee. Zeke's cousin had helped in building the church today. Each time Matt looked his direction, Ned had been staring openly at him, then quickly focused his attention elsewhere. Matt wasn't overly alarmed. Ned didn't seem shocked or suspicious. Only curious. He probably wondered how Matt had gotten his limp.

Matt took a swig of cool water and watched Amanda dish thick stew onto a tin plate she then handed to Mr. Wilbur, the last to be served in line. Amanda reminded Matt of a bright butterfly, though the dress she wore was a faded gray. A few women, including Ivy Randall, wore more colorful frocks, but Amanda outshone them all. Her face was rosy and animated, and her eyes sparkled with life.

"Good thing we were able to finish that wall today," Pastor Hodges said from behind.

Matt almost strangled on his water and hurriedly looked away from Amanda. "Yes, Sir." He noticed that Pastor Hodges was watching her. After a moment, he turned his gaze to Matt.

"My daughter had a good idea—getting the womenfolk of the workers to bring a food item, then putting it together in a pot to have us a community stew after the day's work was done. First time I've seen those Hunter children with smiles on their faces due to a full belly."

A grin lifting the corners of his mouth, Matt looked at the two youngest Hunters. Light-haired Audelia and Aubrey Hunter engaged in a game of leapfrog by the shallow stream that ran close to where the church was being built. Not old enough yet to write their numbers or letters, they were the most athletic of the Hunter brood.

"Amanda has a good heart, but she's still childlike in her thinking," her pa continued. "Because of that, her outgoing behavior is apt to get her in a muddle. A muddle that, if I can help it, I'm determined to see she doesn't wind up in."

At the subtle warning in Pastor Hodges's tone, Matt looked his way. Piercing gray-green eyes pinned Matt like a coon in a trap. Matt wished he weren't holding a plate in one hand and a cup in the other so he could tip his hat downward and escape the accusation written there. Did Amanda's father think anything improper had happened at the cabin earlier that week, during the three days Matt was ill?

"Sir, let me assure you, when your daughter took care of me without her ma's help that first day, nothing occurred for which either she or I should be ashamed—nor on any day thereafter."

"I know Amanda well enough to be assured of that. It's not that which concerns me. Amanda's strong in both body and spirit—but she's headstrong, as well, and too young to know what's good for her. A stranger new to town, seeming to be without background or history, might prove too strong a fascination for her idealistic young mind." He focused on the two children frolicking like march hares on the grass and took a drink from his cup. "Am I making myself clear, Mr. Campbell?"

"Yes, Sir. Perfectly clear." The pastor's words made Matt squirm inside, like a worm at the end of a hook, but he didn't move a muscle. This was the opening for Matt to tell something about himself and his family. To relieve the man's mind and prove to him that he was a wholesome character of moral upbringing, worthy of taking an interest in a preacher's daughter.

However, Matt couldn't say a word—though he wished

with all he had in him that he did have the right to say those things. As he'd done on numerous occasions in the four months since he'd arrived in the hollow, he remained silent, the silence only serving to further condemn him.

Amanda came their way, a plate of pie in each hand. "I brought you dessert," she said, her green eyes sparkling with vivacity and trained on Matt. "The way it's disappearing, I wasn't sure there'd be any left. I hope you like strawberry pie, Mr. Campbell."

Matt roused a smile and took the offered plate. "Thank you, Ma'am. I do at that."

Her smile dimmed as she searched Matt's face, then looked at her father. "Pa?" She held out his pie. "Is anything wrong?"

"Of course not," her father said, somewhat curtly. He took the plate from her. "This meal was a superb idea, Amanda. We'll have to do this each Saturday. Hopefully the idea of free food will bring more volunteers to help build the church, as well as feed the needy."

Amanda's brow cleared. "I convinced Mrs. Hunter to take some stew home with her. She refused at first, but when I said it would probably just go to feed the hogs, and after all, she contributed an onion, so it was partly hers as well, she agreed to take some. Let's just hope Mr. Hunter is as agreeable." Her gaze turned Matt's way again. "It's nice to see you up and fit, again, Mr. Campbell. I trust you're fully recovered?"

"Yes, Ma'am. Thanks to you and your ma."

"Amanda, Ivy is trying to get your attention," Pastor Hodges abruptly said.

Amanda stared at her pa strangely but looked over her shoulder. Ivy crazily motioned with one arm for Amanda to join her. Amanda blew out an exasperated breath and focused on Matt. "I best go see what she wants. I hope you enjoy the pie, Mr. Campbell. I picked the strawberries yesterday—the first of the season. Eating fruit fresh is so much better than using preserves from a jar—don't you agree?" Before moving away, she offered another sweet smile, warming Matt clear to his boot tips.

❧

"All right, Ivy. Tell me what couldn't wait during those few minutes I had to catch a breather." Amanda was annoyed. The solitary moment she'd finally found to exchange a few words with Matt had been interrupted.

Ivy frowned. "Zeke's looking for you."

"Is that all?" Amanda rolled her eyes heavenward. "With the way you were flapping your arm at me, I thought some emergency had cropped up." She turned to go, but Ivy touched her sleeve.

"He's upset. I think you should find out what's bothering him. He's over there." Ivy nodded toward the bank on the opposite side of the stream at a place where the water widened a few feet.

"Honestly!" Amanda released a frustrated breath when she saw Zeke near some dogwood trees. He stared in her direction. "Oh, alright. I'll go see what he wants."

Muttering to herself about spoiled little boys who never grew up and always had to have their way, Amanda lifted her skirts a few inches and stepped onto the smooth rocks of the shallow stream. Once she joined Zeke, he grabbed her elbow.

"What did Mr. Campbell say to you?" he insisted.

"That's none of your business." Amanda snatched her arm away. "And furthermore, you have no right to act like some sort of scalawag!"

His smile wasn't kind. "You're getting your name-calling mixed up, Amanda. It's Matthew Campbell who's the scalawag, not I."

"What are you talking about?" She gathered her brows.

"My cousin was outside the bank that got robbed in Liberty a few years back. Amid all the shooting, he got a close look at one of the outlaws as he fled—the man dropped his moneybag in front of where Ned was standing, and the kerchief slipped from his face when he bent to scoop it up. This afternoon he stared long and hard at Mr. Campbell for the first time. Ned said he'd swear on a Bible, in court, that Matthew Campbell—of whom you think so highly—is a member of the James Gang."

Chapter 3

For seconds after hearing Zeke's grim words, Amanda only stared. Then she laughed. "That's preposterous! Matthew Campbell is no more a member of Frank and Jesse James's Gang than I am a follower of the infamous Belle Starr! Can't you just see me toting a gun?" She giggled again.

Zeke frowned. "Laugh all you want, Amanda, but what do you really know about the man? He doesn't talk about himself to anyone and evades any questions people ask. Suppose he's here to stake out our town or something equally despicable? I've heard it said that the James Gang was spotted near here a couple of weeks back."

"Zeke, if he were a wanted man—and I'm not saying he is, mind you—we don't have a bank in this town to rob," Amanda countered, though a niggling doubt began to squirm into her mind. She took a few edgy steps from the dogwood, then faced him again. "Most of the hill folk pay in hogs and eggs and the like. All that aside, Pa's always said a man has a right to his privacy. And I should think that rule applies to Matt Campbell, too."

"Maybe we don't have a bank to rob, but Father has a safe full of valuables. In any case, outlaws don't just rob banks, Amanda. They rob stages and trains and towns—any place they can get their hands on gold or money." Zeke gritted his teeth. "But you've veered away from the discussion. We were talking about Matt Campbell—"

"No, *you* were talking about Matt Campbell. As far as I'm concerned, this discussion is closed." Turning her back on him, Amanda hurried across the rocks of the stream.

She was irritated with Zeke for his outrageous accusations, but even angrier with herself for the doubts that crept in concerning Matt. Why was he so quiet? Was he just shy? Amanda didn't think so. If he were hiding a secret—though surely it couldn't be as terrible as what Zeke suggested—then the first opportunity she could get Matt alone, she would try to find out just what that secret was. Privacy or not, she owed it to herself to discover the truth if she planned to marry the man someday.

≈

Matt strolled along the path, his footsteps making slurping sounds on the soggy earth. A pale sun shrouded by gauzy clouds shone through the branches of a tall maple as if not quite sure it wanted to make an appearance. The cloying aroma of nearby honeysuckle drew the bees, and Matt swatted his hat at one lone, winged insect that seemed more interested in his plaid shirt.

Or maybe it was the lingering sweet smell of soap coming

from the material that drew the bug. Matt wasn't sure what Amanda put in the soap, but it wasn't plain lye. Actually, when he thought about it, his shirt smelled of her—like wild roses—and he could imagine her holding his large cotton shirt in her soft, small hands, folding it with great care, then laying it in the basket to deliver to him, as she'd done the day after the sickness left him. It had been a surprise when she'd arrived at his doorstep and had taken his spare clothing and bed linens to wash. He wondered what her ma had thought about that. Certainly Mrs. Hodges couldn't have been too happy with her daughter, though it was a kind gesture. Amanda had done all she could to make Matt feel welcome in the hollow. Matt supposed with Amanda being the preacher's daughter she'd been taught at her pappy's knee to be charitable to her fellow man.

Tinkling laughter sailed from beyond the bushes, startling Matt.

"Miz Amanda, iffen ya keep up yer gigglin', you'll scare away the fish," a protesting young male voice said from beyond some hawthorn bushes.

"Sorry, Jeb. But if you don't want me laughing, then you'd better stop giving those imitations of your teacher. I shouldn't be laughing in any case, encouraging such horrid behavior."

"Aw, I don' mean no dizespect, Miz Amanda; ya'll know that. Ma says I got me a gift for copyin' people's voices, though she don' know what good such a gift'll do me. So I needs ta find some way to use this here gift. Makin' people laugh's a good thing—don't you reckon?"

"Yes, that's true, Jeb. But you shouldn't use your gift at

other people's expense. And poking fun at your teacher isn't a nice thing to do."

Curious, Matt moved off the path and through an opening in the bushes, making a loud rustle as he parted them. The surprise on Amanda's features must have equaled the surprise on Matt's face to see her sitting on the ground next to Jeb, a fishing pole in her hands. She awkwardly scrambled to a stand, dropping the stick. It fell halfway in the water. Jeb grabbed the pole before it could slide all the way in the river and held it out to her. Her face going rosy, she darted a look Matt's way.

"You won't tell?" she asked

"Tell what?" Matt replied.

She glanced at Jeb, as though uncertain, then focused on Matt again. "I need to speak with you in private." Before Matt knew what she was about, she approached, stopping less than a foot in front of him. Her wide eyes glistened like the leaves after a spring rain. "You won't tell anyone you saw me fishing?" she whispered.

"I won't if you'd rather I didn't," Matt answered, befuddled either by her strange words or her close presence. Which it was, he couldn't rightly say. But suddenly his brain refused to work right. "Uh. . .if you don't mind me asking, why should it be kept secret?"

She blew out an exasperated little breath. "It's the silliest thing, really. Ma doesn't consider it proper for a lady to go fishing. She and Pa grew up back East, where everyone is fussy about things like that, I reckon, though here in the hollow such notions seem odd." She tilted her head to one side. "You don't consider it improper, do you?"

He squirmed. "Well, now, Miss Hodges, I don't s'ppose my opinion matters one whit in light of your ma's wishes."

"Oh, won't you call me Amanda? We're not exactly strangers. And I'll call you Matt." She smiled, her teeth as creamy white as a hawthorn's blossoms in springtime. "Or would you prefer I call you Matthew? Matt is how I think of you, so it would be easier to call you Matt, but I surely understand if you'd rather I didn't. I despise it when people call me Mandy." Her words hinged on bold, but her eyes betrayed uncertainty, making her appear almost vulnerable.

"Matt's fine." He cleared the huskiness from his throat. "I'd best be going. I'm heading to town for some supplies."

"Wait. I'll join you. I should be getting home anyway." She looked toward the river. "Jeb, I'd consider it a favor if you'd take my fish to your ma. Rosalie breaks out in hives when she eats catfish, so Ma wouldn't take too kindly to my bringing them home for supper."

Jeb shook his head. "Thanks jis' the same. But I cain't take no charity. My pappy wouldn't like it."

"Oh, Jeb. Consider it thanks for the pointers you gave. Without your help, I wouldn't have caught those three little fish—it's been so long since I held a pole—so they're just as much yours as they are mine. Either that or throw them back. I simply can't take them." Amanda turned from the boy and moved through the bushes.

Matt waited to see what Jeb would do, then joined her.

"Did he take them?" she whispered.

"He tied them to his catch."

"Good! I know Mr. Hunter's leg has been paining him since that tree limb fell on him last fall, and he can't go hunting as often as he used to. It was a horrible accident, with the way he got caught in that storm. But that's no excuse to let his family go without, even if it means accepting a handout now and then."

"The folks in these hills are proud," Matt countered, thankful she'd taken a different tack in the conversation than where he thought it was heading. He didn't want to tell her how he'd gotten his limp.

Amanda sniffed. "Proud enough to let their children starve, I reckon. I get so weary of their stubbornness—and their superstitions. If Hickory Hollow is going to grow into the kind of town Pa and Mr. Randall are striving for, then a lot more people are going to have to learn to put aside their old ways and work together."

"I reckon so. But you're dealin' with a stiff-necked bunch."

"Don't I know it!" She sighed. "I suppose it'll take a leap of faith to save them."

"A leap of faith?"

"One of Pa's examples from his Sunday preaching. He said when something looks downright impossible, you need to believe beyond what you've done already. You need to spiritually move out in faith and leap over your chasm of troubles, while holding fast to God's promises from the Holy Bible."

Matt rolled the words around in his head.

"At least Ma and I can feed the poor every Saturday, after you menfolk build on the church—those who'll come, that is." She looked at him, her eyes curious as though an idea had just occurred to her. "Are you from around here, Matt? You seem to know something about the hill people."

Uneasy, he looked ahead. "I come from the hills. In Tennessee."

"Oh?" She was quiet a moment. "Have you got any family?"

Matt hesitated. "A brother. Both my parents are dead."

"I'm sorry." Her gaze dropped to the ground. "And do you hear from your brother much?"

Matt stopped walking and looked full at her. "Why do you ask?"

She seemed startled by his abrupt question. "No reason. Just trying to make conversation."

Matt forced his tense shoulders to relax. She didn't know who he was, after all, or rather who he'd been. "My brother and I parted ways awhile back."

"Oh." Her reply came soft.

They continued walking. Matt felt a twinge of guilt for speaking so harshly and broke his usual silence to ask a question of his own. "What made your parents decide to leave the East and make their home in the Ozarks?"

"Pa felt led to come to the hollow and do his preaching here."

"Your pa is a good preacher."

"I think so, too." She smiled at him. "What about your pa? What kind of man was he?"

Relieved that they'd come to the clearing that led to the town's buildings, Matt raised two fingers and a thumb to touch the brim of his hat. "Well, I'll be tendin' to my business now. Have a nice day, Miss Amanda."

He walked on but could feel her intent gaze burn a hole through his back the entire way to the mercantile.

❦

The weather cooperated the next Saturday so that the men could work on the church without getting rained on. Yet what should have been a good turnout, due to fair weather, wasn't. Several men were down with the sickness Matt had grappled with weeks ago, and the total number of workers at the church was five: Matt, Bob and Pete Wilson, Pastor Hodges, and a slow old codger named Frank Whipple, who barely could lift a hammer—much less hoist a heavy stone block—and whose arthritic bones made him shuffle from corner to corner. Matt supposed the idea of free food had lured the old bachelor from his home. Yet Matt knew the preacher was grateful to any and all who volunteered their time, whether young or old.

Matt watched six-year-old Edmund who was "helping" by stirring mortar, then lifting the stick out of the pail and staring at it with extreme interest. With his finger, he poked at a gray glob hanging from the stick.

"Edmund Cornell Hodges." Amanda's soft, stern voice came from behind, startling both Matt and the child. "You'd best stay out of that goop before Ma sees you. You ruined your one good shirt last week—and that's your only spare."

42

Edmund frowned but dropped the stick back into the bucket. Warily, Matt faced Amanda. She smiled, holding out a tray with tin cups on it.

"It's cider—nice and cold. Ma always keeps a jug cooling in the stream. I thought—that is, Ma thought—you and the others might like some."

"Amanda," her father called from the other side of the church wall. "I sure could use some of that cider."

She offered an apologetic smile to Matt and handed him a cup. "Excuse me."

Matt relaxed once she'd moved away, and he swallowed the cool apple drink in several gulps. Since the day he'd caught her fishing, Amanda had come around a few times while he worked, often shelling out a barrage of questions involving Matt's history that Matt didn't feel he could answer. Worse, the more time he spent in her company, the more he experienced a keen desire to share some of his past with her. Not the kind of information that could get him strung up with a rope, but the regular, everyday sort of conversation that people engaged in all the time. Amanda was pleasant company, but to tell anyone even a little of his past could prove dangerous.

As he feared, when Amanda finished handing out the refreshment, she returned to his side, supposedly to keep an eye on Edmund. The boy squatted a few feet away from Matt and watched a big black bug crawl down a limestone block.

"It sure is fine weather to be outdoors." Hugging the empty wooden tray to her chest, Amanda inhaled deeply, as if by doing so she could drink down the sun's golden rays. Maybe that would explain why her face shone with such vitality. Sunshine dwelled inside her soul.

She turned laughing eyes his way, her grin laced with mischief. "Of course, on a day like today, I'd much rather be fishing."

Matt smiled. "The fish might not be biting this late in the afternoon."

"Oh, fiddle-faddle. Fish'll eat when they're hungry, just like people do, I expect." Her gaze briefly dropped to the ground as if she were weighing her words. "Matt, would you consider coming along? After supper, of course. I reckon you know of a lot better fishing spots than I do."

Matt wondered how she'd arrived at such a conclusion, since in the short time he'd been a resident of Hickory Hollow he'd only been fishing twice. "You sure you want to go this late in the day? The best time would be early morning."

"Wonderful!" she exclaimed brightly. "Then it's settled. We'll meet at dawn at your cabin day after tomorrow. We can't go tomorrow, of course, it being the Lord's Day and all. Oh, no—wait. Monday is washday, and I promised to help Ma with her visits to the sick this week, too. Thursday then."

Matt blinked, stupefied. Had he agreed to go with her? "Well, uh, I don't know—"

"Oh, don't back out on me now," she hastened to say. "Jeb's coming, too. It's for his family's sake I'm doing this. Whatever I catch, I'm going to make sure he takes home, like last time. Please, come with us." Her expression was guileless, entreating him, but her soft words made Matt's heart pound with strange foreboding.

"Say that again to my face!" The sudden shout erupted from one of the Wilson boys and stymied whatever reply Matt might've given. He turned to see Bob facing down his brother, his hands clenched, his face an angry beet red.

"Alright, I will." Pete's usually easygoing features appeared as if they'd been etched in stone. "I said, Miss Ivy's too smart to have anything to do with a slow-witted ox like you." Pete emphasized each word. "And I'll be the one dancin' with her at Tom and Mayflower's weddin'."

Bob growled and swung his fist, connecting with Pete's jaw. Pete jerked a few steps backward, then lunged at Bob, wrapping both arms around his waist and driving into him like a locomotive. Both men hit the ground, upsetting a bucket of mortar. Their heads came close to cracking against a huge stone block. Amanda gasped. The boys' ma cried out.

Matt pushed his empty glass into Amanda's hand and sped toward the dueling brothers. With a good deal of effort, he pulled Pete off Bob. Another man grabbed Bob. Pete tried to lunge at his brother again, but Matt caught his arm and brought it up hard behind his back. "Stop it! The both of you. You should be ashamed, upsettin' Preacher's doin's like this. No pretty gal is worth fighting over if it means splittin' up kinfolk." Matt growled the words low, but he spoke from the heart.

Once he and Buck had fought over a charming belle who

liked to play brother against brother, like pawns on a chess-board, and had fluttered about, smiling at each in turn, feeding upon their jealous rivalries as a she-cat feeds upon its kill. That had been the start of the trouble between him and Buck.

Pete spat on the ground and wiped the back of his hand along his bloody mouth. His narrowed gaze was fixed on his brother the whole time, but he gave a short nod, and Matt dropped his hold. The other man followed suit and released Bob. The youth picked up his hat from the ground and made as if to go, but Matt wasn't finished.

"Now shake."

Both brothers looked at Matt in disbelief. Their jaws, covered in peach fuzz, set stubbornly, and they crossed their arms over their chests.

"I said, 'shake,'" Matt muttered, not giving an inch. "You've upset the womenfolk with all your carrying-on, and you'd best make it right between you and ease their minds. Or have you forgotten we're trying to serve God and community by building a church here? You two ain't no Cain and Abel, that's for sure, so shake hands and be done with it."

At mention of the women, Pete's gaze went beyond Matt to his ma and a few other ladies staring in their direction. Ivy was absent, and Matt wondered if her presence would have prevented the brawl between the brothers.

His mouth thinning, Pete jerked his arm out toward his brother, clearly reluctant. Bob stared at the proffered hand a minute, then clasped it tight. Pete winced, but the two shook hands, and Matt retraced his steps to Amanda. Her eyes were strangely sad.

"Amanda," her pa called out. "You'd best be going about your business. We men need to do more work on the church before we have our supper."

"Yes, Pa." She gave Matt a lukewarm smile, then turned away, heading for the two women who stirred something in a huge black kettle over flaming logs.

Scratching the back of his neck in puzzlement, Matt watched her go. What had happened to cause such a rapid-fire switch in her emotions? A bleak thought struck.

Did Amanda care for one of the Wilson brothers, who both apparently preferred her friend Ivy? The brothers couldn't be more than sixteen, if that, but folks around these parts married young. Some as young as fifteen. And Amanda certainly was the right age to be a bride. She'd make some man a fine wife one day, Matt was sure. She possessed an inner strength and tenacity mixed with the right amount of gentleness to be a rock-solid support to the man she picked for her husband. And Matt was certain she'd have it no other way. She wouldn't let someone choose her mate. No sirree, not Amanda. She'd be the one doing the choosing. . .and suddenly Matt envied the unknown suitor.

At the sudden sharp and unwelcome twist his thoughts took, Matt set his mouth grimly and resumed work.

Chapter 4

Thin patches of white mist curled between the thickly wooded hills and the valley floor as Amanda, Matt, and Jeb tramped over the mountain in search of the perfect fishing hole. Or at least that was the original plan; with all the walking they'd done, Amanda was beginning to wonder if "the perfect fishing hole" was in another county!

The cooing song of mourning doves occasionally rippled through the damp air, which still held the bite of morning chill. Wildflowers in a rainbow of shades grew in abundance. The hardwood trees had traded their sprinklings of cheery spring buds for lush mantles of greenery that filled the surrounding mountainside.

Earlier, Amanda had sped through her chores. The moment her siblings headed for the little log schoolhouse and her ma had taken Charmaine with her to visit Zeke's mother, Amanda sped from the cabin. She'd been relieved and happy when Matt answered his door with a fishing pole propped on one shoulder. His eyes had seemed wary, but the smile he'd given her and Jeb was friendly enough.

Yet for the past two hours little conversation had flowed between them, and Amanda figured it probably was easier to get a mule to talk than it was Matt Campbell. She still fretted over his remark concerning women the other day, when he'd broken up the fight between the Wilson brothers. He'd said, "No pretty gal is worth splitting up kinfolk." And while she supposed that was true, Amanda couldn't help but feel his meaning went deeper and that Matt had little regard for women in the marrying sense.

Two long blasts from a steamboat whistle broke through the forest stillness. Amanda hurried to a clump of trees and moved a leafy bough aside. Through a willow's branches on the riverbank, she could just make out the majestic, three-storied side-wheeler a few hundred feet away, as it glided along the water, its massive wheels churning up white froth.

"Isn't that just the prettiest sight you ever did see?" Amanda murmured when she heard Matt come up beside her. "One day I'd like to ride on a riverboat so fine and see what life's like beyond the hollow."

"You might be disappointed," Matt said as though to himself.

She glanced his way. "In what? The world beyond or the riverboat?"

Her question startled him into looking at her, and a grin played with the corners of his mouth. "Both, probably. People's expectations are often too high."

"What about you, Matt? Have you seen the world?"

The smile disappeared, and he looked toward the river. "I've seen my share."

The reply wasn't satisfying, but at least he was talking. "And were you disappointed with what you saw?" When he didn't answer, she asked another question. "What about riverboats? Ever been on one?"

"Once."

"Oh—what's it like?" She could barely contain her excitement. "Are there riverboat gamblers with evil designs who prey on defenseless young women?"

He raised his eyebrows. "It sounds like you've been reading those dime novels."

Her face went hot. "Not me. Ivy. She told me all about riverboats."

Matt thought a moment. "I've met my share of gamblers, but you'll find those everywhere. Not just on riverboats."

"I suppose that's true." Amanda looked toward the steamboat that was disappearing from view. "Wishing for a trip upriver on one of those is pointless in any case. Ma would never allow it. She shares Ivy's opinion that riverboats are full of sinful men. Though if I were aboard one, I certainly wouldn't have anything to do with those sorts of people, so she needn't worry."

She let go of the branch, which rustled back into place. Turning, she was about to suggest they go, but was struck speechless by the hopeless longing in Matt's beautiful eyes as he stared at her.

"Matt?"

He seemed to snap out of whatever had him misty-eyed and moved away. "Jeb must've gone ahead. I don't see him."

"He's probably chasing another chipmunk," she said, hurrying to catch up. "He'll find us. Did I say something wrong?" She lifted her skirts and stepped over a lichen-covered boulder in her path. "Is that why you look so upset?" Suddenly she halted. "Oh, Matt. Your pa was a riverboat gambler, wasn't he? That's why you're upset. I shouldn't have spoken so."

He stopped walking and turned, his mouth open as though he would offer a hasty reply. Instead he hesitated, then closed it. "No. He wasn't a riverboat gambler."

"Your grandpappy then? No, that can't be right. Riverboats have only been around for the past fifty years or so, though come to think of it, I reckon it could have been your grandpappy—"

"Miss Amanda. . ." Before Matt could complete the thought, big, wet splats hit Amanda's head and cheek, and Matt blinked one eye as though something had gotten in it. They both turned surprised gazes to the sunny sky. A small rain cloud hovered overhead, as if intent on making itself known. A light shower began to sprinkle upon them.

"Oh, my," Amanda squealed, then laughed.

Matt grabbed her arm. "Come on—before it gets worse."

Together, they ran as fast as they could to a nearby towering oak, whose many leafy branches swept outward and upward, providing shelter to keep them dry. Watching the rain softly fall, Amanda remembered how Jeb's father was wounded when lightning struck a tree, much like this one, last year. She shivered, though there weren't any detectable rolls of thunder or flashes of light in the clouds.

"You're cold," Matt said and propped his fishing pole against the wide trunk. To Amanda's surprise, he looped his arm around her shoulders, drawing her close. Maybe if he were wearing a jacket, he would have put that around her shoulders instead, but Amanda couldn't help but feel grateful that the day was too warm for such outerwear. Being this close to him made her feel safe, content, and sped up her heart a few beats with an emotion still new to her. Was it love?

Feeling as if she were caught up in some wonderful dream, she tilted her head to look at him.

Matt gasped as though suddenly short of breath and dropped his arm from around her. "Don't look at me like that!"

"Like what?" Not understanding his swift change in mood and smarting from the sharpness in his tone, Amanda clutched her elbows. "Did I do something wrong?"

He briefly closed his eyes. "No. I don't reckon you did," he said at last. "You have no idea what I meant, do you?"

She shook her head.

He stared at her with an expression she couldn't define, as though he didn't want to look at her but couldn't keep from it. With wonder, she felt his rough fingertip stroke her jawbone to her chin, then watched his head lower. Cold rainwater dripped off the brim of his hat onto her scalp, but when his soft cool lips touched her brow, she forgot the minor discomfort. "Stay sweet, Amanda," he said, his voice husky.

Feeling suddenly hopeful and a little reckless, she lifted both hands to his rough-whiskered jaw and softly pressed her lips to his. He stiffened, and Amanda, now horrified by her boldness, began to draw away, but his strong arms suddenly wrapped around her waist. His kiss was more fervent than hers had been, and Amanda's heart soared. He must feel the same way about her that she did about him!

Within seconds, he pulled away, the bleak expression in his eyes puzzling her. Why should he look so sad when she felt so happy?

"I shouldn't have done that," he whispered. "You don't want to get hooked up with a man like me, Amanda."

Discouraged, she regarded him. "You're wrong, Matt. Why would you even think such a thing?"

He somberly shook his head and stared up at the sky as though he couldn't stand looking at her any longer. Steady splashes of water hitting the leaves and ground were the only sounds heard. Amanda relived the last few minutes over in her mind while she stared at his sober profile. He obviously cared for her; otherwise he wouldn't have kissed her—would he? Why should he think he wasn't worthy of her? Unless. . . unless Zeke's hateful words about Matt being an outlaw were true. Yet the man Amanda had grown to know was far removed from her idea of an outlaw.

"It's beginning to clear," Matt said. "We should find Jeb."

The shower had ended as quickly as it began. Amanda followed Matt from beneath the shielding oak, feeling as if the small rain cloud had drifted into her heart and watered down her joy in the day. Matt's sudden interest in Jeb's whereabouts was odd, considering the boy often roamed the foothills alone and didn't answer to anyone but his pappy. In fact, the youth probably knew this mountain better than anyone in the hollow. Not too surprising, Jeb spotted them before they ran across him.

"Come see what I found!" he yelled from a nearby covering of pines. A flash of gray broke through the underbrush as he beckoned in a wide motion with his arm, and half of his moon face could be seen. Then both the face and the gray-sleeved arm disappeared, and a loud rustle followed as Jeb darted back through the forest.

Amanda and Matt left the well-beaten path and moved in the direction they'd last seen him. A new sense of excitement winged through Amanda, and she wondered what treasure Jeb must have found. Rarely had she seen him so enthused about anything.

The trees stood close, blocking her vision of what was up ahead, and she didn't see the small clearing with the aqua-blue spring until she'd almost come upon it. Jeb excitedly pointed to a midsized bluff of jagged gray-and-tan rock, only one of many bluffs scattered throughout the area. Wild ferns and undergrowth grew tall against the coarse stone, almost shielding the black hole at the bottom.

"I ain't never seen this cave before," Jeb exclaimed excitedly. "You reckon it's linked to the one over yonder, acrost the mountain a ways—the one that has water comin' out the hole and runnin' into the stream?" As he talked, he moved toward the cave. "That one you cain't get in 'cuz it's too high. But this one should be easy enough, I reckon."

"Be careful, Jeb," Matt warned. "You don't know what might be waitin' inside. A grizzly. A copperhead. . ."

"I agree with Matt. Come away from there."

Amanda wasn't sure why, but she felt a niggling sense of danger, though she couldn't put her finger on what seemed wrong. As always, the forest was eerily quiet, except for the occasional rustles in the undergrowth or the distant shriek of a hawk or other bird. Yet today the thick wood seemed almost too quiet. Perhaps it was the presence of the cave that bothered her. Amanda never had liked caves, which were scattered throughout the mountains as thickly as fleas on a sheepdog.

Jeb paid them no heed and tromped on ahead. Amanda shared an exasperated look with Matt, then followed the boy, stepping over the smooth, gray rocks that lined the muddy ground at the front of the bluff. Up close, the cave's black entrance was taller than a man but not quite wide enough to stretch her arms out when she touched the sides. She put her hand to the coarse rock at shoulder level but moved no farther. Cool air drifted out, brushing against Amanda's face and stirring her damp tendrils. Shivering, she looked away from the gaping hole that led to who-knew-where.

An orange-and-black-spotted reptile, about six inches long with the tail, rapidly skittered along the face of the bluff, near her fingers. She squealed and jerked her hand away.

Jeb laughed. "Aw, it's jis' a salamander, Miz Amanda. It

won't do you no harm."

"Thanks," she said drolly. "It only scared a year's life out of me, is all." She eyed the creature with disgust. It had halted its rapid pace and seemed to regard Amanda with black, beady eyes.

"We need to be heading back." Matt's voice came abruptly from behind, startling her. She looked his way. His gaze was caught up in the trees near the spring. His jaw was tense, his manner alert.

The hairs on the back of Amanda's neck prickled. "Matt, what's wrong?"

He looked at her. "Nothin'. We just need to head back." He took a firm hold of her elbow and turned her in the direction from which they'd come, as though afraid she might refuse. "Jeb, you, too."

Startled, Amanda darted a glance over her shoulder at Jeb, who shrugged, obviously as ignorant to what was bothering Matt as she was.

"But. . .aren't we going fishing?" Amanda sputtered.

Matt didn't answer but kept walking, pulling her along with him. For a man who limped, he certainly was keeping a fast pace. Amanda didn't have time to think about his odd behavior, struggling as she did to keep up with him.

❧

On the evening of Mayflower and Tom's wedding, Matt gathered his few belongings and left the cabin for what would be the last time. When he'd kissed Amanda yesterday in the rain, he had wished it could have been the first of many kisses. Because of that, he was doing the best thing for all concerned and leaving Hickory Hollow. For good.

It would be hard not to see her once more, not to look into those clear green eyes or hear her sweet voice. Yet Matt knew Amanda, and he knew his heart. With the strong way he felt about her, the love he now recognized he had for her, Matt figured it would take little persuading on her part to get him to stay. For her sake, he couldn't allow that to happen. She was different from the scheming women he'd known. Women like Maryanne, who with one word or look could rip a man's heart to shreds. Amanda was sweet. Headstrong at times, but sweet, and as innocent as a lamb.

Pushing all bittersweet memories of Amanda aside, Matt settled his hat more firmly on his head and closed the door. He had one last order of business to take care of before leaving the hollow. If the rumors he'd heard were true, then Buck was on this mountain. And sure as shooting, those squashed cigar stubs Matt had spotted near the cave entrance had been his brother's, as well as the empty whiskey bottle underneath the bushes. He knew he'd seen movement in the trees and didn't think it belonged to a moonshiner using the cave for a still. A moonshiner would have confronted Matt, Amanda, and Jeb with a shotgun before they'd so much as stepped into the clearing; whereas an outlaw might have hidden in the trees until it was safe to come out—unless he knew he'd been spotted. Then there would have been shooting. No, it wasn't any moonshiner spying on them. Which meant only one thing.

The gang must have found another hideout.

Matt rubbed his sore hip, his fingers brushing against the ivory-handled butt of the Colt .44 revolver in his holster. Scowling, he looked at a nearby bluff, remembering the day he'd been shot by one of the boys, though he didn't know which one had done it. The impact of the bullet in his leg and the fiery agony of splintering bone had knocked him off his horse. Once he hit the ground, he'd rolled and gone over a short bluff, much like that one, and been left for dead.

Wouldn't Buck and the others be surprised to see how alive he was?

Chapter 5

Haunting strains of a dulcimer mingled with the twanging of a banjo and the merry strings of a fiddle as the people danced and clapped and stamped their feet, locking arms from time to time in the rollicking mountain reel. Laughter and smiles abounded, but Amanda didn't feel one bit joyful. Not after the talk she'd just had with her pa.

Spotting Zeke, she curled her hands into fists at her sides and marched over to where he stood on the fringes, watching the merriment. He raised his brows when she stopped in front of him. "Care for a dance?"

"Don't you talk to me about dancing," Amanda fumed. "How dare your pa take the land for the church away from my pa! He promised it to him. Your pa had no right to go back on his word."

Zeke regarded her, a patronizing look on his face. "Now, Amanda, don't fret so. Nothing was signed. Father recently realized he'd made a mistake—a business error, if you will—in issuing the use of that land to your father. Your pa can build his church elsewhere on the mountain. Father told him that."

"Build elsewhere? The church is already halfway to being built, Zeke. Maybe nothing was signed on paper, but there's such a thing as a gentleman's agreement—yet your pa's obviously no gentleman!"

She whirled away, but Zeke caught her arm before she could take more than two steps. "Marry me, and I'll persuade Father to give us that land for a wedding present. Then you can give the deed to your pa. I'm sure I can get Father to agree. I know something about his affairs he wouldn't want Mother to know." He grinned slyly.

"You'd blackmail your own father?" Amanda asked incredulously. She sobered. "Zeke Randall, I wouldn't marry you if you were the last man to draw breath in all of Hickory Hollow." Zeke's face grew tight, and she jerked her arm from his hold. "You're just like your pa. You think you can order everyone around, and if that doesn't work, then you try and buy people or bully them to get what you want. Well I'm not a woman who can be bought—or bullied!"

"It's Matt Campbell, isn't it?" he sneered. "Ever since he came to the hollow, he's been nothing but trouble, messing in our affairs."

"*Our* affairs? Oh!" She stamped her foot, wishing it was his shoe she was stamping instead. She didn't believe the man's gall. "We don't have any 'affairs' between us—never did—and this has nothing to do with Matt. It has to do with something you obviously know nothing about. Integrity and honor and. . .and. . .well, just doing what's right!"

Noticing they were drawing unwanted attention from those dancing nearby, Amanda bustled away. Before she could reach the edge of the clearing, she met Ivy. Her eyes were troubled. "Amanda, I'm so sorry about what my father did. I had no idea. . . ."

Amanda's anger waned a bit. Ivy was the only Randall with any shred of decency; one reason the two of them had been friends since they were children. "I don't blame you." She darted a look up the mountain. "But if I don't get away from here, I'm sure to embarrass my parents. I need to calm down. If they should ask for me, tell them I'll be back shortly."

Ivy frowned. "You're going to see him, aren't you?"

"Just tell them!" Amanda stomped up the path. She had no doubt that the "him" to whom Ivy so disdainfully referred was Matt. Amanda didn't understand what Ivy had against him; he was so nice to everyone. Knowing that, Amanda wondered why he hadn't made an appearance at the wedding. He and Tom seemed to get along well.

As she neared his cabin, she relaxed. She wished to speak with Matt about this latest occurrence, even if he only gave his usual scant replies. Simply being in his presence made her feel better.

At the door, she knocked, waited, then knocked again. She frowned, remembering that spring morning when she'd found him ill. Wondering if she should peek inside, she suddenly noticed fresh boot prints in the mud. Many of the hill people were trappers and hunters and took to wearing knee-length moccasins, but Matt favored boots, so she assumed the prints were his. They led over a path that wound higher up the mountain.

She thought a moment, looking in the direction of the wedding celebration, though she couldn't see the clearing from this point. But she could hear faint strains of music floating over the air. It was doubtful her parents would look for her or be concerned; Ma left early to help deliver a baby, and Pa had gone home, discouraged by Mr. Randall's news. The cruel buzzard could have at least waited until after the party to break it to her pa.

Amanda looked up the mountain and decided to follow the tracks and find Matt. She was still too angry to rejoin the others.

The birdsong in the trees was noisier than usual, as if the feathered creatures were complaining about the exuberant music from the clearing. Amanda climbed higher, crossed a ridge, and took another path that ascended, leading around the mountain. The tracks moved along the same path Jeb had taken them on their quest for the perfect fishing hole they'd never found.

The prints veered off the path, deeper into the thick wood. Amanda hesitated, then followed, realizing Matt must have gone in the direction of the cave. Why? He didn't seem to have any interest in exploring it when they were there yesterday. Cautiously she walked over the damp, black soil, avoiding stepping on a stick that could snap and give away her presence, though why she felt she should be so secretive, she didn't know. Yet, just like that other day, something didn't feel right.

Before she reached the clearing, she heard the rise and fall of men's voices. Surprised, she moved closer so she could hear, pressed herself against a thick trunk to hide, then cautiously peeked around the bark.

About twenty yards away, Matt stood facing a young bearded man the same size as he in both height and form. His hair was almost as long as Matt's, and like Matt, he wore the same type of boots. A wide-brimmed felt hat was pulled over his forehead. A gun belt was strapped around the stranger's waist, and Amanda noticed that Matt also wore his guns.

"So, what did you come for then?" the man groused. "You gonna spout that same religion garbage to me?"

"No," Matt replied. "We had the same mother, and she taught us from the same Bible. You know the gospel same as me, Buck. That's why I had to leave the gang. I couldn't abide the stealing and killing anymore."

Amanda gasped. What Zeke had said about Matt being an outlaw must be true!

The man named Buck grunted. "You were a fool to face 'em down and tell 'em you were turnin' over your share of the gold and givin' yourself up. If you'd gone through with it, you woulda been hanged."

"What's the difference?" Matt asked dryly. "A rope or a bullet—both bring about the same end. Death. Only whichever one of the others shot me when my back was turned didn't succeed in killing me."

Crossing his arms over his chest, Buck regarded Matt. "What makes you think it was one o' the others?"

"Who else? Oh, no." Matt's voice went hoarse. "Not you—my own brother?"

At Matt's distress, Amanda's heart wrenched.

Suddenly a large, dirty hand clapped over her mouth, and someone grabbed her around the waist from behind, pulling her hard against him. "Now, whatcha have to go and snoop 'round this neck o' the woods for?" a young man's voice rasped near her ear. "You should be home, like a good little girl, tendin' your chores and mindin' your own business."

Amanda tried to scream and struggled, kicking back with her heels toward her attacker's shins, though he stood with his feet planted apart so it was hard for her to make contact. Matt ran into view, a long-barreled revolver in his hand. His eyes widened when he saw her, but his gaze immediately veered to the man holding her, and he raised his gun to aim.

"Let her go, Jesse," Matt ordered. "It's me you want. Not her."

The ominous click of another gun's trigger being cocked sounded to their left. Amanda's eyes flicked that way. A slender man with a hawk nose and sandy hair and beard casually stood, his gun trained on Matt.

" 'What fools these mortals be,' " he said quietly, quoting Shakespeare. "Drop the gun, Matt, and kick it away. Buck might have missed your heart last time, but my aim is true, as you know."

Matt hesitated, then let the gun fall and did as ordered.

The man holding Amanda released her with a little forward push and moved to pluck the weapon from the ground, then took a stand near the gunman. Like the other man, he trained Matt's gun upon them, motioning with the barrel for Amanda to move next to Matt. The second gunman's hair under the hat was darker, his features boyishly handsome, but the blue eyes that glittered in the smooth face were hard and unyielding. Both men wore long soldiers' overcoats and appeared to be in their early twenties.

"Well, Frank," the one who'd grabbed Amanda said, his tone almost cordial. "What do you reckon we ought to do with these two?"

The bearded gunman looked at Amanda and smiled, though the expression wasn't pleasant. "You know more about these things, Jesse. You decide."

Amanda gulped a shaky breath, faint with the knowledge that struck her. Frank. . .Jesse. . .

She was a prisoner of the James Gang.

Hands and feet tied, Matt leaned his shoulder against the cave wall. Amanda was also tied, but her hands were bound in front of her, whereas Matt's were tied behind his back. The small fire Frank had started once it grew dark flickered eerily on the tan stone around them, making huge shadows. The flames produced little warmth for Amanda and Matt, who sat about fifteen feet inside the cave entrance. Still, the fire did give off light, which offered some comfort amid the high-pitched squeals of the bats. The black winged creatures flew from wall to wall, obviously upset to have their peace disturbed. Matt knew they were harmless and told Amanda so, but he noticed her dart an anxious glance at them from time to time and shiver when one swooped too close.

Jesse strode toward them, a bowl of something steaming in his hands. He hunkered down beside Amanda. "Squirrel stew," he said with a grin, watching her. "Best eat it while it's hot. Never let it be said that the James brothers let their prisoners starve. Especially when the prisoner is such a purty young thing."

Amanda scowled and turned her face away. From behind Jesse, Frank chuckled. " 'Frailty, thy name is woman,' " he mocked.

Jesse set the bowl down and stood. "We got a stubborn one here, all right."

He rejoined Frank and Hugh, another gang member who'd recently arrived. All three men stood at the entrance and conversed.

"An outlaw who quotes Shakespeare," Amanda muttered, her bitter gaze on Frank. "How amusing."

Surprise made Matt speak. "You know Shakespeare?"

"Ivy has a book of his plays and sonnets," she said, still not looking at him. She hadn't looked his way since they'd been forced into this cave at gunpoint, hours ago. Not that he could blame her.

Matt sighed. "You better eat. You need to keep up your strength."

"What about you? I notice they didn't bring you any."

Matt didn't say he was certain that the brothers had decided his fate. Where they planned to send him, he wouldn't need food, but at least Amanda would be safe. The James brothers had never harmed or killed a woman, not to his knowledge, and when Matt had mentioned that Amanda was a preacher's daughter, a look of grudging respect lit the brothers' eyes. Jesse and Frank's pa had been a preacher. But he'd left the ministry for the gold fields when Jesse was just a boy and had died there. Perhaps his pa was the reason Jesse carried a Bible wherever he went, though the life-changing words obviously had never entered his heart.

"Go on and eat," Matt quietly encouraged.

Amanda awkwardly picked up the bowl with one hand, managing to bring it to her mouth. In the process she sloshed some liquid on her dress and scowled. The round neckline had gotten snagged on a low branch during their trek to this cave, though the tear was modest. But an angry red scratch could be seen on her collarbone. "It would've been nice if they could have untied me first," she mumbled between sips. "I can barely feel my hands anymore."

"Amanda, you don't know how sorry I am that you got involved," Matt said forcefully, keeping his voice low so the others couldn't hear. " I'd do anything I could to undo the past."

In the scant firelight, he saw her brow soften. "I know. I heard what you said to your brother before I got caught. I can't say as how I understand why you got involved with them in the first place, Matt, but I can tell you're not one of them anymore—and I surely don't blame you for what happened to me." She glanced at the stony ground. "It was my own stupidity that got me in this pickle. Like Ma says, I'm too willful for my own good."

"I reckon it'll take quite a leap of faith to get us out of this one, huh?" His words were light, meant to relieve some of the dread she must be feeling.

Surprise, then excited certainty swept across her face, filling him with awe. Most women would be in tears by now or cowering against the wall. But not Amanda. In the dim firelight, her eyes seemed to crackle, regaining their vibrancy.

"You're right," she exclaimed softly. "That's exactly what's needed. Thank you for reminding me." She closed her eyes, and the sweetest expression came across her features as her lips began to move and she murmured words Matt couldn't hear.

Uncomfortable, he shifted his gaze to the boot tips of his tied feet. He couldn't pray; not when he felt such bitterness. His original desire in finding Buck was to persuade him to leave the gang and give up this life, which was no life at all—always on the run, always hiding out. But all such notions fled after Buck's revelation. Buck hadn't come right out and said he was the one to shoot Matt, but he'd implied it. His own flesh and blood tried to kill him! How could Buck have done such a thing?

I forgave you all your sins; do likewise to others, My son.

Matt blinked hard at the soft urging that tugged at his spirit. No. . .he couldn't. Yet he had no choice. Not if he wanted to stay in God's favor. God forgave Matt for all the robbing and shooting during his wild days with the gang, when he'd been an uncertain, bitter youth of seventeen. . . .

Matt swallowed, his mind forming a wordless plea for strength to do what the Lord willed him to do.

After Buck finished his stew, he brought a bowl over to Matt. "You need to eat, too," he said gruffly.

Wary, Matt regarded him. His stomach was coiled in knots, and he doubted he could get anything past them. Buck also seemed tense, his eyes not able to meet Matt's, but he didn't move away.

"Were you the one who shot me?" Matt asked quietly, needing to know.

Buck paused for a few nerve-rending seconds before answering, "Yes."

"Why?" Rolled into that one word was all the frustration, hurt, and bitterness Matt had felt since he suspected his brother had betrayed him.

"Hush up!" Buck darted a glance toward the front of the cave, where the others sat and conversed, then looked at Matt again. "I did it to save your skin, you fool," he growled quietly. "If one of them had shot you, you think you'd be sitting here now?"

Matt drew his brows together. "I don't understand."

"Jesse said you had to be stopped, and I volunteered. After I shot you, I rode back to where they waited and let 'em know. I figgered when you came to, you'd find yourself wounded—yes. But you'd be alive. How was I to know you'd roll over that bluff? But it turned out to be a good thing, 'cause Jesse wanted to see for sure you were dead. So I took the boys to the edge of the bluff where they could view your body. I guess they figgered no one could survive that fall."

"Did you think I was dead?"

"Naw, I knew you were breathing. I climbed down to check before I rejoined the others." At Matt's stunned expression, Buck added, "Who do you think sent that old hermit your way?"

"You?" Matt asked hoarsely, something making sense that never had before. Like how quickly the hermit had found him and stopped the bleeding. He swallowed over a tight throat. "You had no idea that hermit was a doc, did you?"

Surprise lit Buck's eyes. "Well, that explains how you survived."

"God took care of me, Buck. Even then."

The admission made Buck look away, and the strong need to try again and talk sense into his brother rose up in Matt.

"Buck, you're not like those two. So why keep riding with them? Give it up. If not for me or you, do it for Ma's memory. I know we had some bad blood between us on account of Maryanne—and I'm sorry about that—but you're all the kin I got left. And I don't want to see you danglin' from the end of a rope."

At mention of the cruel young belle who'd brought animosity between them years ago, Buck's mouth tightened. He set the bowl of stew down with a dull clunk and stood. Before moving away, he stared at Matt awhile longer, then moved to the fire to light a cheroot. Matt closed his eyes, leaned his head back against the cold rock wall, and took his own leap of faith.

⁂

Shivering, Amanda watched the bats dart past eerie flickers of light and shadow on the strange formations of stone around her. From deep within the cave's bowels, she detected the hollow sound of trickling water and remembered Jeb's comment about this cave possibly being linked to one with a stream. With all the rain they'd gotten, what if there was a flood? She'd heard older residents of the hollow spin yarns about flash floods in caves. Grimacing, Amanda stared at a pile of brittle bones. Would she and Matt get out alive, or would these outlaws leave them behind until they shared the fate of whatever animal had huddled near the opposite wall long ago?

Minutes earlier, Jesse, clearly the leader of the gang, had given orders to both Hugh and Buck before looking Amanda's way. "Sorry we have to leave you tied up like this, Miss. But I'm sure you understand why we can't let you go. We'd prefer not to have your kinfolk come lookin' for us 'til we're a fair piece from here."

"You're not actually going to leave us in this place?" Amanda's eyes were huge. "Defenseless against any wild critters that might wander inside?"

"Considering the circumstances, there's little else to do." Frank grabbed a burlap sack and slung it over his shoulder. In the eerie semidarkness, his eyes glittered like black pebbles. "Remember, Miss Hodges, 'He's mad that trusts in the tameness of a wolf.' "

"Enough of the Shakespeare," Jesse muttered, grabbing his shotgun. "Let's get the horses and get on outta here." A short whispered conversation among the four outlaws at the mouth of the cavern followed before the James brothers exited the cave.

As Amanda watched, the man named Hugh spat on the ground, said something to Buck, then he, too, left the cave. Buck continued to look out the entrance, his tense stance betraying his nervousness. Suddenly he turned, whipped a hunting knife from his belt, and rushed toward Amanda and Matt.

Matt gasped, his eyes wide in horror. Amanda's blood ran cold. *Jesus, help us!* The cry winged through Amanda's soul.

Buck dropped to his knees once he reached them. The knife arced, the gleam from the fire bringing out yellow glints on the deadly blade, which came down with force toward Matt.

"No!" Amanda screeched.

"Hush up!" Buck threw her a disgusted glance. "Are you trying to get us all kilt?"

For the first time, Amanda saw the ropes around Matt's legs had been cut. Buck quickly did the same to the rope tying his brother's wrists, then faced her. Amanda barely had time to think before he'd sawed through her ropes. Uncomfortable heat tingled through her hands and feet as blood rushed back into them. She felt as if she were being pricked with dozens of pine needles.

"If you two have any sense at all," Buck muttered, "you'll sit like you was. I doubt Hugh'll look close enough to see what I done. When I give the word, you both run outta here like a bear was chasin' you for its evenin' meal."

Matt drew his hands back behind him and crossed his wrists, his eyes gleaming with something suspiciously close to tears. "Thanks, Buck."

Buck sheathed the knife, a smile on his whiskered face. "You don't think I'd let my little brother and his woman become a victim of what they'd planned, do ya? Maryanne's history; it ruffled my feathers is all. When I shot you that day, I was only tryin' to save yer hide."

"I realize that now," Matt said quietly.

Buck stood. "Stay alert, and wait for my signal."

"Buck?"

"What now?" Matt's brother turned and looked at him.

"About what we talked on earlier. Think on it some?"

Buck hesitated, then nodded.

Amanda watched him move to the fire, glad that Matt and his brother were obviously on good terms again, also glad Buck was on their side. God was working it all out, and she couldn't help but feel convicted regarding her lapse into fear earlier. Remembering what her pa preached about in the book of James concerning the double-minded man who would receive nothing from the Lord, she realized she couldn't pray for one thing, then believe another. If she was going to pray that the Lord would deliver them from evil as His Word said He would, then she'd better start speaking right words and believing them, too.

Amanda smiled at her fellow prisoner. "We're going to get out of here alive, Matt. God's taking care of us."

An awed expression came across his face, but he only nodded.

She wished she could slide over and put her hand in his, but that might not be the best thing to do, considering they had to pretend they were still tied up. It had felt good to hear her being referred to as Matt's woman, but even so, Amanda was curious about the girl Maryanne and what she'd been to Matt.

Hugh returned to the cave and glanced at the two sitting against the wall before he crouched in front of the fire. He and Buck shared little conversation. Hugh slowly ran both sides of his knife along a piece of whetstone, then tossed the stone aside and began to whittle on a stick. Buck wiped his whiskered jaw and stared into the sputtering flames, as though something were bothering him.

"Hugh! Buck!" Jesse's voice abruptly sounded outside the cavern, raspier than usual. "Get on out here, and make it fast!"

Both outlaws scrambled to a standing position and looked at each other. Hugh ran from the cave. Buck stared at Matt, his expression grim. Alarmed, Amanda shot her gaze to the cut ropes, loosely wrapped around her wrists and ankles for effect, then looked Matt's way.

His eyes somber, he slowly shook his head.

Chapter 6

Buck gave Matt one last look before leaving the cave after Hugh. Matt understood what his brother didn't say. If Jesse saw their cut ropes, Buck was a dead man. Yet Matt's first concern was Amanda and getting her out of here. *God help us all,* he silently prayed as he hurried to stand.

After sitting on the cave floor for hours, his hip ached something fierce, but he forced himself to act. He helped Amanda up, then moved with her toward the entrance. Since Jesse had taken his gun, Matt grabbed the shotgun that Hugh had left and plucked up Hugh's knife for good measure, tucking it in his boot.

"If anything happens to me," he whispered to Amanda, "run and hide."

A loud rustle came from some nearby bushes. Matt turned his head in alarm and watched as a tall, shadowed form materialized and approached. Matt raised the shotgun. "You might as well just stop right there. I'm takin' Miss Hodges outta here, and ain't nobody gonna stop me."

"I ain't aimin' to stop ya, Mr. Campbell," a cheery young voice said. Jeb walked closer, into the firelight. "I come ta help."

"That was you who cried out for Hugh, wasn't it?" Amanda said from behind Matt, amazement in her voice. "I thought the voice sounded too raspy to be Jesse's, but it sure fooled them. Oh, Jeb, you're wonderful!" She moved forward and gave the embarrassed youth a hug, then straightened suddenly. "But where are they?"

Jeb held up a thick branch and grinned wickedly. "Them two got what was comin' to 'em, I reckon."

"Jeb!" Amanda gasped.

"Aw, no call to look like that, Miz Amanda. I didn' kill 'em. But they sure is gonna have some powerful headaches come mornin'."

"We better leave while we can," Matt said. "Though with how dark the mountain is, it'll be dangerous walkin'."

"No, it won't," Jeb shot back. "I got me a lantern. Left it over yonder." He pointed toward the pines. "I came back yestiday and been watchin' 'em ever since."

"Your ma must be worried something fierce," Amanda gently rebuked.

"No, Ma'am. I tole my pappy I was goin' a-huntin'." He grinned again. "And I reckon I did—caught me two skunks, leastways. Guess my gift for copyin' people's voices done some good, after all."

"It most certainly did," Amanda said with a smile.

Jeb looked beyond the spring. "I reckon they'll be out 'til

we can git help. Too bad I couldn't ketch the others, but my stick weren't gonna hold up to no shotgun, an' they had horses, b'sides."

With Jeb carrying the lantern for a guiding light, Amanda walked beside Matt down the mountain. She wished there was a law official in the hollow, but no such person existed. No jail did, either. If trouble arose between the hill people, they battled it out among themselves. Or the tough men who worked for Zeke's father intervened.

As they walked, Amanda had time to think. "Who's Maryanne?" she asked casually.

Matt's head turned her way, and he seemed to hesitate. "She's a girl Buck and I both liked once. Like Buck said, she's history."

Amanda decided to be content with that. She really didn't want to know too much about any other woman associated with Matt, especially if she was no longer part of his life. Amanda was here with him now, and she intended it to stay that way.

After more than an hour's walking, they neared the clearing. Through the trees, the church's three rock walls glowed in the moonlight. More than a dozen torches flamed across the black night and appeared to be coming closer.

"Uh-oh," Jeb muttered. "Looks like there be trouble."

Curious, Amanda walked with Matt into the clearing. Spotting her father in the row of men moving their way, she halted. "Pa?"

"Amanda!" He hurried to her and clasped her shoulders.

"Did he hurt you?"

"Grab that no-account and string him up with a rope," Zeke yelled. "We'll show him how we deal with his kind!"

Three men grabbed Matt by the arms. Matt's shotgun fell, but Jeb picked it up before anyone else could.

"No!" Amanda broke away from her father, moved a step Matt's way, then swung back around to face her pa. "Aren't you going to stop them?"

"Amanda," he said haltingly, as if he were in pain. He reached out to touch the torn flap of her dress.

"No—you don't understand." She shook her head, then again looked toward Matt. Zeke and the others were pushing him toward a sturdy oak with low-hanging branches. The search party had turned into an angry mob yelling for Matt's death.

"Pa—you gotta stop this!" Amanda cried. "Matt didn't do anything. You can't just stand there and let them kill an innocent man!"

Not waiting for his reply, she picked up her skirts and ran toward the group. "Wait!" she yelled. "He didn't do anything!"

The men paid her no heed, and she doubted they could hear her over all their shouting. In the eerie half ring of fire from the torches, she watched as someone threw the rope over a branch and pulled one end down. *Dear God, I know You promised to deliver us from evil, and I'm aiming to keep my mind on that promise. But how do I get them to listen?*

Her gaze darted to Jeb, who stood near the church about thirty feet from the others. She ran to him, grabbed the heavy shotgun from his arms, and cocked it. Aiming the barrel toward the sky, she pulled the trigger. A shot exploded through the night. The stock slammed against her shoulder from the impact of the rifle going off, threatening to knock her off her feet, but she stood her ground. Unnatural silence filled the air as every man looked her way.

She lowered the gun, keeping hold of the slender barrel in one hand. "Now, if you'll just listen, I'll tell you what happened. Matt didn't hurt me. We've been held prisoner by the James Gang."

"The James Gang!" someone exclaimed. "What would they be doin' on our mountain?"

"I'll tell you what they're doing," Zeke spoke up. He pointed at Matt, who stood silent, his manner resigned. "He's one of them. He was sent to spy on our town."

"No," Amanda countered. "That's not true! Matt was a prisoner just like me. They tied us both up, but we got away."

"My cousin saw him rob the bank in Liberty," Zeke argued.

Several men began to murmur and eyed Matt. "That true?" asked a gruff-looking man with a long beard. "You one of Jesse's gang?"

"I was," he said quietly.

"That's all we need to know," one man called out. "Let's get this over with!"

Amanda watched in horror as the thick rope was looped around Matt's neck.

"Lynch the thievin' skunk!"

"Hang him good!"

"No!" Amanda lifted the heavy rifle and sent another wild shot into the air. This time she hit a branch, which fell to the ground with a rustle, almost hitting one of the men. He jumped and scurried a few feet away. Again she had their undivided attention.

"How can you talk about hanging a man who's done nothing but good for the hollow? Mr. Wilbur," she said, looking at a scrawny man, "Matt fixed your wagon wheel when it broke off and you were stranded on that cart path. And Mr. Conners," she said, directing her words at a grizzled-haired man, "he helped you get those boulders off your land so you could plant seed." She motioned with the gun to the walls behind her. "Matt's the only one of you who's given up every Saturday in helping build our church. Though if Zeke's pa takes the land, I don't know what we'll do."

"What?" Mr. Wilbur turned to Zeke. "What's she blabberin' about?"

Zeke looked uncomfortable. "Nothing we can't discuss later. The point is, what are we going to do about him?" He threw a malevolent look Matt's way. "Don't forget," he said, addressing the others, "it could have been one of your daughters or sisters out there tonight instead of Amanda."

"And I told you," Amanda shot back, "nothing happened."

Mr. Wilbur and Mr. Conners looked undecided, as did the other men.

"I say we let Matt speak," Pete Wilson piped up. "Let him tell us why he done what he done."

"Yeah," Bob Wilson added. "Why'd you go lookin' fer the James boys tonight, if you weren't up to no good to begin with?"

A hush settled over the area. Matt's somber gaze sought Amanda's, and it was as though he was speaking only to her. "What I did in riding with the gang was wrong, and I'm not saying it wasn't," he said slowly. "I'm not excusin' my behavior. But I need to tell you something so you might better understand.

"Durin' the War Between the States, my ma argued I was too young to join up with the Confederacy, saying she didn't want to lose two sons to the cause. At the time I would've given anything to fight. Then, the last year of the war, my parents died. I was almost seventeen. My brother, the only kin I had left, came home not long after. He'd met the James brothers when he served under Anderson's guerilla band and brought them with him. They talked about avengin' the South and fightin' against the persecution of the North, and I decided to ride with them. I was angry, bitter at God for taking away my parents, and bitter that the South had lost the war."

He shook his head. "Only the bank robbin' and train holdups didn't seem much like helping the South, and I didn't like the shootin' and killin' that came with it, either. My ma raised me on the Bible, and I didn't feel right about what we was doin'. One day I'd had enough. I told the gang I was leaving and taking back my share of the gold—that I was puttin' myself at the law's mercy. Only before I could get far, one of the gang shot me. That's how I got my limp."

Her heart full, Amanda loosely cradled the shotgun, stepping closer to the oak tree, her eyes never leaving Matt's.

"An old hermit, a doc, found me, cut the bullet out, and nursed me back to health. He'd been as bitter as me, havin' lost a daughter after the surgery he'd done on her didn't spare her life. But he was closer to God than to most people, and durin' those six-and-a-half months I stayed at his cabin, he pointed me back to the Lord."

"If that's true," Mr. Conners said, "how come you was with the gang tonight?"

"I wanted to talk some sense into my brother. I wanted him to leave the gang."

"Yes," Amanda agreed. "Everything Matt said is true. I followed him, without him knowing it, and heard it all. Then later, after Buck cut our ropes and Jeb knocked two of the outlaws out, Matt's only thought was for my safety."

"My Jeb knocked two outlaws out?" Mr. Hunter said from within the crowd, pride in his voice.

"Sure did, Pappy!" Jeb called out. "And they're still up there, I reckon."

"Well, what are we standin' here for?" Pete Wilson said. "If there's a gang to be caught, let's kitch 'em. I could use some reward money."

"We'll split it betwixt the all of us," one man said gruffly. "Fair's fair."

"Wait!" Zeke motioned to Matt. "What about him? He's an outlaw, too. You heard him admit it!"

Amanda's pa stepped forward into the ring of firelight. "From the way I hear him tell it and what I've seen of his character thus far, I believe this young man is truly repentant and has received just punishment for his mistakes. Earthly punishment, that is. God has already forgiven him for his crimes."

Amanda's heart leapt for joy, and she could have run over and kissed her pa then and there.

"I reckon that's good enough fer me," Mr. Conners said and turned to go.

"He's the preacher," Zeke argued. "Of course he's gonna say something like that!"

"My pa is an honorable man," Amanda defended him. "He wouldn't say something if it weren't so."

Mr. Conners scratched his jaw, then looked at Amanda's father. "Preacher, you willin' to stand by what you said and keep an eye on Matt here 'til we kin look into it?"

"I'm willing."

Mr. Conners nodded and joined Jeb at the foot of the path. The others followed.

"But. . .but," Zeke sputtered.

"Let it go, Zeke," Bob Wilson said and moved to join the rest of the men, leaving only Zeke and Matt underneath the tree.

Zeke glared at Matt, shifted his gaze to Amanda, and tossed the end of the rope he still gripped away from him. It swung madly in the air. "This isn't over, Campbell," he growled, then stormed off in the direction of his home.

Amanda's pa cleared his throat. "We best let your ma know everyone's all right."

Amanda glanced at him. "Give us a minute alone, Pa?"

He paused, looking between the two, then nodded and left.

Awkwardly holding the rifle, Amanda closed the distance until less than a foot stood between her and Matt. In the light of a torch someone had stuck in the ground, she could see a smile flicker on his lips as he held out his hand for the shotgun. Gladly, she relinquished the heavy weapon to him.

"You're amazing," he said quietly. "I have you to thank for my life."

"I only used a shotgun once before, but my aim wasn't good. I put a hole through Ma's sheet hanging out to dry instead of hitting the can." She felt giddy with the gentle look in his eyes and wasn't quite sure what she was saying.

Suddenly she frowned, noticing the rope still circling his neck. She stepped closer to lift the noose over his chin and forehead, then tossed the vile rope to the ground. Picking up his hat from where it had fallen, she brushed it off and set it on his head. Her gaze met his, and she smiled.

"Amanda. . ." His voice was hoarse. "I don't deserve a woman as fine as you."

"Nonsense," she murmured. "Besides Pa, you're the most honorable man I know. Any woman would consider it a privilege to grow old with you. In fact, now that there are no longer any secrets between us. . ." Her words trailed away as she shyly lifted her face to his. "There aren't, are there?"

Matt grinned. "No. You know everything there is to know about me now. . .except for how much I love you."

Amanda thrilled to his words. With his free hand, Matt drew her closer and dipped his head, tenderly covering her lips with his.

Indian summer appeared to be visiting the mountain valley, though an earlier bout of cold weather had painted the hardwoods in bright hues of reds and yellows, amid the constant evergreen of pines. The day was warm and bright, perfect for the dedication of the new church.

Amanda stood beside Matt, hand in hand, as they stared up at the finished building of stone with the wooden double doors and gray roof. Narrow rectangular windows ran along the sides and at the front. A steeple perched on top, and Zeke's father had promised to donate a bell soon. Once the townsmen discovered Mr. Randall's decision to seize the land, they'd ridden on horseback one night, carrying torches, and gathered outside the lumberman's home, while Mr. Conners confronted him, saying, "We Conners don't take to a man who don't honor his word." Some of the hill people agreed, saying it less kindly, and Amanda had heard there'd even been threats.

The next morning a surly Mr. Randall approached Amanda's father with news that he'd reconsidered and the preacher could have the land. After that, more townspeople began to show up on Saturdays to help, as if the incident had jarred them into realizing that by working together, they could make a difference. The frequent rains ceased, and the church went up faster than Amanda would have believed possible.

"There for awhile I was wonderin' if your pa's dream would ever be realized," Matt said. "It feels good to see it happen."

Amanda smiled at him, so thankful for this man beside her. Next week, her own dream would be realized when she and Matt would become man and wife. It seemed fitting that theirs would be the first wedding to take place in the new church.

Remembering how she almost lost him the night the mob tried to hang him, she held his hand more tightly. Amanda had learned that once the posse arrived at the cave, they'd found no signs of the outlaws, but they did spot the two sets of cut ropes, proof that Matt was telling the truth. Then, two weeks ago, a stranger rode into town with a letter for Matt, one he was asked to deliver. The blank envelope contained a brief missive from Buck, stating that he'd left the gang and telling Matt not to worry about him any longer. A huge worry did seem to lift off Matt, making him smile more often, but both he and Amanda never ceased to pray for his brother.

"Amanda?"

Ivy's faint voice came from behind, and Amanda turned in surprise. Since Zeke had left town the morning after Matt had almost been lynched and hadn't been heard from since,

Ivy and her family had treated Matt and Amanda with contempt, which stung deeply.

Ivy looked as perfectly put together as ever, with her light-colored ringlets bouncing beneath a fashionable hat that matched her blue dress. Yet her eyes were troubled. "You've heard I'm going back East this week, to be a companion to my grandmother?"

Amanda gave a short nod, and Matt gently squeezed her hand.

"I may not always understand you or your choices," Ivy said, flicking a brief look Matt's way. "But I'll always love you like you were my sister. And I don't want to leave with ill feelings between us."

"Oh, I don't want that, either!"

Teary-eyed, the women hugged. Ivy was the first to break away. She swiped a finger underneath her eye and solemnly stared at Matt. "I won't tell you to take care of her, because I know you will. And I won't tell you that you're getting the best girl in all the hollow, because I think you know that already." She lifted her chin. "But I will tell you this: If ever I hear that you've done anything to hurt her, I'll be back here and on you so fast it'll make your head swim!"

Matt grinned. "You're a loyal friend to Amanda, Miss Randall, and you're welcome in our home any time."

"Yes, well. . ." His words clearly flustered her, and she gave him a polite smile. "Thank you."

"Ivy!"

The stern bellow came from her father, and Ivy turned an

anxious glance his way. She looked at Amanda again and clasped her hand. "I'll write. Good-bye."

Pensive, Amanda watched Ivy hurry to rejoin her parents, who stiffly stared at Amanda and Matt. Amanda knew Mr. and Mrs. Randall considered it an affront for her to refuse Zeke's offer of marriage and that they blamed her for their only son leaving the hollow without word to anyone. What leap of faith would it take to bridge the distance between families?

Matt gently tugged her hand, and she looked his way. "They're starting to gather," he said quietly. She nodded, and they joined the crowd of people at the corner of the building.

"Well, Matthew," the elderly Mrs. Conners said from behind them. "Now that ya'll be gettin' yerself a wife, I reckon there be no call for me to bring ya my strawberry per-serves."

Amanda whirled to face the gray-haired woman. "That was you?" She could feel Matt's curious look, but she smiled. "Oh, no, Mrs. Conners. Please, do! You make the sweetest preserves in all of Hickory Hollow. I could never make them so fine. Maybe you could show me how?"

The woman beamed and nodded, and Amanda faced the church again.

"What was that all about?" Matt whispered.

Her heart light, Amanda's smile only grew wider.

Amanda's pa took a place at the front, a twinkle in his eye that Amanda hadn't seen in a long time. "It gives me great pleasure to stand among you here today, to tell you that God does indeed fulfill His promises," he said once the buzz of voices died down. "When the Lord first showed me to build this church of stone, a lot of you questioned why we shouldn't make it from lumber instead."

A few men chuckled, and some nervously darted a look Mr. Randall's way. Grim-faced, he didn't move a muscle.

"In all honesty," her pa continued, "I never foresaw the many obstacles that would arise—the complications that would beset us—and it took a great leap of faith not to let circumstances overwhelm me." His voice filled with emotion, he looked at Matt. "I think it fitting that my soon-to-be son-in-law, who had such a hand in bringing this day about, should continue with the honors. Would you mind reading the dedication, Son?"

Matt paled, but he released Amanda's hand and moved forward, his limp more pronounced, proof he was nervous. Her father clapped Matt on the back, and Matt took off his hat, holding it against his heart as he faced the cornerstone.

"Despite all manner of hardship that rose against us," he slowly read aloud in a strong voice, "we, the people of Hickory Hollow, through the Lord's divine favor, have prevailed. From this day hence, may future generations who look upon this spot remember not the adversity that threatened to tear us apart; but rather let them recall the unity that bound us together, as one body, in building this House of God. On this eighth day of November, in the eighteen hundred and sixty-ninth year of our Lord, this church is hereby dedicated to God's glory, consecrated for His service, for all generations to come. So be it."

A cheer arose, and Amanda's eyes blurred with tears. Underneath the dedication were inscribed the names of all those men who helped build the church. Matt. Zeke. Her pa. The Wilson brothers. Mr. Whipple—all of them.

Her father held out his hand to her mother, who went to join her husband, and they led the townspeople up the steps and into the church for its first meeting. Matt rejoined Amanda, drawing her close to his side. His eyes were gentle. "This is a happy day for Hickory Hollow."

"For all generations to come," she agreed with a contented sigh, slipping an arm around his waist. "For our sons and daughters. And for our grandsons and granddaughters. Because finally, we're a town built in unity."

Matt took her other hand and brought it to his lips, and Amanda looked at him with all the love in her heart. Then, together, they walked into their new church home.

PAMELA GRIFFIN

Pamela lives in Texas and divides her time between family, church activities, and writing. She fully gave her life to the Lord Jesus Christ after a rebellious young adulthood and owes the fact that she's still alive today to a mother who steadfastly prayed and had faith that God could bring her wayward daughter "home." Pamela's main goal in writing Christian fiction is to help and encourage those who know the Lord and to plant a seed of hope in those who don't, through entertaining stories. She has six titles with Heartsong Presents and several novellas published by Barbour Publishing and other companies. Pamela invites you to check out her Web site: http://members.cowtown.net/PamelaGriffin/

Shirley, Goodness, and Mercy

by Kristy Dykes

Dedication

To my hero husband, Milton,
who is my collaborator in the deepest sense of the word—
he's believed in me, supported me, and cheered me on
in my calling to inspirational writing.

*The eyes of your understanding being enlightened;
that ye may know what is the hope of his calling.*
EPHESIANS 1:18

Chapter 1

Hickory Hollow, Missouri, 1894

Sitting on a grassy knoll overlooking her grandfather's church in the verdant valley below, Shirley Campbell smoothed her serviceable brown skirts and replaced a hairpin in the chignon high atop her head.

This was something she never did—sit and while away time. But her beloved grandmother's burial that morning prompted her mother to give her some time away from the never-ending farm work.

"Oh, Grandmother," she whispered as her eyes misted over, "I loved you so. You were the only one who truly understood me. We were like knitted souls, you and I." A tear trickled down her cheek followed by a deluge, and she wiped her face with her hanky and kept it at the ready instead of tucking it back in her waistband. "Such good times we had together. How will I make it without you?"

Holding her well-worn copy of *Little Women*, she stroked

its cover as reverently as if it were the family Bible that held a prominent place in the Campbells' farmhouse.

"How you used to enjoy it when I would read to you from these pages."

When her grandmother came down with the heart ailment, she asked for Shirley—of all the grandchildren—to come and help her one afternoon a week. Shirley soon found out that her grandmother didn't want help with dishes and sweeping. As the preacher's wife, her grandmother was besieged with offers of help from the saintly ranks. No, what Grandmother really wanted was for Shirley to read to her from the pages of *Little Women,* of all things.

Where Grandmother got the book, Shirley never knew, or why she wanted Shirley to read to her at all, she never could fathom. But from the very first, Shirley devoured the heartwarming tale of the four charming young ladies and their doting mother in prim and proper New England—a world away from Hickory Hollow, Missouri, both in distance and in deportment. She had read *Little Women* so often in the past year, she knew certain passages by heart.

Shirley envisioned the plucky heroine, Jo March, and quickly found the description of her in the opening pages of the book:

> *Jo was very tall, thin, and brown, and reminded one of a colt. . . . She had a decided mouth, a comical nose, and sharp gray eyes which appeared to see everything, and were by turns fierce, funny, or thoughtful.*

Her long, thick hair was her one beauty.

"Sounds like me." Shirley smiled as she thought of Jo, the fledgling writer who every few weeks would don her scribbling suit and "fall into a vortex."

"Does genius burn?" Jo's sisters would ask when they popped their heads in the door of her attic writing room.

Shirley flipped to the passage about Jo's literary endeavors and read aloud:

> *When the writing fit came on, she gave herself up to it with entire abandon. . .while she sat safe and happy in an imaginary world, full of friends almost as real and dear to her as any in the flesh.*

Shirley found the entry she loved about the girls' devoted mother. Marmee, they called her:

> *She was not elegantly dressed, but a noble-looking woman, and the girls thought the gray cloak and unfashionable bonnet covered the most splendid mother in the world. . . . The first sound in the morning was her voice as she went about the house singing like a lark, and the last song at night was the same cheery sound.*

She could see Marmee in her big armchair surrounded by her adoring daughters, encouraging them in their pursuits: Meg in her role as little mother to the younger girls; Jo in her writing ambitions; Beth in her piano playing; and Amy in her artistic leanings. Marmee was their comrade, but more than that, she was their encourager, their champion in the relentless quest of their goals and aspirations.

"Oh, to have a mother like Marmee March." Immediately, Shirley felt ashamed for voicing such an errant thought. Her mother was a good mother, a wonderful mother, but she was. . .she was. . .what was Mama? How best to describe her?

"Ah, Mama." Pictures of her mother appeared before her eyes as if they'd popped out of the picture book she treasured as a tyke, the only book she ever owned as a child, the book that was torn up long ago by her sister Gladly, though Shirley now had a few books she could call her own such as *Webster's Dictionary* and *Shakespeare's Plays*.

Thinking of Mama—Mama at the washtub on Mondays, scrubbing clothes and bed linens and white curtains, getting the dirt out with a vengeance, then starching and ironing each item, then folding and putting them away, week in and week out with never a letup in her strict regimen.

Mama at the woodstove morning, noon, and night, turning out mouthwatering meals and cakes and pies and other delectable dishes.

"Be sure and get Amanda Campbell to bring her strawberry pie," folks were known to say. Or her pecan pie or her cinnamon peach cobbler or a host of other sweets she could whip up in the blink of an eye.

Back to the mental pictures. Mama beating the rugs.

Mama tending the garden. Mama sewing the family's clothing. Mama getting her brood to Grandfather Hodges's little stone church in the wildwood and, before Shirley took over the children's Sunday school class, Mama herself teaching it, making sure the Campbell children as well as the other youngsters hid the Holy Scriptures in their hearts. Mama visiting the poor of the community and the infirm in the congregation, sometimes bringing them good things from her kitchen.

Mama, Mama, Mama. . .always working, always going, always doing, a constant buzz of activity, like a honeybee on a hyacinth, never just being. . .or feeling. . .or dreaming. . .like Shirley often did.

Oh, it wasn't that Shirley shirked her work. She could turn out a meal almost as fast as her mother, and her fancy stitchwork was praised all over Hickory Hollow by friends and family alike. After all the chores were done that a farm demanded, she helped Grandfather Hodges nearly as much as Mama did with what he called divine service. Besides comforting the sick and bruised of heart, Shirley corralled all the children under the hickory trees every Sunday afternoon in the warm months and taught them Sunday school lessons, and they couldn't wait to get there every week to hear her.

"Shirley makes them Bible stories come alive right before our eyes," the tykes told their parents.

Most certainly, she always did her part wherever and whatever the workload required, but as she toiled every day, she thought and she dreamed and she saw and she felt. . . .

"You've got your head in the clouds, Shirley," Mama was prone to say. "That won't stand you well in life."

Shirley had tried to talk to her mother once, a few months back. She confided in her about how she saw and felt things so deeply, how she dreamed and aspired and longed for—what, she knew not. But she was hoping her mother would know and could help her.

"Mama, at times it seems my musings and longings are otherworldly," she told her, "so far away, something distant and unattainable, yet so yearned for. Oh, what does it all mean?"

She even gathered the courage to tell her mother about the stories that bubbled up inside her and ached to be shared with the world.

Mama only said, "Fiddle-faddle, Shirley Campbell. Such as that won't find you a good man. You'd best forget about that froth and frippery and put your head to getting yourself a husband. After all, you're eighteen now, soon to be nineteen."

Shirley rolled her sleeves a mite higher and unfastened the top button of her high collar to let in some air. Oh, if only she had the time to get those stories down on paper. Paper? Well, not the fancy, store-bought kind. They could never afford that. But she'd be willing to write them on plain brown wrappers and old envelopes, if only she had the time.

Maybe she could get up earlier and write before breakfast. But she was already getting up at dawn, like Mama and Papa did. And if she got up before break of day, there would be no light. And her mother would never allow her to waste lamp oil for. . .for froth and frippery. She winced, thinking of those hateful words Mama used to describe her. . .her dreams.

No, getting up before dawn wasn't the answer. And neither was writing on Sunday, the day of rest. She let out a little snort. By the time she got back from morning service, ate dinner, then headed back to teach her Sunday school class, the day was over. The last moments on Sunday evenings were consumed with helping Mama tend the children. Always the children were clamoring for Shirley's attention in the everyday busyness of life—her little brothers and sister washed, dressed, and fed, over and over again, and sewed for and cooked for and readied for school.

Perhaps she could find a few minutes every now and then and get her musings recorded. She knew with a surety that she would never find large blocks of time to devote to her writing endeavors. It would have to be in bits and snippets. Yes, that was the answer. And when a sufficient number of days passed, she would have whole stories fleshed out.

So happy did she feel, so grateful she was for a resolve to her dilemma, she laughed as she hugged her knees to her, almost like it was Grandmother she was embracing, and her heart beat hard in its perch in her chest. For if she could get her stories written down—it was a long shot, yes, but perhaps—she could become an authoress.

Like Jo March!

The thought was so strong and so weighty with all its implications, for a moment she almost couldn't breathe. Somehow, some way, certainly so, she could become an authoress.

Like Louisa Mae Alcott!

With childlike abandonment, she leapt to her feet. Hugging the book to her, she dashed through the wild spring daisies. So hard and so fast did she run, she panted like Papa's hunting dog on a chase, hurting from the stitch in her side.

But she kept on running with not a care in the world, and she called out to Jo March and to Louisa Mae Alcott and told them that one day, she, too, would be joining their elite ranks, and it seemed they answered her back.

Determination and diligence are the pathway, my dear, and if you possess those, you will succeed in your quest.

Their advice thrilled her, for indeed, she had a goodly portion of both.

When she came to a tall stand of hickories and pines and beeches with a magnolia or two among them, she halted to catch her breath. With wonderment, she noted that the singing of the birds was almost as loud as the singing in her soul.

For a long eon she stood there, drinking in the serenity of the sight, robins and jays zipping between the towering hickory trees and lush chortleberry bushes, the hummingbirds buzzing in profusion about the honeysuckle vines, and she reveled in all that was being birthed in her heart and soul, thanking the heavenly Father for this revelation.

Presently, still clutching *Little Women,* she came to the meandering brook that bordered Grandfather's church far downstream. She stopped for a moment and read Miss Alcott's short biography in the front of the book:

Louisa Alcott's first story was published when she was twenty. When she was twenty-three, things began to improve. A book of hers sold well. She went to Europe a few years later, and then came her great success: the publication of Little Women in 1868. Good Wives, Little Men, and Jo's Boys followed. These four books made her name and her fortune.

In awe, Shirley took up her trek beside the gently flowing, crystal-clear, gurgling brook, visions of grandeur appearing before her eyes. . . .

Miss Shirley Campbell, authoress, being feted at a tea among society's cream of the crop.

Miss Shirley Campbell, authoress, autographing her books at a book signing in a large city.

"Shirley," someone called from a far place.

Miss Shirley Campbell, authoress, speaking before a distinguished crowd at a university.

"Mama's needing you, Shirley," came the voice again, this time with a whine. "Why'd you stay gone so long?"

Miss Shirley Campbell, authoress, hobnobbing in the North and the South and the East and the West with the literary greats of the United States—no, the world.

"Mama said to come right now. There's a horde of people eating at Grandmother's house, and we've used every plate in her cupboard, as well as our plates from home—not to mention all of Aunt Charmaine's. Mama said you and I are to do the dishes and to be quick about it."

Shirley looked over and was startled to see her sixteen-year-old sister Gladly on the other side of the brook. It was as if she had dropped down from the sky. Only Gladly was no angel.

"Gladly?" Shirley said blankly, taking a deep breath, trying desperately to climb down from the dais at the university where she was standing, trying to disengage herself from the places she had soared.

"If you don't come right now, Shirley Campbell," Gladly yelled, "I'll tell Mama your wits have gone a-woolgathering again."

Suddenly, Shirley was disengaged. . .

from the high-society tea. . .

from the big-city book signing. . .

from the university. . .

and from hobnobbing with the literary greats.

She was also disengaged from her dreams of becoming an authoress.

They were dashed to the ground. For after all, she was only Shirley Campbell, a plain-looking, little-educated farm girl from Hickory Hollow, Missouri, with nothing but a life of drudgery ahead of her.

"Just like Mama's," she said under her breath. With an audible groan, she turned and crossed the brook pell-mell over the large, flat stones Grandfather had positioned decades ago when he was building his church. Now she used them to make her way to. . .to. . .the work that awaited her.

Chapter 2

The Reverend Forrest Townsend drove his horse and buggy down the street to the social for the young people of his congregation, thinking about the letter he had received in the mail from the Reverend Hodges in Hickory Hollow. He planned to answer it first thing tomorrow—a firm no.

What the Reverend Hodges requested—as well as how he requested it—was far off the beaten path. Why, pastoral changes were simply not carried out in the manner he suggested. Forrest's late father, a bishop in the church, would highly question the reverend's tactics. There were procedures and protocol to follow.

As Prancer *clip-clopped* down the road, Forrest envisioned the Reverend Hodges's unusual letter, the missive that seemed to be branded in his mind:

Dear Rev. Townsend,
   I've come to know of you and your ministry through

the church conference. I reside in a little place called Hickory Hollow. I have highly admired you—and your father before he passed on—and I've heard nothing but the very best about you.

Twenty-four years ago, we built and dedicated our little church in the wildwood to the glory of God. Now I am old. My wife passed away, and I can no longer shoulder the burden of pastoring. I know this town is not as big as the one you are now living in, but Hickory Hollow has a host of good people with big hearts.

I am writing to ask if you will accept the pastorate of my church. I believe you will find ministry here rewarding and fulfilling. Because I started this church, my heart is tied up in it, and I want the very best for it. I feel that with your fine qualities and capabilities, you are the man who should fill my shoes.

Of course, I want God's will in the matter. As I prayed, I felt strongly impressed that you could be the one—if God deals with your heart. Will you seek the Lord about this matter and then let me know your answer? I would deeply appreciate this.

One last thing. Please do not share this matter abroad. No one in Hickory Hollow knows of my intentions.

Sincerely,
Preacher Anson Hodges

Riding down the road, Forrest looked at the lovely brick homes that lined the street. Why would he want to leave

First Church of Harrisonburg? He had been here two years, and he didn't see any need to change pastorates. The congregation had grown, and besides, it was situated prominently on Main Street. The Reverend Hodges's place of ministry was a church in a wildwood. Why move down and take a little country congregation when he could continue serving this fine city parish?

He thought of the ramifications if he were to accept the Reverend Hodges's offer. In their church conference, the bigger one's congregation was, the higher one could climb on the ladder of ministerial success. There were positions of prestige available in the conference such as becoming a bishop, a leader of ministers as his late father had been, and there were certain steps one took to achieve a role such as that. Perhaps a lofty position was in his future. Frankly, he hoped so. Pastoring people got tiresome at times, whereas pastoring pastors was an enticing thought. The size of the congregation he served definitely had bearing on his future, so why leave his city church?

He turned down another street and continued on his way, thinking about his swelling membership and the finances that accompanied it. Perhaps he would send an offering from his church fund to help the Reverend Hodges's church. That was how he could assist the church in Hickory Hollow. He wouldn't have to move there to help them. Sending money would suffice. Perhaps one of the burdens the Reverend Hodges was facing was a lack of funds. Perhaps that played a role in his intended resignation.

"If I send him some money," Forrest mused aloud, "maybe that will buoy him up and help him continue in his pastoral ministry until a future date."

Forrest had it all figured out. He was a man of action, who put foresight and forethought into things. He knew how to run ministries and programs in churches. He prided himself on that. Of a certainty, his plan to send funds to the little church in the wildwood was the answer to this situation.

"Giddyap," he said gingerly, realizing he'd let Prancer slow to a walk. "Let's go, Girl. Miss Euphemia Devine is waiting." As his horse set off at a clipped pace, Forrest wondered what Miss Devine would think of the Reverend Hodges's request.

If things were to develop between him and Miss Devine, how would she take to moving to a country town when she was a city girl? She was born with a silver spoon in her mouth and had never lacked for anything, especially the fashionable things of life. Her parents doted on her and kept her steeped to the lips in finery.

From the moment Forrest had first met Miss Devine, he had admired her. She was an intelligent, well-bred young woman, and besides that, she was a feast for the eyes with her delicate blond beauty and piercing blue eyes. A regular snow maiden, she was.

Lately, he'd allowed time for serious matrimonial musings. He would make sure he married a woman who could contribute to his ministry. That was important to him—at the top of the list even. He smiled. Miss Devine would be a fine asset to his pastoral ministry.

Long ago he'd made up his mind that whatever woman he chose must have a keen appreciation for the Lord's business. That was the main requirement he was looking for, and Miss Devine fit the bill admirably. She was a chaperone for the young people's group and had given of her time untiringly in this endeavor.

He smiled again. Things were well on their way to turning out splendidly for him in the matrimonial department, namely with Miss Devine.

That was another reason he would never accept the Reverend Hodges's offer. He could not envision Miss Euphemia Devine as a country parson's wife. She would miss her china-painting lessons and her charcoal portraiture club and her gracious entertaining of society women. No, he would not ask that of her.

And the last reason he would not consider the Reverend Hodges's request was because he didn't care to live in Hickory Hollow. It was a rough sector of the state—or at least it used to be. Everyone knew that, years ago, outlaw gangs had holed up around Hickory Hollow and caused a lot of trouble. Their evil influence was probably still lurking, and he certainly didn't want to take on any more trouble than was necessary.

He would not give the offer another thought. But what he would think about was Miss Devine—with pleasure. Within a quarter hour, she would be sitting beside him on the buckboard, wearing her frip and finery that always made him proud. They would ride in the moonlight to the young people's social, enjoying genteel conversation and occasional covert glances between them.

When the time was right, he would ask for her hand in matrimony.

He smiled as he thought about Webster's definition of "divine," a word that so closely matched Miss Euphemia's surname, "Devine." He had looked it up last night on a whim to get an exact definition.

"Superb. Heavenly. Proceeding directly from God."

He smiled again. "Most apropos, Miss Devine. Divinely inspired? Giddyap, Prancer," he called with gusto. He thought about the verb "divine." Webster's said it meant to perceive intuitively. "I divine that a divine girl is in the future for me. I wonder if she'll be a Devine girl?"

With that welcome prospect in mind, he threw back his head and chuckled heartily.

Chapter 3

"You're doing what, Pa?" Shirley's mother exclaimed, her rocker suddenly motionless.

Shirley could only watch the interchange between her grandfather and her mother on the porch, where all three of them were sitting on Saturday afternoon, her and Mama shelling pecans. Well, her anyway. Mama's hands were momentarily stilled from their busyness, rigid in tight fists, and words were flying too fast for Shirley to get one in edgewise.

"You can't mean this," her mother said, provocation in her voice. She put her bowl of pecans on the floor with a plunk.

"Yes, I do mean it. I'm resigning." Grandfather had that unwavering look to his eyes, and his jaw was firmly set.

"But Pa, you're a strong man yet, even with the years on you. There's no need to do this—"

"I don't have the will or the inclination to continue pastoring." None of them was rocking now. It was as quiet as a schoolhouse on a summer day.

"But we all help out at the church, Pa. You know that. Shirley, Matthew, Edmund, me, all the others—"

"This church needs more than piecemeal parcels. And it needs more than Hodgeses and Campbells and Randalls. If it's going to grow, it's got to have fresh ideas and a new young preacher to lead it."

"But you started this church. You gave it your heart and soul—"

"And it won't be easy leaving it—as its preacher, that is. I'll always live in Hickory Hollow. I'm moving out of the parsonage and in with Edmund and his family, but I'll still attend church every time the door's opened."

"Who could possibly take your place?" Mama's eyebrows were upside-down U's.

"His name is the Reverend Forrest Townsend." Grandfather paused, amusement written in his eyes. "That's what city folks call preachers. 'The Reverend.' Remember that, you hear?"

"You've already secured a replacement?"

"When will the new preacher arrive?" Shirley managed to interject. "I mean, the new reverend?"

"On Thursday of next week. I plan to resign to the congregation in the morning. I figure on having my things out of the parsonage by Monday afternoon, and you womenfolk can clean it Tuesday and Wednesday. He can move in on Thursday—"

"Maybe you can get the Randall women to help you,"

Mama said, sounding a little angry.

Shirley thought about her mother's peculiar comment regarding the Randalls, and her mind wandered to the feud that started years ago when Mama and Papa began courting. Zeke Randall, Mama's former suitor—or at least he thought he was—hadn't liked it one bit when Papa came along. Not long after, Zeke left town. Later, after Mama and Papa married, Zeke came back with his uppity new wife, and through the years there'd been contention between the two families, all of it instigated by the Randalls. Thankfully, Zeke's sister, Ivy, who lived in the East, had continued to be Mama's best friend.

"It'll take a leap of faith to make things right between the Campbells and the Randalls," Mama said when the feud would flare up occasionally.

"A new preacher in Hickory Hollow. . ." Mama's words trailed off, jarring Shirley from her musings.

Grandfather let out a long sigh. "Ah, Amanda, the apple of my eye. Did you think I'd keep preaching until my toes turned up?"

"I suppose I did." A sob shook Mama's voice. "It never crossed my mind that any other preacher would stand behind the pulpit you built with your own hands in the church you and Matthew carved out of the woods. And then, with Ma dying and all. . ." Tears trickled down her cheeks, but she made no move to wipe them away.

He reached over and patted her hands, which were limp now, then handed her his handkerchief, and she dabbed at her tears. "This is for the best. You'll see. The town is growing.

And the church needs to grow, too. I believe the key will be a new young preacher. And this one is known across the Missouri conference for his innovative ways."

"Grandfather's right, Mama," Shirley chimed in. "This new preacher—what's his name, Grandfather?"

"The Reverend Forrest Townsend."

"The Reverend Forrest Townsend will probably institute new programs and attract new people," Shirley went on. "And then he'll generate more workers for divine service."

"And after the Reverend Townsend builds up the congregation," Grandfather said, "maybe he'll add wings onto the church for more space."

Shirley's mother picked up her bowl of pecans and began to rock, and Shirley and her grandfather began rocking, too. "Perhaps you're right, Pa."

"That's my girl."

The rockers shifted back and forth, and Grandfather hummed "Blessed Assurance," and the pecans came loose from their shells under nimble fingers, and the perfume of flowers borne on a gentle spring breeze filled the air.

"As I said earlier," Grandfather said, "this is the best thing that's happened to our church in a long while—getting a new young preacher. . .I mean a reverend." He paused. "And it might be the best thing that ever happened to you, Shirley."

"What do you mean, Grandfather?"

"The Reverend Townsend's not married."

"He's not?" Her mother's face was as bright as a ray of sunshine.

"What does that have to do with me?" Shirley spouted, fighting the consternation she felt rising inside of her. She had to be respectful, she reminded herself. That was her raising. But it was hard. Why was everyone trying to get her married off? Then her conscience assailed her. Well, not everyone. But certainly Mama was. And now Grandfather. "Where is Rev. Townsend from?" Shirley asked sweetly, trying to distract them.

"Harrisonburg. Listen well, Shirley. You couldn't find a finer husband in all the world than the Reverend Townsend."

I'm not looking for a husband, Grandfather, especially not a preacher-husband. I'm looking for. . .oh, what am I looking for? The authoress visions were back, parading before her mind's eye.

"You're a whole year older than I was when Matthew Campbell came to Hickory Hollow," her mother said, a sentimental look in her light green eyes. "And it didn't take me long to find out he was the man for me."

"Shirley?" Grandfather asked, a gentleness in his tone.

"Yes, Sir?" Shirley studied the black veins on the brown hull of a pecan.

"Rev. Townsend couldn't find a finer wife in all the world than you, Girl. You'd make a fine preacher's wife, just like your dear departed grandmother. Saint and sinner alike loved her to pieces."

"If Shirley'll mind her p's and q's," her mother said, "I believe she can lasso this new preacher—"

"I don't want to lasso the. . .the reverend." Shirley jumped up and set her bowl on the floor with a thud, a few pecans jumping over the rim and landing on the porch. "I don't want to lasso anybody. I want. . .I want. . ." She dashed across the floorboards and jerked open the door. "I. . .oh, never mind. You wouldn't understand. Neither one of you."

The door slammed behind her.

❧

That evening, as Shirley lay abed beside Gladly, with little Milcah snuggled in the trundle to her side, she made a firm resolve. *I'm staying as far away as possible from the Reverend Townsend. I want nothing to do with him.*

Being a preacher's wife was the ultimate life of drudgery, worse than farmwork even, and she wanted better things for herself—and for her family. Besides that, even if being a preacher's wife somehow fell to be her lot in life, she couldn't do it. She was simply unequipped. For sure, she would steer clear of the Reverend Townsend. She would resign her afternoon Sunday school class immediately. That way, she would only see him at Sunday morning services. That would suit her just fine.

Why, I wouldn't marry a preacher if he was the last man in the world.

Chapter 4

S o this is the girl I've heard so much about," Forrest said of the young woman standing beside the elderly Reverend Hodges. Forrest was in the doorway, greeting his new parishioners in Hickory Hollow as they filed by. He smiled—broadly. "Let's see, Rev. Hodges," he said, "didn't you tell me your granddaughter's name is Shirley?"

"That's right. This is my granddaughter Shirley Campbell. Shirley, this is the Reverend Forrest Townsend." He nudged Forrest in the ribs. "You'll have to get her to tell you how her mother came to name her Shirley."

Forrest thrust out his hand for a shake, but for some reason the young woman didn't respond in like fashion. "It's a pleasure to meet you, Miss Campbell. Your grandfather's given me a glowing report of you and your dedication to the Lord's business." This was a woman he wanted to get to know—and know well.

With hesitation, the young woman finally shook his proffered hand, then released it as if she had touched a hot coal. "Thank you, Preach—" She stopped abruptly. "Reverend."

Her look was polite but unfriendly, and her tone was definitely clipped.

Forrest fiddled with his tie. What was wrong with Miss Campbell? Her grandfather had raved about her, going on and on about her duty and her devotion and her distinction, that she was of noble character, honorable. Yet she was indifferent and most decidedly inelegant—and without proper decorum it seemed.

"I'm delighted to make your acquaintance," Forrest said, forcing cheer into his voice, trying with all his might to dispel the sudden dampening of the pleasant spring air.

Rev. Hodges slipped his arm around the young woman. "Shirley, I told Forrest the day he was moving into the parsonage that you were sure to be along any time. I told him, 'If there's a church activity going on, Shirley'll be there if nobody else shows up.' Only, you didn't show up."

She looked at her plain brown shoes that peeked from beneath her plain blue skirts. "I–I. . ."

Forrest felt the need to put the young woman at ease. "Well, Miss Campbell, as I said earlier, it's a pleasure to meet you. Your grandfather has my curiosity piqued. One of these days, you'll have to tell me whom you were named after."

"Not named after," the young woman spoke up, almost in rebuke. "How I came to be named Shirley."

"It's a unique story that'll bring you a chuckle or two," Rev. Hodges said.

"I see." Forrest rocked up and down on his feet, toe to heel, heel to toe. He was indeed seeing a number of things. First, he was seeing that for some reason Miss Campbell had no use for him. That was all right. He had no use for her, either. Second, he was seeing a drab young woman. Oh, she wasn't drab in her looks so much. In fact, she was quite attractive with her thick swath of dark hair and her exquisite features and her piercing gray eyes that seemed to read your thoughts. But in dress and deportment, she was as countrified and unpolished a woman as ever he'd come across, a woman who would never be of interest to him.

His mind flitted to Miss Euphemia Devine and her winsome, charming ways. She could come up with witty sayings at the drop of a hanky. The belle of the ball was a good way to describe her. But it was no use thinking about her. She let him know in no uncertain terms that she thought his move to Hickory Hollow was folly.

"There you are, Reverend," called the Widow Ford from the bottom of the steps. She was adjusting her hatstrings under her double chin, which jiggled every time she talked. She dabbed behind her ears with her handkerchief, then moved it around to the back of her neck and rubbed hard like a waterfall was back there. Forrest had to squelch a smile as he pictured a Niagara Falls of perspiration gushing over her.

"Are you almost ready, Reverend? I'm about to wilt in this heat, April though it is. Wonder what August will bring us?" Mrs. Ford touched her rotund midsection. "I hope my gall bladder doesn't get to acting up on me again." She shook her head from side to side, and her double chin jiggled all the more. "My baking hen will be baked clean off the bones if we don't get home soon. Are you finished talking yet?"

"Have a good day, Reverend." Miss Campbell whisked

down the steps and in moments was out of view, and Forrest could only wonder.

"I asked, are you coming now?" the Widow Ford piped up.

"Why, yes, Mrs. Ford," he said distractedly, still thinking about Miss Campbell. "I'll be right along."

"Then I'll be on my way and get my baking hen out of the oven. You'll be there directly, Reverend?"

He nodded. "And thank you for your gracious invitation to join you for Sunday dinner. I'm looking forward to spending time with you."

"Same here, Reverend." She turned, her voluminous, out-of-date skirts swishing, and made her way down the walk.

The elderly Reverend Hodges nudged Forrest in the ribs, twinkles dancing in his eyes. It was a mannerism Forrest was quickly growing familiar with. Why, if Rev. Hodges continued this practice, Forrest would have sore ribs at every turn.

"That's the last time you'll be able to say you're looking forward to spending time with the Widow Ford," Rev. Hodges said, the twinkles still in his eyes.

"I don't catch your drift." Forrest had to force his thoughts back to the Widow Ford and to what the Reverend Hodges was saying. He was still brooding over Miss Campbell's abrupt departure.

"The Widow Ford's known for her organ recitals."

"She plays the organ?" Forrest came alive. "That's wonderful! Why didn't she play this morning? Singing to organ accompaniment is much better than a cappella."

Rev. Hodges nudged him yet again. "Organ recitals, Forrest. Liver. Heart. Spleen. Gall bladder."

Forrest threw his head back and laughed, finally catching on. "Every church is blessed with at least one of those."

Rev. Hodges winked at Forrest. "The Widow Ford is a kind old soul, but oh, the pains she bears—and she recites every last one of them."

In a jovial mood, Forrest clasped his hands together and looked heavenward. "Lord, give me patience." In his heart, he meant every word.

❧

Forrest thought about his new pastorate in Hickory Hollow as he drove toward the Widow Ford's house. The church was small, but it was growing on him. When he'd first read Rev. Hodges's letter of invitation, he thought to answer with a firm no. But he finally decided that taking a small church and helping it grow into a big one would be an excellent entry on his list of ministerial accomplishments.

The parishioners were growing on him, too. All except one—namely, Miss Campbell, who thought she was Miss Panjandrum when she was nothing but a country mouse. He recalled their conversation—or rather, lack of one—on the church steps a half hour ago. Why had she acted that way? It was a snubbing if ever he'd seen one.

"Hmmmph," he snorted. "Miss Campbell is playing that age-old game of Hard to Get. I can play it, too. Only my game won't have the same goal Miss Campbell's obviously does. Why, I wouldn't have her on a silver platter."

Chapter 5

Standing in front of the discolored mirror that hung over the bureau in the cubbyhole of a room she and her two sisters shared, Shirley drew her long dark hair into its usual chignon and pushed her combs firmly into the sides.

"My one beauty," she said, peering closely at herself. "Just like Jo March's hair." She fluffed the front part, silently thanking the curl papers that they had done their job. She endured the torture devices every Saturday night and for special occasions. Today was one of those—the Sunday school picnic.

"If only I'd been born with beauty." She put down her brush and tidied up the top of the bureau. "But when the Good Lord was passing out looks, I thought He said, 'Books,' and I said, 'Give me plenty of those.' "

She smiled at her little joke. As she looked down, she saw a smudge on one of her cuffs and brushed it away, grateful to see the dirt disappear so easily. She was wearing her second-best shirtwaist, and she had nothing else presentable to change into except her best, which she had to save for Sunday.

She wondered why Mama wanted her to go to the Sunday school picnic. She had quit teaching her class right before Rev. Townsend came and had no connection with Sunday school now. Mama could've told her to take the children and come back home. The corn was in, had been all week, and Mama needed her. They had worked like Trojans, the lot of them—even little Milcah. Mama had set the tyke to shucking ear after ear so she could can some of it to use next winter. The rest would go to market. So why was Mama wanting her to go today?

Rev. Townsend, of course.

Shirley thought about their new preacher's looksome ways. His hair was as dark as hers, and his eyes were about the same shade of gray. But that was where the likeness stopped. Where she was plain, he was perfect with his handsome features, his fine chiseled jaw, and his even, white teeth. Besides that, he was tall and robust and cut a dashing figure in his expensive suits and ties—sometimes string, sometimes cravat-style.

She pondered over their differences again. In the looks arena, she was a wren. He was a cardinal. In the brains arena, she was a simpleton. He had the knowledge of the world. In the deportment arena, she was raw, green, a slow coach. He was a brilliant-cut diamond.

Her mother must be intending to thrust them together at every opportunity. Matchmaking Mama. That was what she should be called. Shirley didn't even feel a smile coming on at that thought. It only conjured up a frown.

"If you don't hurry up, Shirley Campbell, we'll be late for

the picnic," her sister Gladly whined through the wall. A sharp rap sounded on the door.

"Hold your horses, Gladly. There's plenty of time." Shirley put on her frumpy-looking hat, lamenting her lack of a new one. But it was not to be. There were simply too many mouths to feed in the Campbell household for such things as that. Perhaps she could replace the ribbons come fall, when the crops were in and accounted for. That was what she had done for two years in a row without complaint, though her mother had detected her desire for a new one.

"I never cared much for fripperies," Mama whispered to her when they were purchasing new ribbons last year, "but when you get married, maybe your husband can buy you a new hat—or two or three—if that's what you think will truly make you happy."

In the last year or so, there had been a reference to marriage in nearly every conversation between them. Not that Shirley didn't want to get married someday. Of course she did. She wanted love and marriage and children, what all women wanted. But the key word was "someday." Before the inevitable someday came around for her, she wanted to see her goals and aspirations fulfilled. Her thoughts drifted to the high-society tea, and the book signings, and the university dais, and the literary greats.

"Shirley!"

"I'm coming." She grabbed her frayed reticule from the hook on the wall, resolving to keep it turned toward her skirts so no one would see the worn spots.

"Yes, I'm coming," she whispered to the dreams of her

heart as she dashed out the door.

৯৯

Forrest made his way out of the sanctuary and into the churchyard, greeting his parishioners who milled about the grounds. Children's voices called out to each other from both sides of the church, and the smell of good things to eat wafted through the air. He noted that even old Mr. Wilbur, a vet from the War Between the States, was there. Sunday school picnics were always well attended. Too bad Sunday school wasn't. But he would soon change that.

In the distance, he saw Miss Campbell alight from her wagon, her brothers and sisters clambering down almost before she got it stopped. When she approached with a basket on her arm, he took a step toward her.

"I'm surprised to see you here, Miss Campbell," he said. He prided himself that he kept the acrimony out of his voice. He had been teaching her class for each of the six weeks since he became pastor. The thought filled him with chagrin—he, the parson, having to contend with twenty-seven wriggly, writhing, hot, and sweaty children—with no help. Didn't country churches know that pastors didn't teach children's classes? That there were more important things for pastors to do? Apparently not.

"Since you gave up your Sunday school class, I assumed you wouldn't be attending today," he added.

"I had to bring my brothers and my sisters," she said, her tone clipped as usual. "Mama and Papa—neither one could bring them. The corn is in."

"I see, Miss Campbell." This time, the acrimony was

125

evident. *Forrest, you're the pastor. "Be ye kind, one to another, tenderhearted, forgiving each other,"* he quoted silently. He forced a smile. "We welcome you."

She touched the basket at her arm. "Where shall I put this?"

He pointed to sawhorse tables on the side of the church, under a canopy of hickories. "Over there."

She made her way to a table, delivered her basket to three young matrons from the congregation, and came back to the front of the church. "Rev. Townsend?" She held her reticule in front of her, her fingers working furiously, squeezing each fringed knot at the bottom.

He noticed spots that were badly frayed on her small bag and couldn't help but compare it to Miss Devine's showy accoutrements. She had the good fortune to be born on the sunny side of the hedge. Obviously, Miss Campbell didn't.

"I was wondering. Do you need any help. . .with the games?"

"I hadn't planned on games."

"No games at a Sunday school picnic?" Her eyebrows shot up above her light gray eyes.

He tried not to stare. Was she criticizing him? He'd been to plenty of Sunday school picnics, and he knew very well that there were games of all sorts and sometimes wagon rides. But those were picnics he didn't have to plan. This picnic, he decided, would be just that—a picnic. They would eat and visit, and then they would go home.

"May I organize some games?"

Conscience pricking you, Miss Campbell? he thought but didn't say.

"I was thinking of Blind Man's Bluff and Mother, May I? And maybe a few more," she persisted.

"Certainly. I welcome your participation." *In more ways than one. Why don't you take your class back and relieve me of this burden?*

"Thank you, Reverend. I'll get a game started, then." She looked at him as if waiting for his permission.

"Yes. Meantime, I'll ask the ladies to prepare the food for serving. After we eat, you can have one more game, and then we'll dismiss." *Thank the Lord.*

❧

All afternoon, Shirley led the children in games and frolics to their hearts' content. She even let them wade in the creek, hovering over them like a hen over her chicks, making sure not a one suffered an injury. That was how it was when she taught their Sunday school class, watching them as intently as if they were her brothers and sisters.

Though she hated to admit it, she admired Rev. Townsend for taking on the challenge of teaching her class. He loved children as much as she did.

"Let's have a play party," shouted a snaggletoothed, red-headed little boy. "Let's do Skip to My Lou."

"Yes, my favorite," called out a flaxen-haired young miss.

"All right, children," Shirley said. "One last game. A play party, it is. Form two lines, please." She touched the snaggle-toothed boy on the shoulders. "Timothy is first in this line." She pointed to a spot six feet away. "Millie will be the first in the other line. Everyone else, get behind them."

The children scurried to form two lines, and on a lark, Shirley joined the first one.

"You're playing, Miss Shirley?" a little girl said from behind, delight in her eyes.

"Yes, I thought to. Now, children. Settle down. I need to get a head count." That done, she realized the second line was a person short. This was a partner game.

From out of nowhere it seemed, Rev. Townsend stepped up and joined in. "I'll make it an even number."

Shirley was surprised. "You will?"

"Yes."

"But we skip."

"I understand."

"And we sing."

He nodded.

"You know how to play Skip to My Lou?"

"Of course. I've seen it done many times."

She swept her gaze away from him, wondering. Why would he want to participate in a children's game? Ah, because he taught their class. He was trying to build camaraderie with them, and that made her admire him all the more. A city preacher who would skip with country children? Why, he was ten feet tall in her eyes.

"It's time to begin, children," she announced. "You know what to do."

She led them in the song, and as they sang lustily, a child from each line formed a partnership with a child from the other line and skipped down the center aisle, holding hands. When their turn was finished, two more formed a partnership and took their turn skipping and holding hands down the center aisle.

Flies in the buttermilk, shoo, shoo, shoo!
Flies in the buttermilk, shoo, shoo, shoo!
Flies in the buttermilk, shoo, shoo, shoo!
Skip to my Lou, my darling.

On and on the play party went, the children singing at the top of their voices.

Little red wagon, painted blue,
Little red wagon, painted blue,
Little red wagon, painted blue,
Skip to my Lou, my darling.

The singing and skipping grew more frenzied.

Skip, skip, skip to my Lou,
Skip, skip, skip to my Lou,
Skip, skip, skip to my Lou,
Skip to my Lou, my darling.

When the line moved on and Shirley was the next person up, she was startled to see that Rev. Townsend was going to be her partner. How could that be? He'd been at the end of the line when they started.

The children yelled for them to go on with the play party, and she and the reverend came together, locked hands, and began skipping down the aisle. Suddenly, the words of the song stung her ears.

Bart's come a-courtin, yes, yes, yes!
Bart's come a-courtin, yes, yes, yes!
Bart's come a-courtin, yes, yes, yes!
Skip to my Lou, my darling.

Panting, she and the reverend came to a halt at the proper place but said not a word. When Shirley looked up at him, he was peering at her, his chest heaving up and down from the strenuous activity. For a moment, their gazes were locked, and she could think of nothing to say. A tingly feeling took hold of her heart.

To her side, she felt more than saw the children dispersing, running this way and that, calling out cheery good-byes, and in the distance, she knew that wagons were pulling out. But her attention was fixed on the reverend, and his on her.

"Preacher, looks like we have a prophecy being fulfilled right before our eyes," old Mr. Wilbur said from behind them, laughing like a hyena.

Neither responded.

"I said, 'Looks like we have a prophecy being fulfilled right before our eyes.' You know—the song."

A little gasp gurgled up in Shirley's throat as she caught his meaning. The song talked about courting.

"A prophecy, Mr. Wilbur?" Rev. Townsend said at last, breaking their intense stare.

"That's right, Preacher. A prophecy. It means, 'a prediction of something to come.' "

"Every minister knows what the word 'prophecy' means,"

Rev. Townsend snapped. But his brows drew together as if he were perplexed.

Shirley was convinced her face had turned scarlet, as surely as if she were looking in a mirror. Courting?

"Isn't your first name Bart, Preacher?" Mr. Wilbur stroked his white waist-length beard, amusement lurking in his gaze. "Like in the song?" He belted out, "Bart's come a-courtin, yes, yes, yes!"

"No, it's Forrest," Shirley blurted, then felt flustered. She should've let Rev. Townsend answer for himself.

Mr. Wilbur chuckled. "Forrest is your middle name, right, Preacher?"

Rev. Townsend's expression grew sheepish, and he gave a boyish grin. "As right as rain. My full name is Bartholomew Forrest Townsend."

"Well, well, well," Mr. Wilbur said, stroking his beard again, smile twinkles in his eyes. "That's a deep subject."

Shirley blushed once more, could feel the intense heat in her face, and said a hurried good-bye to the reverend. As she walked toward the wagon, she smiled. She wouldn't have told Mr. Wilbur that her middle name was Louise for all the tea in China.

Chapter 6

"Hurry, Milcah," Shirley crooned to her little sister. "It's almost time to leave for church. Put your socks on, and I'll button up your shoes for you."

"Yeth, Thirley," came the little girl's lisping reply.

Shirley continued dressing. She pulled her shirtwaist over her head and fastened the tiny buttons up the front, then put her lace collar around her shoulders.

For nearly four months now, ever since last April, when the Reverend Townsend had come to Hickory Hollow, their paths had crossed over and over, though inadvertently. It started with her taking her class back after the Sunday school picnic. Her conscience had simply gotten the best of her—she would never forget the hurt look on Grandfather Hodges's face when she withdrew from it. Teaching Sunday school again had brought about several conversations between her and the Reverend Townsend. She recalled one in particular. . . .

She arrived on the church grounds one Sunday afternoon,

and as she alighted from the wagon, she saw him coming out the church door.

"You certainly handle Deacon Hunter's children well," he said. "Something I could never seem to accomplish when I was teaching your class."

"Thank you," she replied shyly, taking a quilt and a basket from the wagon and walking toward the hickories. "I keep them busy mostly." Under the canopy of trees, she grasped hold of the quilt by two ends, and in a flash he was at her side, grasping the quilt by the other ends, and they shook it out and spread it on the ground.

"I tried that, too," he said, "keeping them busy. But it didn't work for me. Those Hunter children are as rambunctious as ever I've seen." He rolled his eyes.

Shirley gave a shrug and smiled as she smoothed one end of the quilt. "I've been known to send the two older ones for a pail of drinking water two and three times in an afternoon, and the next three children I use as play actors for my Bible stories. The two little Hunter kiddies give me very little trouble if they know I've brought cookies."

He rolled his eyes again. "I never thought of that. Imagine. Seven children under foot. And every one of them going in different directions. I don't know how Mrs. Hunter manages."

Shirley didn't say anything. She knew only too well how Mrs. Hunter managed. The same way she did. And Mama did. There were seven children in the Campbell family, too, six still living at home. Shirley let out a little sigh. One simply did what one was expected to do. And one did the best job possible. It was as plain as that.

"I don't think it's the assignments you give the Hunter children that keep them corralled. I think you have a keen knack for handling kids, Miss Campbell, and I commend you."

Now, as Shirley stood in front of her bureau smoothing her collar, she recalled the warm feeling that had seeped over her that day as Rev. Townsend complimented her. It was affirmation she rarely received, and it felt like water to a dying plant.

Another duty she had taken up was cleaning the church. She was surprised when her mother suggested it and was willing to release her from house and farm work for three hours every Saturday afternoon. That as well had prompted occasional conversations with the reverend in regards to special cleaning needs for certain events.

Then, at the box supper last week, he'd purchased her dinner, his bid the highest. That was when he asked her to tell him the story of how she came to be named Shirley. . . .

"When my mother was a little girl," she told him as they sat side by side at a sawhorse table under the hickories in the churchyard, "she heard my grandfather reading the last verse of Psalm 23 one Sunday morning."

He paused from eating, his fork in midair. "The one that says, 'Surely, goodness and mercy shall follow me all the days of my life: and I will dwell in the house of the LORD forever?' "

"That's the one. My mother mistakenly thought the verse said, 'Shirley,' not 'surely.' "

He threw back his head and laughed heartily.

"When they got home from church that day, she announced to my grandparents that someday she was going to name her little girl Shirley. When they asked why, she told them it was straight from the Bible, that Grandfather had read it that morning. Grandfather put two and two together, and he and my grandmother got a big chuckle out of it."

"And that's how you came to be named Shirley." He swung his head from side to side, smiling. "How intriguing."

"The other children in our family have equally unusual names, and they're all biblical."

"Oh? And what are they?"

"Peesultree's the oldest—"

"That is unusual."

She could feel smile twinkles dancing in her eyes. "It's from the book of Psalms. Grandfather used to pronounce the word 'psaltery' as 'peesultree.' It wasn't until a visiting minister heard him say it that he had any inkling he was mispronouncing it."

The reverend let out a belly chuckle.

"Mama was taken with the sound of Peesultree, and that's how he got his name. He's two years older than I am and works in Springfield. I come next. Then there's Gladly, which is biblical, too."

"It's found throughout the Psalms."

"Yes. Mama said it sounded lyrical. Then there's Moses, Mordecai, and Malachi, all boys of course. And then there's little Milcah, our baby sister."

Now, as Shirley put the finishing touches to her chignon, she continued thinking about Rev. Townsend. Every time their paths had crossed—inadvertently, she reminded herself—they found common interests and even laughed together.

She remembered the children's midsummer program they worked on in tandem, choosing the songs to be sung and the Scriptures to be quoted, even collaborating on the writing of the play, which was deemed a success by all who saw it.

That last thing brought joy to her heart—the writing of the play. As she'd promised herself on the day of her grandmother's funeral, she had carved out bits and pieces of time to write. So far, she had completed four stories.

Just as it was said of Jo March in *Little Women*, so it could be said of her, and she quoted the lines:

> *When the writing fit came on, she gave herself up to it with entire abandon. . .while she sat safe and happy in an imaginary world, full of friends almost as real and dear to her as any in the flesh.*

She smiled, her mind back on the new friend who had become real and dear to her in the flesh—the Reverend Townsend.

Her face grew warm, recalling old Mr. Wilbur on the day of the Sunday school picnic, talking about prophecies being fulfilled when she and Rev. Townsend skipped-to-my-Lou while the children sang, "Bart's come a-courting, yes, yes, yes."

Perhaps Mr. Wilbur's words were prophetic after all. There had been no formal courting, but she and Rev. Townsend had enjoyed a lot of fellowship these last four months. Her heart had grown tender toward him, and she sensed the same thing had happened in him.

A hard tremble shook her. *You've been silly to dally with a man so terribly wrong for you.*

"Thirley, I've got my thockth on," little Milcah said. "And my thewth. I'm ready for you to button them up."

Still tremulous, Shirley strode over to where her sister was sitting on a rag rug in front of the bed. She knelt before her and pulled Milcah's shoe buttons through the loops with the button hook, one by one, noting the fraying across the toes and the worn spots in the soles.

"Is the preacher thweet on you, Thirley?" little Milcah asked.

Shirley felt a lump rise in her throat. "Why do you ask that, Dearie?"

"Becauth I heard the Widow Ford thay it."

The lump grew to boulder size, and she took a deep draught of the morning air flooding through the curtains. "I–I. . ."

"I heard Mama thay it, too."

Shirley started working on the second shoe. One button. Two. Three. Four. Up Milcah's ankle she went. So everyone was talking about her? About the two of them? That there was something going on between them?

Jumbled thoughts rose in her mind. Of course she was

flattered by Forrest's attentions. She corrected herself—Rev. Townsend's attentions. She had no claim on him and therefore no right to use his given name, even in her thinking. But it rolled off her tongue with. . .enjoyment? "Forrest," she said distractedly.

"Ithn't that Preacher Townthend' name?" little Milcah asked.

Enjoyment? Yes, that was what she felt when she was with him, she admitted to herself. And affection? Her hands shook as she continued buttoning little Milcah's shoe.

"Thirley, did you hear me? Ithn't the preacher'th name Forretht?"

The shoe buttons fastened, Shirley sprang up, little Milcah's questions sinking into her befuddled mind. "I think so. Now hop up, Dearie. It's time to go."

All the way to church, Shirley's heart beat in time with the horse's hooves and just as loudly it seemed, and her breath came in short spurts.

Affection? she questioned herself earlier, when she was thinking of Rev. Townsend. Her heartbeat speeded up. *Affection? Most decidedly.*

But it can't stay, she told herself sternly as she remembered the vow she once made. *I wouldn't marry a preacher if he was the last man in the world.*

Marriage to a preacher—reverend, she corrected herself—meant a life of drudgery, like her grandmother had led. Shirley had her dreams and goals and aspirations. She wanted a life surrounded by interesting people in stimulating settings. And she wanted material comforts for her beloved family. Living totally immersed in divine service—as a preacher's wife—offered nothing of the sort.

Sorrow filled her heart at the forthcoming loss of her real-and-dear-in-the-flesh friend. But nevertheless, she resolved to keep her vow.

I will not marry a. . .a reverend.

Chapter 7

As Forrest looked out over his congregation, waiting for the service to begin, his heart skipped a beat when his eyes came to rest on Miss Campbell. They had been in each other's company numerous times over the past months, and long ago he had given up his mistaken notion that she was a drab country mouse.

On the contrary, she was full of vim and vigor and amusing thoughts and feelings that he had become aware of in his tender discovery of her.

He tapped on his bottom lip. She had blossomed before his very eyes, like a flower budding forth. But then perhaps she hadn't. Perhaps she had always been in full bloom, but he had only recently come to see it. Yes, that was definitely the case. She was a magnolia and always had been, like the ones that dotted the church grounds under sprawling limbs, and her fragrance was just as sweet. Sweeter, in fact. He drew in a deep, throaty breath, thinking about Miss Campbell and the luscious scent of a magnolia.

He once thought Miss Devine was a snow maiden, but Shirley was the real snow maiden. She was the perfect example of the Proverbs 31 woman, and he was as smitten with her as ever a man could be. It wasn't because she would be an asset to his ministry. It was because she was a woman uniquely created for him.

That last thought warmed his heart. God had been watching out for him, as an earthly father cared for his son, when He sent him to Hickory Hollow, Missouri. God knew that there was one Miss Shirley Campbell, whom He was preparing for one Forrest Townsend. Shirley was the one in a thousand for him and for him alone.

He smiled, recalling pleasant times spent in her company. He thought about the day she told him the amusing story of how she acquired her name, as well as how her brothers and sisters acquired theirs.

"Pssst, Reverend," whispered a voice from the choir loft behind him. "It's time to start the service."

Forrest was so startled, he dropped his Bible. "Thank you," he whispered as he swooped down to pick up the holy book, then stood and strode across the platform, his long legs carrying him quickly.

"Shall we bow our heads in prayer?" he intoned from behind the oaken pulpit.

⁓

This is going to be painful, grievous even, coming to church every Sunday and seeing him. Shirley's hands were perspiring so profusely, there were wet marks on the hymnal where she was grasping it.

141

My heart is his, she admitted to herself. *But my will is my own.*

And what am I going to do when I see him at afternoon Sunday school every week? And what about when I clean the church on Saturdays? Oh, Lord, help me.

All through the sermon, she managed to keep her mind on the latest story she was developing. If she concentrated on him and his sermon, she might. . .what might she do? She didn't know. She only knew that she had to keep her thoughts clear of him.

As she filed out the church door after the service was over, she gave him the perfunctory handshake and smile but avoided his eyes and whisked a few steps beyond him, hoping he would be too busy with the church people to take note.

"Preacher Townsend," bellowed old Mr. Wilbur from behind her. "The Bible says, 'Surely, goodness and mercy shall follow me all the days of my life.' You already have goodness and mercy. When are you going to get Shirley? When are you two going to get hitched, Bart?"

Shirley was mortified. Should she turn and greet the old gentleman in politeness and try to change the subject? Or should she keep going and act as if she hadn't heard?

It was decided for her.

"You make an excellent point, Mr. Wilbur," he said, enthusiasm dripping from his voice.

Had Shirley been looking at him, she knew she would see his face aglow with affection, his eyes warm with the tenderness she had become familiar with.

"Perhaps we need to talk to the lady to find out," he said softly.

Shirley rushed down the steps and crossed the church-yard lickety-split. She was glad Papa had the wagon at the ready. She climbed on board, and all the way home, her heart was in the same state it had been in on the way there—beating in time with the horse's hooves and just as loudly.

Chapter 8

The next Saturday, Shirley rode toward the church faster than she should've, but it couldn't be helped. "Giddyap, Girl," she said to Old Glory, and the wagon surged forward.

She didn't want to run the risk of seeing him when she went to clean the church today. Most Saturday afternoons, he made visits in homes, so she felt relatively sure that she wouldn't see him. But one never knew. Perhaps he would get back earlier than usual. If that happened, she must be done cleaning and out of there. But to accomplish that, she had to hurry.

She pulled up in the churchyard. In her quick perusal of the parsonage across the way, she was relieved to see that his buggy was gone. Good. Out of sight, out of mind, as the old saying went. That would be her discipline from now on. The stirrings in her heart were simply too strong to be trusted. She must stay away from him as much as possible. Then, when sufficient time passed, her heart would calm down.

Perhaps the Widow Ford would keep him inordinately long this afternoon, rehearsing her gall bladder attack of last week. She smiled, knowing the elderly lady was lonely and just needed a caring ear.

Perhaps Mr. Wilbur would detain him. But that thought dismayed her. Mr. Wilbur liked to talk about courting and prophecies and matrimonial things.

Perhaps Deacon Hunter's wife would invite him to stay for supper. For sure, there would be plenty of time to clean the church if that happened.

As she climbed down from the wagon, Shirley laughed, envisioning Deacon Hunter's wriggly, writhing, screeching children around the reverend as he sat at their large plankboard table, forks a-flying and spoons a-pinging, giggles and chatters accompanying a number of knocked-over glasses with milk a-flowing. At least that's the way it was the last time she'd supped with them. In light of the remarks he made about the rambunctious Hunter children when she came to know him better, she laughed even harder.

For two hours, she worked her heart out cleaning the church, polishing the altars and pulpit, sweeping the floors, dusting the benches, and spic-and-spanning the windows.

In the hot August weather, beads of perspiration formed on her forehead, so hard and fast did she toil. All the while, she formulated a new story in her head. She had found a nifty little literary device—that of utilizing her work time by tooling out her stories. Then, when she found a minute to herself, she wrote them down.

She dashed outside, poured out her cleaning water, then rushed back inside the church and gathered her cloths and bucket and broom, making ready to put them in their closet and be on her way pell-mell.

"Miss Campbell, I've been wanting to get a word with you."

Startled, she dropped the items in her hand, and they clanked on the hard wooden floor.

"Miss Campbell?"

Her back to him, she froze like a statue. He was the last person she wanted to see. Why was he here, anyway? He was visiting church members, wasn't he?

"I didn't mean to frighten you. Please forgive me."

She knew by his voice that he was directly behind her where she stood near the altar. Evidently he had come in the front door of the church and walked up the aisle. She felt hot and cold all at once and knew not what to do. Turn around and greet him? Greet him as she picked up the items so she wouldn't have to make eye contact with him?

Instinct kicked in. She dipped to the floor and gathered the bucket and the broom. "I wasn't expecting you, that's all, Reverend."

In his gentlemanly way, he dipped, too, and swooped up the cloths. They arose together, and when they faced each other, he tucked the cloths into the bucket on her arm. "I got back a little early from my pastoral rounds. The Widow Ford is fit as a fiddle today." He chuckled. "So I arrived back sooner than I thought. I've been wanting to see you all week,

Miss Campbell. But woe is me, our paths perchance did not cross. Ah, the misery."

Keeping her eyes on the floor, Shirley toyed with the bucket handle. Was he making fun of her? He knew her literary pursuits. He knew the words he was speaking were Shakespearean and not used in everyday vernacular. She had confided her dreams and hopes and aspirations to him. Now, she felt naked in his presence.

"Art thou in Grub Street? Thou wast so engrossed when I came upon thee."

She glanced his way. Yes, he was making fun of her. Every writer knew that Grub Street was the London abode of literary hacks in the seventeenth and eighteenth centuries. Why, the nerve of him.

He chuckled. "Let's see. You were writing—in your head. I've seen you like this many times. You're present in body, but your mind is far from here, spirited away to other worlds. Isn't that true, Miss Campbell? Does genius burn?" He leaned against the pew behind him, his arms folded across his chest, his smile still lurking, his eyes twinkling.

"I–I. . ." She felt silly for stammering and even sillier for not being able to give him a quick comeback. Oh, to have the pluck of her sister Gladly, a speed-of-lightning thinker who could deliver a retort that burned the ears.

"Please don't think I'm making light of your giftings. For that's what your writing is, you know. Giftings. From God Himself." He paused as if he were deep in contemplation. "God has equipped you with something unique, Shirley," he said, his voice exuding tenderness as he spoke her given name. "The rare talent of writing. Many people seek to write, and some foolishly think they have the gift. But few ever accomplish anything. You are going places in the literary world, mark my words, all for the glory of God."

She swallowed hard. *Not if I marry a. . .a reverend.* The lump in her throat grew bigger, and she willed herself not to let the tears in her eyes escape down her cheek. But what kind words, what affirming words. Why, no one had ever said anything of the sort to her about her writing. Suddenly, without warning, the stirrings in her heart for him grew to tidal wave proportions. *Oh, Forrest. . .*

"Will you sit down? I have something of great import to ask you."

She looked into his eyes but quickly averted them. Her heart was too telltale. He might read what it was saying.

"Please? Surely you can spare a few minutes." He sat down on a nearby bench and patted the spot beside him.

She hesitated, dreading this tête-à-tête. If only. . .

She smoothed the sides of her hair and took a seat behind him on a bench all to herself. She couldn't chance closeness right now.

He turned around to face her and propped his arm across the back of the bench. A puzzled look filled his eyes, but then he brightened. For nearly a quarter hour, they talked, him mostly, about the two new Sunday school classes that were recently formed due to church growth. The Lord's business, he called it. He told her the Sunday night sing-along he was planning would attract a large crowd and that he intended to have more special events, a strategy he used with success in Harrisonburg.

She smiled and showed interest at appropriate times and even added to the conversation when she could muster her courage. But for the most part, she sat there, her heart hurting beyond words.

Affection? she'd questioned herself earlier. *Is that what I feel for him? No,* she answered now. *Love. I feel love for him.* She blinked hard to keep her eyes from misting over. *But,* she told herself sternly, *I must purge it from my heart.*

"From what your grandfather says, the Hickory Hollow church has never had a sing-along service before."

She tried to force her mind to think of high-society teas and book signings and the university dais—and all that this would bring to her family, but it refused to obey. *Forrest, Forrest, Forrest!* her heart shouted.

"Did you hear me? Are you back on Grub Street?" He smiled a boyish grin, and she thought her heart would melt and slide down the seat. "That's all right with me," he continued, his heart-melting smile seeming to radiate from the very sinews of his soul. "I'm proud of your pursuits—and accomplishments. That's just one of many reasons why I came to love you. . . ."

Love? She nearly bolted out of her seat. She wished she could be translated like Phillip in the Bible. But instead of getting up, she willed herself to stay still. Her heart was beating so hard, her lightweight cotton shirtwaist was vibrating at the movement, and her breath was coming so short, she felt faint.

"Miss Campbell. . .Shirley. . ." In a flash, he was sitting on her bench, a space between them, his long, Bible-thumping fingers an inch away from her shoulder. "I'll say this in language you adore." He let out a long sigh.

A love sigh, she fleetingly thought.

He cleared his throat and recited:

> *"If I could write the beauty of your eyes*
> *And in fresh numbers, number all your graces,*
> *The age to come would say, 'This poet lies;*
> *Such heavenly touches ne'er touch'd earthly faces.'"*

For sure, she was going to swoon. His sweet, rhythmic words were straight from a sonnet of Shakespeare's.

"From the moment I laid eyes on you, I knew you were a part of my destiny."

She resisted the urge to grab the cardboard fan in the hymnal rack and fan her face. Rather, she clasped her hands rigidly together and kept staring straight ahead, as she had been doing all along.

"When your grandfather introduced us on the church steps, something leapt within me, and though I resisted at first, I came to know you and love you. Let me hasten to add that the reason I resisted you was because I thought you were resisting me. I thought that your quiet ways signified you weren't interested. I didn't know the real you back then, the you down inside that sees and feels and knows things so deeply. And so tenderly. . ."

He trailed his finger across the top of her hand, and she felt as if she had died and gone to heaven.

His hand properly back on the bench again, he leaned in a little closer.

"She's beautiful, and therefore to be woo'd;
She is a woman, therefore to be won."

Another tear threatened at his beautiful Shakespearean language, but she kept it in check.

"Shirley, 'come live with me and be my love. . . .' "

Marlowe verses? She smiled despite her pain. This man was simply sent down. What an apropos analogy. He really was sent from above to Hickory Hollow, to do the Lord's business. And to woo her? She resisted the thought.

In another flash—he could certainly do things swiftly— he was on his knees in front of her, and she squelched a smile at his big hulking stature bent up like a screw jack in the narrow space between the benches.

Her breath was coming in short snatches again. She knew what a man on bended knee meant. This couldn't be happening. Here. Today. Right now.

"I'm asking for your hand in marriage, Shirley. I'm proclaiming my love for you, oh Beautiful Eyes with numbers of graces. Wilt thou have me as thy wedded husband? Wilt thou be my wedded wife?" He took her hand in his and kissed the back of it, then gently released it.

This time she bolted up out of her seat on the hard wooden bench—couldn't help doing so—and rammed right into him, where he knelt in the narrow space.

"I—I'm s—sorry," she stammered, feeling like Joey in the Harlequinade. "I didn't mean to. . ."

He bolted up beside her, brushing at his knees.

She felt like a cornered fox on a hunt and looked every which way. She would never be able to look him in the eyes again, not after today, not after this.

He backed out of the narrow space and came to stand in the aisle. "Apparently, I caught you off guard."

Holding onto the back of the bench, she edged away and came to stand in the aisle several feet from him.

"You obviously don't share my sentiments," he said.

She looked down at the floorboards she had swept only three-quarters of an hour ago. She wanted to speak. She wanted to proclaim her love like he had done—in the same fanciful, heartwarming language he used. She would never forget his sweet words for her entire life. But she couldn't say a thing. It was as if her mouth was sewn shut as tightly as the lace collar she had placed stitches in last evening.

"Please. Let me spare you further embarrassment, Miss Campbell." A hard steeliness gripped his voice."I wish to make a pact with you."

She looked at him, wide-eyed.

"At last, you've looked at me. I should feel privileged, I suppose. All these months, as I came to know you and fall in love with you, I thought of you as a snow maiden. You know as well as I do that that's the epitome of womanly perfection." The disgust in his tone grew intense. "Well, you're no snow maiden, Miss Campbell. You're an ice maiden."

She let out a little gasp, couldn't help it. *Dear Lord, please help me to keep my resolve. Please help me to be strong in the greatest trial of my life.* But the Lord wasn't helping her, or so it seemed. She was withering inside, dying a thousand deaths.

"Here's what we'll do, Miss Campbell." His jaw was rigidly set, his eyes narrow slits—almost menacingly so. "We'll go about our lives as if none of this transpired today. We'll be pastor and parishioner and nothing more. We'll be polite in passing, Christlike in demeanor. I think we both have that down to a science. But underneath, we'll both know the truth. You abhor me." He swallowed hard, still staring intently into her eyes. His look said it all. *And I abhor you.*

She turned on her heel and fled out the door in such deep despair, she didn't know if she would live another day.

Chapter 9

Shirley shivered in the crisp autumn air and pulled the covers up to her chin, being careful not to disturb Gladly at her side. Night after night, she was given to lying awake, unable to sleep, wallowing in her misery.

Her heart was as bleak and barren as Missouri's winter weather that would soon be upon them—cold, frigid even. Her writing was the same way. Or lack of writing, she should say. Ever since the day of the proposal, she hadn't written a word on paper—or in her head. It was as if the day her heart died, her aspirations did, too. Oh, that was a fine turn of events. She had refused him in order to pursue her dreams. Now, she had neither him nor her writing. Why did life have to be so hard?

"Forrest, Forrest, Forrest," she whispered under her breath. "How my heart longs for you."

She contemplated her dilemma. Maybe she should give in and marry him. He was dashing, almost debonair so to speak, and gentle and courteous. He was suave even, with his love of

Shakespeare and literature. But could she marry someone who, because of his chosen profession, would force her to live a life of burdensome servitude to lackluster people? Marrying him would mean living in Hickory Hollow right on, her dreams dashed, the grandeur in her head gone, divine service claiming her every waking, breathing minute the livelong day.

She had eyes. She knew how Grandmother had lived, a preacher's wife at the beck and call of the congregation. Could she do that? What was the answer to her dilemma?

A chill ran up her backbone. *Forrest would never have me now.* On that fateful day when she'd refused him—more by action than answer—he made it quite clear to her—more by tone than words—that he wanted nothing further to do with her. Like Pontius Pilate when he washed his hands of Jesus, so Forrest washed his hands of her. He would just as likely take to her now as to Deacon Hunter's seven wriggly, writhing, screeching youngsters. He disdained them, she knew, just as he now disdained her, and that was how things stood between them.

She must never contemplate her dilemma again—whether to marry him or whether to cling to her dreams. There was no dilemma.

There's only oblivion, tortuous oblivion, she thought as she finally drifted off to sleep.

Chapter 10

Forrest rode down the lane, his first thoughts about Miss Campbell hitting him with full force. "I wouldn't have her on a silver platter," he said.

He remembered saying that when he assumed she was playing the age-old game of Hard to Get. But at the Sunday school picnic, he assured himself he had been mistaken, and that's when the tenderness for her took root in his heart.

After that, she resumed teaching her Sunday school class and asked his advice on everything from the location of the class to the midsummer social. When she started cleaning the church, that brought about more conversations between them. It seemed everywhere he turned during those months, she was at his elbow, her face all sunshine and smiles, her talk dotted with Shakespeare and lexicon language.

He shook his head from side to side. All that time, she had indeed been playing Hard to Get, and he didn't have sense enough to see it. Now he knew her for what she was, an ice maiden, what he'd called her to her face.

He winced, lamenting his harshness and remembering that he was a gentleman who should have shown better manners—and besides that a minister. But it simply couldn't be helped. He'd bared his heart to her, and she'd squashed it in the ground as if it were a weed to stamp out.

Well, he would take care of that. He had learned his lesson and learned it well. He would raise up a shield over his heart and never lower it for one Miss Campbell, even if she came begging at his feet.

He smiled, envisioning that very scene. He knew there were few unattached men in these parts. He knew he was clamored for. After all, he had fair looks and a pleasing personality, and beyond that he was a minister, a man everyone looked up to, especially maiden ladies and young widow women. When Miss Campbell experienced a dearth of suitors, a drought of Cupids, a dry spell of troth plighters, she would look his way again. And it would give him distinct pleasure to refuse her.

Absently, he yanked on the reins, and Prancer jerked back. "I'm sorry, Prancer. Didn't mean to give you a toothache or most certainly a neck ache. I'll be more careful, I promise."

On Prancer trotted, toward town. Today, Forrest was to meet with the editor of the newspaper. He was going to convince him to write an article about the city pastor who had willingly taken a little country parish and, because of his expertise, had seen attendance mushroom in only six months.

"While I'm at the newspaper office, I think I'll take out an ad that says, 'Beware of Miss Campbell. She steals your heart and stomps it in the ground.' "

He snorted like Prancer often did. Miss Campbell was flighty, frivolous, and farcical. Of all the young women in Hickory Hollow, why did he have to be drawn to her? Why didn't he have the wisdom to steer clear of her? Why, she had no substance, no depth of character.

He heard a clap of thunder and looked up, but the sky was cloudless, with not a hint of rain on the horizon or a whisper of wind in the air, despite it being a cool fall day.

Forrest. . .

He looked around. Had someone called his name? But there was no one on this deserted country road. He was a good quarter mile from the nearest house.

Forrest. . .

He heard his name again. What was the meaning of this? Into his mind popped two references in the Bible where men's names had been called out of the blue. One instance was Samuel, when God called him to be a prophet. The other was the apostle Paul, only he was known as sinful Saul. What was going on?

Forrest, you've been flighty, flimsy, and farcical.

"What do you mean, Lord?" Immediately he knew it was the Lord speaking to him, just as it had been with Samuel and Saul.

You have no substance, no depth of character.

Forrest was in anguish. "Haven't I given my all to You, God, and dedicated myself to Your business?"

For what reasons? For what gain?

"Lord. . ."

Like a parade, things appeared before his mind, a long string of incidents. . . .

Forrest, at first refusing to pastor the Hickory Hollow church because he thought it was beneath him. . .

Forrest, finally accepting it—only because he thought it would help him climb the ladder of success. . .

Forrest, looking for a wife more for how she could enhance his ministry than for herself. . .

Forrest, enduring people instead of enjoying them—because he thought it would bring benefit to him and his career.

"Father, forgive me," he cried out.

Suddenly, rain began to fall, a driving one with force, and he pulled his muffler more tightly about his throat. What to do? He saw that he was passing the Widow Ford's house.

"What a thrilling proposition," he said as he turned into her yard. "I guess I'll have to wait out the storm hearing the details of her recent stomach ailment." Guilt assailed him. "Oh, Lord, will I never change? Have mercy on me."

In minutes, he was standing on the Widow Ford's porch, rapping on her door, the rain falling in sheets. No one came. He rapped harder. Still no answer. "Mrs. Ford," he called. Then louder. "Mrs. Ford." He saw a note pinned to a cushion on a rocker:

Bertha,
    Please leave the jars of applesauce and the layer cake

*you promised me on the porch. Doc Brewster said part of
what ails me is that I don't get out much, though I can't
imagine why he would have such silly surmisings.
Staying in bundled up against the weather in winter
and away from people's germs in the summer is the best
way to prevent illness. But when I looked out this
morning and saw sunshine, I decided to try his advice.
'Course you're always saying the same thing. I've gone to
see my sister. I'll be gone all day.*

*Obligingly,
Gloramae Ford*

Forrest didn't know whether to laugh or cry, figuratively
speaking, of course. Mrs. Ford wasn't here, so he wouldn't
have to endure her litany of maladies. But because she wasn't
here, he would have to proceed on and brave the rainstorm.
When he got to town, he would be a cold, wet mess, in no
condition to talk to the editor of the newspaper.

He looked around the minuscule porch. Surely she
wouldn't mind if he stayed here and waited out the rain. He
wouldn't go inside, despite the chill in the air. He would wait
on the porch, even if the rain set in for the entire afternoon.

And during that time, he would make his peace with the
Lord.

His heart contrite, Forrest fell to his knees in front of
Mrs. Ford's rocker, his elbows on the caned bottom, his
hands clasped together.

"Lord, I'm a sorry excuse for a minister. I've been accusing

Shirley of being hollow, and yet I'm the real culprit. I saw a mote in her eye, and there's a beam in mine. She has a speck of pomposity, and I have a wagonload. Oh, Lord, wash me clean. Change me."

A sob caught at his throat. "Make my heart and motives pure. I–I've been a baseless fabric of a vision when I needed to be a bedrock. How could I expect to lead a congregation when I'm nothing but a brass farthing—a tinkling cymbal, as Thy Word says?"

Tears misted his eyes, something that hadn't happened to him in a long time, perhaps since childhood. "Lord, I ask Thee to take away my sins of pride and arrogance and vainglory. Forgive me, Father. Let me take on the humility of Christ and be clothed in His righteousness."

In his mind's eye, he envisioned himself in a white robe, pure and clean before the Father, and into his soul came a joy, full and real and powerful—like the gushing of a geyser. He laughed and laughed, a peace as sweet as honey flooding over him, seemingly from his hairline all the way down to his shoes.

"Thank You, Lord." He paused, enjoying the quiet stillness, the rain long stopped. Out of the corner of his eye, he saw a rainbow. "I've been newborn," he fairly shouted as he arose and dusted the knees of his trousers.

"What's that you say, Reverend?" came a woman's voice from out of nowhere it seemed. "Who's got a newborn? Surely you didn't find one of those at the Widow Ford's house?" She cackled.

Forrest was startled as he turned to face the road. Miss Bertha Brown, an elderly spinster in the church, was making her way up the front walk, her arms laden, a black parasol tucked under one armpit.

He ran down the steps and took the cake plate from her. "Good afternoon, Miss Brown."

"Afternoon, Reverend. I told Gloramae I'd bring her some things to cheer her up." She held out the sack she was carrying, and jars clanked inside. "I've told her a thousand times if she'd take exercise like I do, even in cool weather, she'd do a heap better."

"You walked all the way from your house? Two miles?" No wonder he hadn't heard a wagon.

"That's mighty right. These legs were made for walking, Reverend, even through the puddles." She patted the sides of her skirts. "Now, what's that you said about a newborn?"

A quarter hour later, Forrest was on his way to town—after hearing all about Miss Bertha Brown's daily exercise regimen, and her apple-a-day routine that she claimed kept her in good health, and her morning prunes that she insisted kept her skin unwrinkled—and he hadn't minded one bit.

On this leg of his journey, he was a changed man.

Chapter 11

Shirley sat on the settee in the parlor, ready for church earlier than any of her family, lamenting about losing the two great loves of her life.

"Matthew, my darling," came her mother's gentle voice from her bedroom nearby. "Will you button me up the back?"

Her father's deep musical laughter wafted down the hall, and Shirley could see him in her mind's eye, his blue-gray eyes and his still-dark hair and his endearing limp. "I can think of nothing I'd rather do, Amanda, my dear," he said.

A girlish giggle was her mother's only response.

"On second thought, there is one thing that would please me more," he said, his voice husky.

Another giggle. Another laugh. The sound of lips meeting lips in a tender kiss. "This is what I was talking about." Lips met lips again.

Shirley jumped to her feet and shut the parlor door, envisioning her mother and father locked in a warm embrace, what she'd seen many times during her growing-up years. But she didn't want to think about that now—it was too painful.

"I'll never have the joy of experiencing that," she whispered, tears coming to her eyes. "They say there's only one great love of your life, and I rejected mine."

Later as Papa pulled the wagon into the churchyard, she wondered how it would be to see him. As time had passed, she'd thought it would grow easier. But she was wrong. Her heart was bleeding this morning.

As she dawdled toward the church, taking her time in her dread, she saw a group of people clustered around the left corner of the building. Some were pointing at something while others were engrossed in animated conversation.

"Shirley," called her grandfather, his face lit up with enthusiasm. "Come." He was waving at her, beckoning her to proceed his way.

"Yes, Grandfather?" she asked as she approached.

He pointed to the cornerstone. "Jeb told me Rev. Townsend wants to have a dinner-on-the-grounds to celebrate the twenty-fifth anniversary of our church. He says we're going to have it the first Sunday of November. Look at the cornerstone." He pointed downward.

Silently, she read the words on the smooth square of limestone set in the jagged-edged stones all around it:

On this eighth day of November, in the eighteen hundredth and sixty-ninth year of our Lord, this church

is hereby dedicated to God's glory, consecrated for His
service, for all generations to come.

"Will you write a history of the church?" her grandfather
asked.

"That'd be a right nice thing to have," Jeb Hunter chimed
in. "We could keep it in the permanent records, so's nobody
would ever forget the hard work that went into the building
of it. And since I'm on the board of the church—"

"Who would've ever thought that Jeb here—" her grandfather smiled and gestured at Deacon Hunter "—would grow
up to be a deacon?" He punched Jeb in the ribs.

Jeb grinned. "The Lord works in mysterious ways, His
wonders to perform. Anyway, as I was saying, I believe I
could get the church treasury to kick in some money for a
writing tablet for Shirley to work on and some fancy paper
to copy it on when she's done."

"Will you, Shirley?" her grandfather asked. "I know you
don't have much time, and it's only two weeks away. But I'll
speak to your mother about it."

Shirley silently reread the poignant words on the cornerstone. Write? She hadn't picked up a pen for eons. She hadn't
been able to. Her wellspring was simply dried up. But maybe
this was the priming it needed. In fact, she had been praying
that the Lord would give her a rebirth in her writing.

"Will you, Shirley? I can tell you the details. And you
could talk to some others in these parts. You could make it
like a story, kinda like one of them you're writing all the time,

165

only this one would be true. Will you do it, Girl?"

A story? Her breath came in short snatches as she relished the thought.

"If you'll write it, I'll ask Rev. Townsend if I can read it that Sunday. What a day of rejoicing that will be, to think back on the founding of our church. The people'll be pleased with a written church history, I'm certain. And so will Rev. Townsend." Her grandfather paused and lowered his voice, a knowing look in his eyes. "It might take a leap of faith for you, Shirley, but the Lord'll help you."

She brightened. Leap of faith? She'd heard her grandfather preach about a leap of faith all her life. It meant that a person needed to leap over their chasm of troubles while holding fast to God's promises. Leap of faith? That's what she sorely needed.

"Yes, Grandfather," she eagerly said. "I'll write the church history. Or at least try." She turned and made her way pell-mell toward the sanctuary, her mind awhirl with facts and dates, determined to write to the best of her ability. Suddenly, she stopped dead in her tracks.

I hope a broken heart doesn't impede my flow.

⁓

"Here's the Bible, Shirley," her grandfather said Tuesday morning. "Your grandmother's and mine." He pushed the large, leather-bound volume across the kitchen table where they were sitting.

"It'll be a help, I know." Shirley was already opening the thin, finger-smudged pages, being careful not to tear them.

He nodded. "Like I told you, your grandmother wrote down some important dates in there." He dipped his head toward the Bible. "Anything else you need to know before I go?" He shifted in his chair.

"No, Sir. While you talked, I took enough notes to write a book, I believe." She smiled as she looked at her sheaf of scribbles, hastily jotted down as he told the story of the building of the church. "But if I need clarification, I'll let you know."

"What mighty big words you use, Girl." He arose and reached to hug her.

"I like to read Webster's." She not only read Webster's, she studied the words and their definitions diligently.

"Your mother used to read the lexicon, too. When she was young."

"I never knew that." All she knew about her mother was that her middle name was work.

"Speaking of your mother, she assured me that you can take as much time as you need with your writing."

Shirley nodded. "Yesterday, I drove all over Hickory Hollow talking to church members and taking notes." She got to her feet and slid her chair under the table.

"Well, I'd best be going. I'll be praying for you, that the Lord'll quicken your mind and anoint your words. Did you know the Good Book says, 'my tongue is the pen of a ready writer'?"

She marveled. "I've never read that verse before, Grandfather."

"Psalm 45:1."

As she followed him to the front door, she wasn't thinking about the verse in Psalms, wonderful though it was. She was thinking about Mama and why she used to read the lexicon.

☙

For two hours, Shirley sat at the kitchen table, poring over the Hodgeses' family Bible and the copious notes she had taken as her grandfather talked. In the Bible, in her grandmother's handwriting, were dates of when and how the land was acquired, notations of when the work began, who worked on the building, how Mr. Randall tried to take back the land, and how long the actual building of the church took.

There was even a detailed account of the dedication day and the very first dinner-on-the-grounds, complete with the naming of every singer and every dessert on the long sawhorse tables. That account was in a different handwriting than the other items.

"Who wrote this, I wonder?" Shirley said under her breath, gazing intently at the storylike notes, so well written she felt like she was there observing it. Yet it had occurred two-and-a-half decades ago.

"Did you say something, Shirley?" Her mother was at her side, peering over her shoulder, a knife in one hand, a potato in the other, a long brown peel dangling in a spiral floorward.

Shirley pointed to the account. "I was reading about the church dedication day—"

"I wrote that. . . ." Her mother's voice trailed off, and she had a faraway look to her eyes.

"I didn't know you liked to write, Mama."

"I never was any good—"

"But you were. Your story made me feel like I was there. I could almost hear the Blackstone brothers singing, and I could almost taste Grandmother's cinnamon-peach cobbler swimming in heavy cream."

"Fiddle-faddle." Her mother walked briskly back to the tin sink on the drainboard and resumed her potato peeling. "You'd best be getting through with your writing this morning. Your father will be in directly for dinner, and we need to get the table set."

"May I have another quarter hour?"

"All right, then."

※

Shirley's eyes watered and her breath came in staccato puffs as she read the words on the last page of her grandparents' Bible. It wasn't about the church. It had nothing to do with it, in fact. It was a journal-like entry in her grandmother's handwriting, sort of her treatise on being a preacher's wife:

In many ways, Anson and I have been wealthy.
We've been surrounded by a great cloud of witnesses,
God's dear people who have brought us joy and enriched
our lives. I thank God every day that He chose me to be
a preacher's wife. What a privilege! What an honor!
I was unworthy, unequipped, and frankly, unwilling.
Then the Lord showed me this verse: "The eyes of your
understanding being enlightened; that ye may know
what is the hope of his calling," in Ephesians 1:18.

Suddenly, it was as if my eyes were opened, and I embraced this high calling with all my heart, and that's when the joy came. I soon found out that whom God appoints, He anoints, because He equipped me with all that I needed. After living a lifetime in divine service, I can confidently say that I wouldn't trade my life for all the riches and fame in the world.

"Have you ever read this, Mama?" Shirley asked, a tear slipping down her cheek. "What Grandmother wrote on the last page of her Bible?"

Her mother was pulling a pan of biscuits out of the oven with a stove cloth. "About a thousand times—like everything else in there." Her face was red from the heat, and she set the pan down and wiped her forehead with the corner of her apron.

"This is astounding." Shirley ran her hand over her grandmother's words. How could her mother have read this that many times and been so unaffected? This was the most earth-shaking thing Shirley had ever read, and she felt like dancing a jig at the liberating sensation that enveloped her.

Her mother looked over at her, as if she were studying her. The otherworldly musings that often enveloped Shirley seemed to envelop Mama, too. After a long moment, she finally broke the silence. "Shirley, honey, can you clear the table? And sometime today I'd like to talk with you. I have a lot of things to tell you."

"Yes, Mama." Shirley scooped up the Bible and her

writing materials and dashed out the door, wondering what Mama would say to her. "I'll be back in a few minutes to set the table."

⁓

In the quiet of her bedroom, Shirley dropped to her knees in front of the bed, thankful that Gladly was spending the day with their cousins. Otherwise, she might be afoot.

"Lord, I submit my will and my way to Thee." Her tears fell thick, and she didn't bother wiping them, just kept her hands clasped and her gaze heavenward.

"My eyes are opened at last. It was really You I was fighting against, not the ministry and being a preacher's wife. Please forgive my stubbornness." Joy tears replaced the tears of contrition, and gladness bubbled within her.

"Dear Lord, I embrace what I know is before me. . .being a preacher's wife in divine service. I promise to serve Thee and Thy people with all my might and being, as Thou givest me the strength and power. In Jesus' name. Amen."

She swiped at her eyes with her hanky and arose from her knees, as happy as she'd ever been, happier than when the love tingles were developing for Forrest.

"Forrest!" she shrieked. She reeled, feeling like a load of limestone had hit her. She fell to her knees once more.

"Dear Lord, Forrest doesn't want me anymore." The tears were back, and she writhed inside. "He detests me. I can feel it every time I'm around him. Oh, what a mess I've made of things."

Daughter, be not afraid.

"Lord? Is it truly Thee speaking?" She was in awe.

It is I. Be not afraid.

She felt the comfort of the Lord. But then her doubts returned. "He'll never have me." A sob gurgled up her throat. "I love him, Lord. What am I going to do?"

Daughter! I will work it out. Trust Me.

The Lord, the King of the universe, had spoken to her? "Thy will be done," she said softly.

Her grandmother's Scripture verse filled her mind, her heart, her being: " 'The eyes of your understanding being enlightened; that ye may know what is the hope of his calling,' " she quoted, then smiled, feeling as if she could conquer the world.

"Shirley!" came her mother's voice.

"Thank You, Lord, for Thy peace so sweet. I can hear the joybells ringing in my soul." Then loudly, she replied, "I'm coming, Mama."

Chapter 12

That evening, Shirley sat at the kitchen table writing, the lamplight shining on her tablet. The tablet was nice. Deacon Hunter had said she could keep it when she finished this project—a pleasant thought. The church even threw in some extra money to pay for lamp oil in case she needed to work after dark—a kind gesture.

She glanced down, pleased to see five pages filled, with not one line blank. She was nearly done with the story of the history of the church.

She pondered the experience that had happened in her bedroom that morning. She was so overcome by the magnitude of it, she had walked on clouds all day, the story formulating and building in her head. Perhaps that was what made it especially fine, even if she did say so herself.

"About through?" her mother asked over her shoulder. She was ready for bed, her heavy wool wrapper around her, her hair in a long braid.

"Yes, Mama. What I've not finished tonight, I can do

tomorrow or the next day."

Her mother sat down at the table and pulled her chair close. "I've been wanting to talk with you. I–I'm proud of you, Shirley." A smile lit her face so caressing, it was a hug itself. "For writing like that." She touched the tablet. "And for all the other writing you do. I'm right pleased for you."

"You are, Mama? Proud of me?" Shirley was aghast and thrilled at the same time. Her mother had never said anything like this to her.

"I am, Dear."

"That means more to me than you can know." She paused and drew in a breath. "May I ask you a question?"

Her mother shrugged, but she smiled again. "I suppose."

Shirley contemplated her words as she stared down at the tablet. "Mama, when you were a girl, did you have a deep desire to write? Like I do now?"

Her mother sat, not saying a word. Long moments passed.

Shirley looked over at her, wondering, knowing her mother had heard her. She was less than three inches away. "Mama?"

"Yes, I did."

Shirley was trying to digest this astounding news. Why had Mama never shared this with her?

"I used to read the lexicon—"

"Grandfather told me."

"I wanted to write. Stories came to me, especially when I would lie down at night. Sometimes they were so vivid, I couldn't sleep."

Shirley nodded in understanding. "Why didn't you keep on writing?"

"Life never led me that way."

"But couldn't you have done something about that?"

"Shirley, every person who loves God is called to walk a certain path." A romantic look filled her eyes. "For me, that path was to be the wife of Matthew Campbell and the mother of Peesultree, Shirley, Gladly, Moses, Mordecai, Malachi, and Milcah." She laughed softly in the dim lamplight. "That was my calling."

"Why didn't you ever encourage me in my writing endeavors?"

"Because I've had such a good life with your pa that I wanted the same thing for you. I was afraid if you pursued writing, you couldn't have the love of a good husband like I enjoy. But now I see that I'm wrong. A moment ago, I said God has a path for each of us to walk. Shirley, your path is twofold."

"Twofold, Mama?"

Her mother nodded. "Writing and being a wife—a preacher's wife at that." She smiled broadly. "The Reverend Forrest Townsend's wife."

Shirley felt that familiar tingly feeling on the inside.

"Somehow, Jesus will fix things. He will bring all of this to fruition in your life."

"You know that, Mama? Why didn't you talk to me about this sooner?"

"It only came to me this week, the surety of it." She

touched the family Bible with Grandmother Hodges's entry in it, and a knowing look filled her eyes, a wise look.

Shirley was a chatterbox all of a sudden, asking her mother things she'd never dared, about writing and about men, Forrest in particular, and Mama answered with God-given wisdom.

Her mother slipped her arm around Shirley's shoulders. "The book you used to read to Ma before she passed on—"

"Little Women?"

Her mother nodded. "That was mine when I was a girl."

Shirley couldn't believe her ears.

"Ma somehow scraped together some money and purchased it for me. She knew I longed to write. I think she discerned that in you, too."

"So that's why. . ." Shirley's voice trailed off.

"Strangely enough, a passage of Louisa Mae Alcott's writing pointed me in the right direction, much as a passage of Ma's clarified things for you."

"Oh, Mama, this is rapturous to hear." If Shirley had been looking in a mirror, she was sure stars would be in her eyes, so joyful did she feel, and she reached over and hugged her mother. "Show me this passage. I'll go get *Little Women* for you." She made a move to get up, but her mother touched her arm.

"No need to get it. I can quote it. It's a saying of Marmee's."

"Marmee's?" Shirley fairly shrieked. She was in a transport of delight.

Her mother nodded, a guilty look crossing her face. "I wish I could've been the mother she was. My own ma was a lot like her—"

"Oh, but Mama, you've been a good mother, a fine mother." A tear rolled down Shirley's cheek and landed on the tablet, blurring the words it fell upon. "I've always felt your love in so many ways. You kept us clean and clothed and fed, and you made sure we memorized the Scriptures like King David did, and you always had such a kind heart. I know that's where I got my compassion for people. That'll stand me in good stead when I'm a preacher's wife...Forrest's wife." The tingles were back, dancing down her spine.

Her mother smiled. "That saying of Marmee's—she was talking to Meg and Jo and Beth and Amy. She said, 'I want my daughters to be beautiful, accomplished, and good; to be admired, loved, and respected; to have a happy youth, to be well and wisely married, and to lead useful, pleasant lives, with as little care and sorrow to try them as God sees fit to send. To be loved and chosen by a good man is the best and sweetest thing which can happen to a woman; and I sincerely hope my girls know this beautiful experience.'"

It was so quiet, Shirley could hear every breath her mother took, a steady sucking in and out. But she couldn't hear her own. She had forgotten to breathe.

Shirley sighed and yawned at the same time, her chest expelling and taking in a great gulp of air, and she jumped to her feet and her mother did, too, and they hugged each other. Embracing, they wriggled back and forth like a fish on a hook. Then they laughed together, the mirthful sounds filling the quiet kitchen.

"Mama?" Shirley finally said, still in her mother's warm embrace.

"What, Dear?"

"You have a beautiful experience with Papa."

"I know." A pause and a giggle. "Shirley?"

"Yes, Mama?"

"You'll soon have a beautiful experience with Forrest."

In response, Shirley only smiled, feeling as radiant as a bride on her wedding day.

Chapter 13

"You want me to do what, Lord?" Forrest exclaimed in response to the Lord's voice He had grown familiar with. He was just finishing his last parishioner call late Saturday afternoon and was headed toward the parsonage. In this nippy November weather, he was looking forward to taking his boots off before a fire and eating the chicken pie the Widow Ford insisted he take home. "Surely You can't mean that, Lord."

That is precisely what I mean, Forrest.

"To go see Miss Campbell?" Forrest let out a snort. "Why would I want to go see her?"

You'll know when you get there.

"She's the last person I want to talk to."

Do you want to be a tinkling cymbal or an instrument of My love?

He swallowed deeply. "An instrument of Thy love, Father." He slowed Prancer and at a wide place in the road made a complete turnaround in his buggy and then headed toward the Campbell home.

"Lord, self is hard to bring under subjection, but I submit my will to Thee yet again. I'm trusting Thee to give me strength and wisdom."

My grace is sufficient for Thee.

"Hallelujah!"

❧

Shirley stood at the drainboard, slicing the huge ham she had just pulled out of the oven. Most evenings, they ate light suppers, but today her father smoked fresh ham meat, and so this meal would be like a feast. Tomorrow, at the dinner-on-the-grounds when the church celebrated its twenty-fifth anniversary, the Campbell family would bring more of the sliced ham plus the trimmings—mashed potatoes with redeye gravy, buttered creamed corn, green beans, and Mama's delectable desserts.

"The preacher just pulled up in the yard," Mrs. Campbell whispered to Shirley. "Why don't you go freshen up? I'll finish slicing the ham."

Startled, Shirley turned, questions in her eyes. Had he come to read the story she wrote about the church history?

Her mother seemed to discern her questions. She patted her arm. "Jesus is fixing things, Shirley."

Shirley nodded, feeling the peace that passed understanding flooding her soul. She pecked her mother on the cheek, thankful for the new bond that had grown between them in the last weeks, then crossed the kitchen on her way to her room.

"Be sure and get my bottle of rosewater off the bureau in my bedroom and use it liberally," her mother called.

"Thank you, Mama."

A quarter hour later, Shirley was washed and dressed in her second-best outfit, her hair freshly done up, the prized rosewater generously dabbed behind her ears and on her wrists. She entered the kitchen to resume her supper chores, as if this were the way she did things every day of the week.

"Here she is, Preacher," Mama announced, smiling broadly. "He was asking for you, Shirley. I invited him to stay for supper."

Shirley floated toward him. She didn't say a thing when she reached him. His eyes seemed to be reading hers, and the look that passed between them was sweeter than words.

"Shirley," he said softly, peering intently at her, his eyes searching her face and caressing her features. "After supper, may I speak with you?" He paused. "Privately?" he whispered.

She nodded shyly. "It would be my pleasure." She swallowed. "Forrest."

"Supper's ready," her mother announced. "Will everyone please gather at the table?"

❧

After supper, Forrest followed Mr. and Mrs. Campbell and Shirley into the parlor, and all four settled comfortably into the chairs and settee.

A quarter hour of conversation ensued, mostly about church and farm work. Then Mr. and Mrs. Campbell took their leave, Mrs. Campbell saying she had to see to the children, Mr.

Campbell mentioning something about a chore in the barn.

Forrest watched in amazement as Shirley got up from her chair and came to sit beside him on the small settee. His breath caught in his throat. He thought he would have to ask her to move closer, but she had taken the action on her own. "Shirley. . ."

"Forrest. . ."

He took her hand in his and kissed it softly.

She trembled in response, and her face lit up.

He didn't say anything. He was enjoying the look passing between them, like what they shared briefly before supper. He studied her face and her luxuriant hair, and he thought about her loveliness and her sweetness and her diligence and the other attributes that endeared her to him. He pondered the love he had for her and the love she had for him.

" 'Let him kiss me with the kisses of his mouth,' " she whispered, smiling up at him, like she was baiting him in the tenderest of ways.

His heart raced. He was surprised—and thrilled—at what she said.

"That's from Song of Solomon." Her voice was as gentle as the cooing of a mourning dove.

"I know." He smiled—broadly—enjoying her tender bantering. Then he did what she asked. He gathered her in his arms and brushed her lips with his.

"Forrest," she murmured as she eagerly kissed him back.

" 'Thou hast ravished my heart. That's from Song of Solomon, too.' "

"I know." She smiled.

In a flash, he was on his knees before her. "I love you, Shirley, with every breath I breathe."

"I love you, Forrest, with every breath I breathe."

"Will you be my wife, to have and to hold from this day forward?"

"I will be your wife, to have and to hold from this day forward."

He was delighted at her boldness. It thrilled him through and through. "My darling. . ."

She made a gesture for him to get up, and he sat down beside her. She snuggled into his embrace and told him how and when she came to love him, and how her repugnance for the role of preacher's wife had kept her from his arms. She related the journal-like entry in her grandmother's Bible and the impact it had on her. She shared about her experience with God in her bedroom, and she told him of the wise counsel her mother gave her.

In turn, he told her about his talk with the Lord on the Widow Ford's porch and how he had a heart change.

"I relish the idea of being in divine service as the wife of the Reverend Forrest Townsend," she said with confidence.

"Divine service?"

"What Grandfather calls the ministry."

I divine that a divine girl is in the future for me, he had once said. At the time, he'd wondered if it would be Miss Devine.

He drew in a deep, heady breath of rosewater as he looked down at the divine Miss Shirley Campbell, memorizing every nuance of her countenance. He took both of her hands in his and held them fast. "A divine girl for divine service."

"How sweet," she whispered.

"And a divine girl for me. Superb. Heavenly. Proceeding directly from God."

"Oh, Forrest. . ."

" 'Shall I compare thee to a summer's day? Thou art more lovely and more temperate.' That's Shakespeare."

"I know."

"I treasure you, my beautiful one. How I thank God for you."

She dipped her chin and smiled. "You make me feel beautiful. You make me feel like a princess."

"You are. You're a King's daughter." He pointed upward.

Long moments of pleasant togetherness passed. Then Forrest broke the silence. "Pending approval from your parents, is it agreeable with you if we announce our betrothal tomorrow at church?"

" 'So smile the heavens upon this holy act.' " She winked at him coquettishly. "That's Shakespeare, too."

"Ah, what a delight you are." Once more, he kissed her, was loathe to release her, but he did. "The first thing I need to do at church tomorrow morning is look up Mr. Wilbur."

"Mr. Wilbur?"

He chuckled. "I need to tell him I finally have Shirley."

She peered up at him, amusement lurking in her eyes. "Along with goodness and mercy?"

He nodded. "All the days of my life."

KRISTY DYKES

Kristy lives in sunny Florida with her husband, Milton, a minister. An award-winning author and former newspaper columnist, she's had hundreds of articles published in many publications including two *New York Times* subsidiaries, *Guideposts Angels*, etc. She's written novellas in two other Barbour anthologies, *American Dream* and *Sweet Liberty*. Kristy is a public speaker, and one of her favorite topics is "How to Love Your Husband," based on Titus 2:4. Her goal in writing and speaking is to "put a smile on your face, a tear in your eye, and a glow in your heart." Fun fact: Kristy is a native Floridian, as are generations of her forebears (blow on fingertips, rub on shoulder). She loves hearing from her readers. Write her at kristydykes@aol.com or c/o Author Relations—Barbour Publishing, P.O. Box 719, Uhrichsville, OH 44683.

Only a Name

by Debby Mayne

Dedication

Thanks to Wally, Alison, and Lauren
for continued support and understanding.

I'd like to thank friends Angela Ivanovskiy and
Ned Johnson for giving up valuable time to critique
my work and helping me become a better writer.

And thanks to anthology mates Pamela, Kristy,
and Paige for all the fun we had with this project.

Grudge not one against another, brethren, lest ye be condemned:
behold, the judge standeth before the door.
James 5:9

Chapter 1

Hickory Hollow, Missouri, 1954

W hy don't you go somewhere so we can have a little peace around here?" Eva hollered at her younger brother, Jack.

He rolled his eyes. "I would if I was old enough to drive. One more year."

"Go for a walk, then."

"I've got a better idea," Jack said sarcastically. "You go somewhere. Mom and Dad always let you have the car when you want it."

Eva started to argue, but then she thought for a moment. *Yeah, why don't I go out for a little while? Change of scenery would do me some good.*

As always, Ted Hargrove handed his daughter the key to the car and gave his standard, "Be careful. Don't try to run the yellow lights."

Eva snickered, grabbed the key, and headed out the door

before Jack could think of something else to say. Man, was he getting on her nerves lately.

The Hargroves had recently moved from Atlanta to Hickory Hollow to be close to the new dam being built on the big lake near town. Eva's father, Ted, had been in partnership with James Randall, who came from one of the founding families of the small community. When James had heard that the Corps of Engineers was about to begin the enormous project that would take many years to complete, he'd talked Ted into working with him. With James's contacts and Ted's business acumen, they'd won the bid for supplying the materials for the foundation of the dam.

As Eva left her family's brand-new, three-bedroom, two-bathroom, two-car carport house in Paradise Acres, the subdivision of tract homes with the slogan "All you have to bring is your family and your furniture and leave the rest up to us," she thought about how different her life was turning out. Nearly two years ago, she'd graduated from high school and enrolled in a secretarial course with hopes of snagging a great job and meeting lots of interesting people. Instead, two months after Eva got her secretarial certificate, her father announced they'd be moving from Atlanta to Hickory Hollow. What a blow. Eva's plans had gone down the tubes. Sure, she could have stayed behind, but she wasn't quite ready to be on her own.

As she wound through the streets leading to the center of the small town, Eva looked around at the scenery. She had to admit, the place was postcard pretty. The hills in the background provided a perfect backdrop for all the foliage in the foreground. Bright green leaves from trees of all shapes and sizes framed clusters of wildflowers that laced the sides of the road. Eva wondered if they'd been planted there on purpose or if they'd taken seed on their own. Whatever the case, the place really was lovely. Too bad she'd had to leave all her friends behind.

With the windows down as her car rolled through town, Eva inhaled the fresh scent of the expansive outdoors. Even with the small one- and two-story stone and wooden structures that housed family-owned businesses, the town appeared natural and unspoiled by modern commerce.

Eva glanced at her watch. She'd only been gone ten minutes, and she'd seen everything she knew how to find.

With a sigh, she parallel parked on Main Street and hopped out in front of the town's only drugstore. As she went inside, the woman at the register greeted her right away.

"You must be from Paradise Acres," the woman said.

Tilting her head to one side, Eva asked, "How did you know?"

The woman offered a good-natured laugh. "We don't get many new folks in town, and most of the ones we do get come from there."

"Oh." Eva glanced around. "Got any candy bars?"

"Sure," the woman said as she came around from behind the register. "Right over here."

"What's there to do around here?" Eva asked after she laid her candy bar on the counter to pay.

"All depends on what you like."

"Well, for starters, is there anything for people like me? I'm twenty, and I don't know anyone in town yet."

"There's always church. We have quite a few young people your age in our congregation, and they all seem to find plenty to do."

Church. That was the last thing Eva would have thought to do. But she didn't want to be rude, so she nodded. "We just might do that."

"Here, let me draw you a map," the woman offered. "That is, if you have a minute."

"Okay." Eva waited while the woman drew the map.

"Here ya go. Just take the first road to your right and go on out of town about two miles. Turn right at the red barn. The church is gray. You can't miss it."

"Thanks," Eva said as she took the paper. "Think it'll be okay if I go there now?"

"Sure, it's okay, but there might not be anyone there. Pastor's on vacation, so his associate is filling in. Nice young man. I don't know if he keeps hours during the week or not, though."

"That's okay," Eva replied. She actually hoped no one would be there. She just needed something to do.

"Oh, by the way, my name's June, and my husband, Lester, is the pharmacist. We own this place."

Eva smiled. "Thanks, June."

"Come back and see us."

"I'm sure I will."

As Eva got into her car, she smiled. She couldn't remember the name of her pharmacist back in Atlanta. Come to think of it, she wasn't sure that she ever actually knew his name.

The directions were simple enough, but once she got out of town, Eva found herself surrounded by a thick forest of hickories and oaks as the road curved, making a ribbon through the woods.

Suddenly, out of nowhere, a red barn appeared on the right. Eva slowed to a stop and studied her map. Now she had to watch for a road that would lead to the church.

Fortunately, although the road was narrow, it was paved, so Eva wasn't worried. She was pretty good at following directions, and she wasn't very far from town.

As the clearing came into view, Eva gasped. There it was. A small, gray limestone church with a wing under construction off to one side of it sat at the base of the hill. A combination of wildflowers and clusters of annuals graced the path leading from the dirt parking lot to the sidewalk.

The scene was absolutely breathtaking. Eva hadn't expected anything so small yet so grand. The church appeared to be very old, and it exuded an inviting warmth, even from the outside.

Eva pulled up beside the one car in the parking lot, turned off the ignition, and got out. As she walked around the yard, admiring the natural beauty of the land, she caught snippets of a human voice coming from inside the church.

She boldly made her way to the front doors and peeked

inside, where it was mostly dark but with a trickle of light coming from the other side. The voice was louder, steadier now. She could tell someone was practicing a speech of some sort, based on stops and starts, with the inflection and tone of a professional public speaker.

Eva let herself in as discreetly as she could. She quietly tiptoed to the back pew and sat down, hoping she wouldn't be noticed. She wanted to see and hear what was going on.

As the man spoke, she recognized verses from the gospels that she'd heard before. Back in Atlanta, her family went to the big church in town—the one where almost everyone went. Her father insisted she and Jack go along because he wanted to make a good impression on his business connections. She'd mostly slept through the sermons, but there were times when she'd listened.

"We're all sinners," the man said in a very gentle tone that lifted as he went on, "but by the grace of God, we've been freed from the ravages of our natures. We have Jesus. . . ." His voice trailed off as he squinted and leaned forward. "Is there someone out there?"

Eva nervously glanced around, although she knew he was talking about her. "Yes, but go on. I'll sit here quietly and listen for a few minutes."

The man chuckled and continued, talking about how Jesus had been sent as our Savior. "Imagine taking your only child and placing him in the hands of your enemy," the man said. "God loved us so much, He was willing to suffer to free us from our sins. And we are all sinners."

Okay, time to leave, she thought as she stood and tried to get to the door without being noticed.

"Where are you going?"

Uh oh. Caught.

"I'm, uh. . .I'm going outside. I wasn't sure if anyone was in here, and I was just curious."

"Hold on a minute, I'd like to talk to you," he said.

Eva didn't see that she had a choice, so she settled back in her seat. The man continued while she listened. He was actually very interesting, and she was able to understand his stories. When he came to a stop, she figured he was finished, so she applauded.

He laughed. "That good, huh?"

"Oh, yes," she said. "It was great."

Once again, she stood to leave.

"Hey, let me walk you to your car." He'd put his notes on the podium and hopped down off the stage.

"That's okay. I can find my way out," Eva replied.

This time, she slid out of her seat and slipped out the door before he had a chance to say anything else. She'd made it to the sidewalk when she heard the man's footsteps as he ran up behind her.

"Hope I didn't scare you away," he said as he made his way to her side.

Now that she saw him up close, Eva noticed that he wasn't much older than she, which surprised her. She thought preachers were old—at least as old as her father.

"No, I'm not scared," she replied as she looked into his

amused eyes. "Not yet, anyway."

"Was it too much?" he asked.

"What do you mean?"

He shrugged and held out his hands. "The pastor is on vacation, so I'm delivering the sermon this Sunday. It's only my second time to preach at this church, so I want to make sure it's perfect."

Now, Eva had to laugh. She couldn't help it.

"What's so funny?"

Eva shook her head. "I never thought about preachers worrying about their sermons. I figured you just told us what the Bible said and we were supposed to listen."

"That's not what I'm talking about. Am I leaving anything out?"

"How would I know?" she asked. "You're the preacher. The expert on the Bible."

He smiled at her and stopped. "Is that what you think?"

"Yeah," she replied. "Preachers know everything there is to know about the Bible."

"Oh, that's where you're wrong," he said, his smile fading. "First of all, I'm still learning right along with everyone else. Every time I read more of the Bible, I learn something new. The light keeps getting brighter as things click in my mind."

"No kidding?"

He cracked a smile, but it quickly faded. "No kidding."

Eva shook her head. "I had no idea."

"I probably don't know nearly as much as you think I know. For one, your name."

"Oh, sorry. I'm Eva Hargrove. My family just moved to Paradise Acres."

He extended his hand. "And I'm Robert Campbell, associate pastor of this wonderful church."

"Nice to meet you, Rob—er, Pastor Campbell."

He chuckled. "Call me Robert, okay?"

"Are you sure that's okay?" she asked. It felt so awkward.

"Of course, it is. Everyone else calls me by my first name." He nodded toward her car. "Is that yours?"

"It's my family's. My dad let me have it so I could get away from my little brother. He's driving me insane." The instant she said those words, she cringed. He must think she was awful.

"I have a brother who does that, too. I sometimes wonder if God put him in my life to test me."

Eva found herself instantly liking this man. He was warm and seemed empathetic. Smiling, she nodded.

"Am I being presumptuous by asking you to bring your family to church this Sunday?" he asked. "Or do you already have a church in town?"

Chapter 2

Eva didn't know what to say. If she told him they hadn't yet settled in enough to find a church, he'd expect to see them on Sunday. Yet if she said they had, it would be a lie. She couldn't lie to a preacher.

He obviously sensed her reluctance because he offered a gentle smile. "You don't have to say anything if it makes you uncomfortable."

That did it. "We'd love to be here on Sunday."

Robert's face lit up. "Really? That's great! Maybe after the service, you can let me know what you think."

"What I think?"

He nodded. "Yeah. You can tell me if I sounded okay."

Warmth flooded Eva. "I really need to get back. My parents have no idea where I am, and they'll start worrying."

"They shouldn't worry around here," he said. "There aren't too many places you can be in Hickory Hollow."

As soon as Eva got back in her car and out of sight of Robert, she studied her map in reverse and made it home in fifteen minutes. Jack was waiting outside as she drove up.

"Where you been, Eva?" he hollered. "Mom and Dad are worried sick."

Quoting Robert Campbell, Eva said, "There aren't too many places I can be in Hickory Hollow."

"You got that right," Jack agreed. He glanced down at the sack in her hand. "Did you bring me a present?"

Eva started to tell him no but thought better of it. *Might as well make this a peace offering.*

"Here," she said. "Just don't eat it before supper. Mom will be furious with me."

Jack grinned back at her. "Thanks, Eva. Sometimes you're okay for a sister."

Eva's mom pounced. "Eva, you were gone long enough. Where were you?"

"I drove around Hickory Hollow."

She watched as her mother stirred something in the pot. "You know it wasn't my idea to move here, right? We had to for your father's business."

The only person excited about this move had been Eva's father. The other three Hargroves had begged him to bid on some jobs in Atlanta. But he was stubborn, and he insisted it would be a fun adventure.

"I know." She had to change the subject. "I found a really neat church."

Her mother's eyebrows lifted. "A church? You went to a church?"

Eva nodded. "It's really small but very pretty. I even met

the associate pastor. He asked us to come there on Sunday."

"Why, of course he did," her mom said with a dubious look. "I'm sure he'd love to have more paying members."

"Oh, Mom, he's very nice."

Eva surprised herself that she'd stuck up for Robert, considering the fact that she barely knew him. But from the short conversation they'd had, she sensed that he wasn't one to invite people to church just to get into their wallets. He'd been sincere.

"Maybe," Mom said. "We'll have to discuss it with your father."

The woman is troubled, Robert thought long after he watched Eva drive away. *She's sweet, but she's not happy.*

He let out a deep sigh as he slowly walked back to the church to gather his notes. It was getting late, and he needed to head back to the tiny old house he was renting in town.

On the way, he stopped off at Taylor's Pharmacy, where June greeted him from the counter. "Hey, Robert, did you meet that very pretty young lady I sent out to see you this afternoon?"

"So you're the culprit." Robert smiled as he picked up a pack of gum, tossed it on the counter, then dug in his pocket for a dime.

"Afraid so. She wanted something to do, so I sent her out to the church. Did you get a chance to chat with her?"

"We had a nice little talk. I invited her to church."

June chuckled. "You young people don't waste any time, do you?"

"I try not to." He put the gum in his shirt pocket, nodded, made his way to the door, and said, "See ya Sunday, June. Thanks for recruiting some new members."

"Any time, Robert. Just let me know when to quit."

As Robert opened his car door, he saw a man with a familiar face approach his car. He'd only been back in Hickory Hollow a few months, but he still recognized quite a few people—particularly those who were supposed to be his enemies for long-forgotten reasons.

He paused. When the man was within hearing distance, he lifted a hand and waved. "Hey, James. I heard you were back in town."

James Randall's scowl was Robert's first clue that the hard feelings wouldn't end without considerable effort. He needed to be cautious and watch for an opening to change things.

"Yeah, what of it?" James replied gruffly.

"It's hard to stay away, isn't it?"

"Money's what brought me back."

Robert wanted to talk to James, to see if he could patch the rift that had started nearly a century ago between their families. The feud between the Campbells and Randalls was well known throughout these parts, but time had passed, and he wanted to bury the hatchet. He'd heard stories of what had started the whole division, but he suspected much of it might have been blown out of proportion over the years. Whatever the problem was, Robert figured it was time to change things—to mend fences.

Deciding he'd just been given an opportunity to explain his presence in town, Robert said, "I came back to preach."

"So I hear." James continued scowling.

"Why don't you come on out to the church on Sunday? It'll be nice to see more familiar faces in the congregation."

James snorted. "Don't count on it. Campbells and Randalls don't mix well."

"C'mon, James, we're grown men. We don't have to perpetuate this stupid feud our families started way back when."

"Who're you callin' stupid?"

James narrowed his eyes and glared, sending a shiver of warning up Robert's spine. Maybe this wasn't the right time to patch things up. Some problems took time to fix, and Robert had all the time in the world.

"I'm not calling anyone stupid. I just thought—"

"That's your problem, Campbell, always has been," James said. "You think too much and don't take action."

Robert remained standing there, staring after the man he was supposed to hate. But he didn't hate anyone. There were times when he didn't particularly care to be around certain people, and this was one of them; but he'd learned that those were the people who needed the extra effort.

Rumors and sightings around Hickory Hollow didn't stay behind closed doors for long. People knew each other's business, inside and out. He suspected curious observers were watching, and his brief encounter with James would be ripe fodder for the gossip mill for the next few days. Oh well, some things can't be changed. Coming back to Hickory

Hollow, he knew he'd have to take the bad along with the treasures.

Robert hadn't been in town more than a day before he'd heard that James Randall had moved back after winning the bid on supplying materials for the new dam, which was supposed to be a huge boon for the town. As much as he loved Hickory Hollow just the way it was, Robert also knew that without progress, the town would die. He'd seen it in other places.

This was why Paradise Acres had sprung up. A land developer had taken advantage of cheap prices and bought a large parcel of what used to be farm land, and they'd built tract houses with amenities like parks and swimming pools. Families were attracted to this because they were able to form their own brand-new communities rather than try to fit in to a place where they didn't have a history.

Robert went home and ate a quick dinner, then looked around for something to do. He'd already read the paper, and he still had some nervous energy.

Since there wasn't anything else to do at this time of day and Robert's adrenaline was still flowing, he decided to go for a drive. He wound his way through the narrow, tree-lined streets of Hickory Hollow and inhaled the crisp, fresh air. It sure was good to be home, even though many of his relatives had either died or moved away. His parents no longer lived here because they'd been offered a small fortune for the family farm. His father had told him it was time they moved on and lived their dream. Robert's mother had always wanted to live in a big city, and now was their chance.

Robert had spent enough time in big cities, ministering to the poor and lost, to know how fortunate the people were in Hickory Hollow. Even though they didn't have all the businesses, restaurants, and elaborate entertainment here, they had something much more important—a sense of who they were. Hopefully, that wouldn't change with progress.

శ్రీ

"Eva, come on in here," her father said. "We're through discussing business. Maybe you and James can talk."

It was no big secret that her parents wanted her and James to get together. "He's a good, honest, hard-working businessman," her father had argued a week ago. But Eva had no desire to date James. She didn't find him attractive or interesting.

James grinned when he saw her. "How ya been, Eva?"

"Fine, I guess." She sat down on the brand-new turquoise upholstered sofa her mother had recently purchased to go in their new home. It still had plastic on it, so it made a whooshing sound as she sank down in it.

Eva's father chuckled. "My daughter met some preacher this afternoon, and she wants to go to church on Sunday. Know anything about the churches around here?"

James squinted. "A little. Which church?"

Eva studied James. She could tell he was nervous.

"It's out by Hollow Creek," she spoke up.

"Yeah, I know the church." James took a sip of the tea Eunice had brought him. "My family used to go there."

"Really?" her father asked with new interest. "Any chance of making decent business contacts?"

James smirked. "You can make business contacts anywhere. All depends what kind of business you want."

Eva could hear his underlying anger, but she couldn't imagine where it came from. With a shrug, she said, "I just thought it would be nice to shop around for a church. It's as good a place as any to start."

"How many churches do you think a place like this has?" her father asked.

"You might be surprised," James replied. "Lots of the farmers and their families come in on Sundays, so three of four have sprung up over the last ten years. Some people spend the day at church."

"Not me," her father said. "I don't wanna hang out at church all day."

"It's been awhile since I've been to church," James finally admitted. "Since I've been back, I haven't had much time for that sort of thing."

Eva saw her opportunity. "Good. Then why don't we all go to the church by Hollow Creek? We can sit together and listen to Robert preach."

James opened his mouth but quickly clamped it shut. A flash of recognition crossed his eyes and just as quickly vanished, but Eva saw it. James knew Robert. She could tell.

Her father let out a long sigh as he stood up from his recliner. "I guess I better let you two young people talk. I have some reading to catch up on."

Once her father was out of the room, Eva turned to James. "Okay, spill it. What's up between you and Robert?"

"I don't know what you're talking about, Eva."

"And I don't believe you for a minute. Do you want to go to church there or not?"

"I'm not sure," he replied. Eva suspected he was being extra careful because her father was the partner with the money. James had the connections, but without her father's money, he wouldn't be in business.

"Either you do or you don't," she finally said. "I want to try that church, and since Robert's preaching on Sunday and I met him, I want to go there. I'm sure Dad will go along with me if I let him know how important it is to me."

With his jaw firmly set, James stared at her for a few seconds. Slowly, he began to nod. "Okay, fine. We'll go."

"You don't have to attend the same church we visit," she reminded him.

"Maybe not, but it would probably be best if I did."

"Why?" Eva challenged him. This was the first time church had come up in conversation since they'd been in the Hickory Hollow community, so she didn't understand why James was acting so weird about it.

"There's no reason not to attend the same church, is there?" he replied, challenging her.

Nothing like answering a question with a question. Eva recognized the evasion technique.

"You can go to any church you want as long as it's based on the Bible, right?" Eva asked, pushing harder to get him to tell her whatever it was he was trying to keep hidden.

They had a minute-long stare-down before he stood. "You need to get off your high horse, Eva. Quit punishing your father and me for uprooting you from Atlanta."

The nerve of that man!

Chapter 3

Robert found himself at the entrance to Paradise Acres, the large stone gate emblazoned with the name in tall, forest green letters. He was about to turn in when he spotted a sleek sports car whipping around the corner. Squinting to see if he knew who it was, he was surprised to see James Randall behind the wheel. James obviously didn't see him as he sped right past, in a hurry to leave.

Turning his attention back to the sign, he thought about how different this place looked now. It used to belong to his great-grandfather and was the first piece of property that had been sold, long before his father sold off the rest of the farm. For years, it sat neglected, until the developers saw the opportunity and dollar signs.

Have to give them credit, though, Robert thought. The neighborhood looked very nice, clean, and crisp. They'd put in sidewalks and streetlights, and all the houses had wide front porches, giving it a feeling of community.

He remembered his conversation with Eva Hargrove earlier. She said her family had purchased a home here in Paradise Acres. Maybe she'd be outside, and he could meet her family.

All the houses had the same basic look but in different pastel colors. It really was a pretty little neighborhood, even though his heart ached at how different things were. He missed sitting beneath the tall oak tree that was now the centerpiece on the playground with brightly colored equipment.

Robert consoled himself, thinking that other children would be able to enjoy shade from the old tree, but he wondered if they'd appreciate it as he had. His grandmother used to bring him freshly squeezed lemonade as he read or daydreamed on hot summer days. In the autumn, he enjoyed the panoramic display of colors the Lord provided as the leaves changed and danced through the air. Wintertime brought the red birds and crisp, biting winds that made him shiver. Spring was amazing, too, because crocus flowers poked their colorful heads through the last of the remaining snow, letting him know a burst of bright color would follow soon.

As he drove through the subdivision, he noticed lights shining through picture windows in the front of almost every house. His heart hammered when he spotted the car driven by Eva a few hours ago. Although he knew she lived here in Paradise Acres and he'd hoped to catch a glimpse of her, he wasn't prepared for the feeling of joy that flooded him. Slowing down, Robert tried to decide whether to stop or keep going. He admonished himself because he always paid follow-up visits to people who'd expressed an interest in the church. Why should this be any different?

Fighting his feelings of panic at the thought of seeing Eva with the long brown hair and bright green eyes, Robert parked, headed up the sidewalk, and lifted his fist to knock. He paused for a few seconds, then held his breath and just did it.

The boy who answered the door was obviously a young teen, but they met eye-to-eye. "Hi, is Eva in?"

The tall, gangly boy with the ducktail-styled brown hair the same color as his sister's turned and hollered, "Hey, Eva, some guy's at the door asking for you."

Robert stepped back, a little stunned at the volume of the kid's voice. "If this is a bad time, I can come back later."

"Naw, she's here. We just got finished with supper, and she's in the kitchen helping Mom with the dishes. I don't think she heard me." He took a step back and opened the door wider. "C'mon in."

Robert took a tentative step inside, then closed the door behind himself. The boy had already run off, leaving him standing there alone, surrounded by bright, plastic-covered, turquoise-and-wood furniture that was obviously brand new. And boxes. Lots of boxes stacked against the wall.

Out of the corner of his eye, Robert saw movement, so he spun to face the doorway leading to another room. When he saw Eva's face break into a smile, his heart did a flip before it pounded so hard he was certain she'd be able to hear it.

"I, uh, thought I might stop by to see about you," he said.

The instant he heard himself stutter, he felt like turning around and running. But he couldn't. He had to pretend to be composed and sure of himself. "Sorry if this isn't a good time."

"Oh, no, it's quite all right," she said as she crossed the room and took his hand. "C'mon in the kitchen and meet my mom. Dad's out back, but I can go get him."

"Are you sure?" Robert asked. Her touch was soft but firm, which was comforting.

"Don't be silly. We're happy to have people over."

Once in the kitchen, Robert saw a woman standing in front of the kitchen sink, a dish towel in her hands, looking like the picture of domestic normalcy. She had the same build as Eva, but her eyes were different, and she didn't seem quite as sure of herself.

"Mom, this is Robert Campbell," Eva said. "Remember that preacher I told you about?" Not giving her mother a chance to respond, she turned to Robert. "Robert, this is my mother, Eunice Hargrove."

"Rev. Campbell?" Eunice said.

"Please, call me Robert," he replied as he extended his hand.

She wiped her hands on the towel and accepted his handshake with a nervous giggle. "If you're sure that's all right. . .Robert."

Eva bounced toward the back door. "Let me go get my dad. Wait right here."

"Are you from here, Robert?" Eunice asked.

"Yes, originally. I moved away, but I felt compelled to

return. When the board of elders at the church found out I was interested in coming back, I was called to be associate pastor of the church."

"That's nice," she replied. "Would you like some iced tea?"

"Sure," he said with a quick nod. "That would be great."

By the time Eunice placed the glass of tea in front of Robert, Eva had returned, dragging her father behind her. "Dad, I want you to meet Robert Campbell."

"So you're the young man my daughter's dying to see on Sunday. Nice to meet you."

Robert caught the shushing glare Eva sent her father, but he pretended not to notice. Eva's brother reappeared, this time with neatly combed hair and a clean shirt, and they met and shook hands. Jack was a lively child, and Robert thought about how much the youth program needed this kind of energy.

He told the Hargrove family all about the church and the programs they currently offered. "I hope to see you there on Sunday. We're small but growing."

"So I've heard. My business partner said his family used to attend church there."

"What's his name?" Robert asked. "Maybe I know him."

"Randall. James Randall."

Robert's insides clenched. He had no idea these people would even know a member of the Randall family, let alone be in business with James.

"Yes, I know James Randall," Robert said, trying his best to hide his dismay.

Eva tilted her head and studied him. He could feel her penetrating gaze, so he tried hard not to look her directly in the eye. He needed some time to digest this new information to prevent further discomfort.

"Good," Ted Hargrove said. "We've already discussed going to your church, and we'll be there on Sunday. I'm not guaranteeing we'll join. I hope you understand. We have to shop around a little before we decide where to hang our tithes."

Robert's chin dropped. He'd never heard it put so crudely.

Backing toward the door leading to the front of the house, Robert forced a smile. "It's been really nice meeting you folks. I look forward to seeing you Sunday."

All the way home, Robert felt a strange sort of knot in his gut. He was torn, but he couldn't deny his attraction to Eva. She was the main reason he wouldn't give up on the Hargrove family. He had to see her again, even if she was the daughter of James Randall's business partner.

❧

Eva hopped out of the car the instant her father pulled into the open slot in the dirt parking lot. She heard her mother say, "How lovely."

James was supposed to meet them here, and her father had promised to sit in the back pew. Eva didn't like being so far back, but since she didn't know anyone at this church yet, she planned to stick with her family.

"This place is small," her father said, not bothering to keep his voice down. "Nothing like our church in Atlanta."

Eunice glanced around nervously. "Do you think they'll like us?" she asked in a meek voice.

"Who cares?" he boomed. "We'll probably never come back to this one. Doesn't look like we'll see many people who can actually do us any good. Most of the folks in here look poor as church mice."

Eva wanted to slink under the seat. Her father might not care who heard him, but she did. She didn't want to hurt Robert's feelings, and the people sitting in the pew in front of them looked very nice. Granted, they had on clothes that looked like they'd come from someone's grandmother's attic, but that was okay.

When Eva heard Robert's voice from behind, she quickly turned around and caught his eye. He winked at her, and her insides fluttered. She sighed.

Robert stopped at each pew on his way to the front, starting with the one her family shared. He spoke to her father, but kept glancing over at her. Eva couldn't help but smile back at him.

Shortly after Robert moved toward the pulpit, James came in. Her father had saved him a seat between himself and Eva.

"Maybe the two of you could share a hymnal," Dad suggested.

"There are plenty of hymnals for each person to have one," Eva informed him.

"Maybe so," he said as he gave her a look she knew too well. "I'm sure the Lord would be happy if you shared."

Eva gulped. What her father was saying without spelling it out was that he wanted her to share a hymnal with James. He wanted them to stand close and hold the same book so their hands would touch. She cringed. She wasn't attracted to James in the least.

Robert reached the podium and lifted his hands, gesturing for the congregation to stand. "Please rise for the opening hymn," he instructed.

James moved his lips, but Eva didn't hear a sound coming out of his mouth. She, on the other hand, sang heartily because she felt that was what the Lord would want her to do.

"Do you have to be so loud?" James whispered as he stuck his finger in his ear.

"Am I that bad?" Eva leaned away and stared at him, waiting for an answer.

"Well, no, I wouldn't say you were bad. I just don't want people staring at us."

Eva grinned. "So you're ashamed of me. I'll have to tell Dad so he won't make you sit next to me in the future."

"Oh, no, don't do that," he said, then took a deep breath, slowly letting it out in resignation. "Go ahead and sing to your heart's content if it makes you happy."

She finished the song, belting out the words even louder than before. James was funny as he flinched on the high notes.

After they were asked to sit, Robert continued the service with announcements and an invitation for guests to stand. Eva stood, but the rest of her family remained seated. James looked up at her as if begging her to sit back down before she was noticed, but it was too late. Robert had already acknowledged her.

He told the congregation who Eva was and said she and her family were there as his guests. He paused before mentioning James, saying he hoped James would return to the church and consider making it his church home.

When Robert softly said the name "James Randall" and paused, several gasps came from the front of the church. Eva was startled at their reaction. There was something about James that she needed to find out—something her dad obviously didn't know. She leaned forward to see if he had noticed the reaction, but her dad was busy flipping through the pages of the hymnal, marking the places of the songs listed in the bulletin.

Robert's message had changed somewhat from what she'd heard earlier in the week. He'd put more emphasis on forgiveness and not holding grudges.

Eva saw James Randall squirm as he listened to Robert elaborating on the message, segueing into the topics of forgiveness and mercy. Yes, something was going on between Robert and James, and she fully intended to find out what it was.

Chapter 4

"W ell?" Eva asked her parents as they stood and waited for an opening in the press of people making their way to the back of the church to greet Robert after the service. "What'd you think?"

Her father shoved his hands in his pockets and jingled his change. "The young man's obviously an excellent speaker. He seems to have this bunch pretty well under his spell." He sniffed. "Very charismatic."

Eva had expected something like that from her father, so she turned to James. "How about you, James?" She lifted one eyebrow and waited.

"I'm not likely to get too involved in this little country church," he replied, not looking her in the eye.

"And why not?" she asked, testing him.

"Eva, honey, why don't we let the men decide these things?" her mother said. "It doesn't really matter what church we go to, as long as we go."

This wasn't the time or place to argue, so Eva kept quiet.

She'd talk about it later, when there weren't so many people around.

The Hargrove family and James filed out as the crowd thinned. James tried to duck out the side door, but it was locked. He had no choice but to leave the way he'd come in—out the main entrance where Robert was standing, shaking hands. He grumbled but shuffled toward the door.

Robert shook her father's hand first and offered a heartfelt invitation to come back. Next in line was her mother, who told Robert how much she enjoyed his sermon. When James reached the door, Robert extended his hand, but James kept walking, his hands in his pockets, a scowl on his face. Eva noticed Robert's expression of concern. Quickly recovering, Robert turned to Eva.

"I was glad to see you and your family here today, Eva. I hope you return." He cleared his throat, glanced over his shoulder at James, and added, "And James, too. He's always welcome in this church."

When they reached the parking lot, James turned to Eva's father. "How about going out to lunch? There's a boardinghouse in town, Granny Palmer's, and they serve the best fried chicken you've ever tasted."

Dad winked at Eva and said, "Tell you what, kids. Why don't the two of you go ahead and eat at that boardinghouse? Eunice and I need to head home. I promised her I'd put some shelves in her laundry room."

"But—" Mom started to protest, but then she caught the look her dad was shooting in her direction. She smiled in understanding. "Oh, okay, that's right. I really do need those shelves." To drive the point home, she added, "I have no place to put the detergent."

"C'mon, Eunice," Dad said as he took her by the arm and led her to the car.

"You don't wanna be with me, do you, Eva?" James said gruffly.

Eva forced a smile at her father's partner. "Whatever gives you that idea, James?"

He shook his head and walked her to his car, opening the door for her before going around to his side. Eva pounced on him the instant he got in, now that they were alone and no one else could hear.

"Okay, what gives, James?"

Without looking at her, he said, "I don't know what you're talking about."

"You and Robert. The two of you obviously have a problem with each other. Or at least you don't seem to like him. Looks to me like he's making an effort to get along with you."

"Can't trust the Campbells," James growled.

"What? Stop being so cryptic. You're not making an ounce of sense."

James sighed. "Okay, if you really wanna know, the Campbells and the Randalls are enemies. Have been for a long time."

"Enemies? Why?"

He shrugged. "It's something that started a long time ago, and I'd rather not go into it."

"Do you even know why?" she asked.

James started the engine and backed out of his space. He was almost to the main road before he said, "No, not really. All I know is that I don't like anyone from these parts named Campbell."

"Do you realize how silly that is?"

"It's not silly," he replied. "It's a fact."

"I won't accept that, James. If something happened a long time ago, why can't you and Robert just laugh about it and be friends? He seems like such a nice guy."

"That's all an act."

Eva groaned. She could tell she was getting nowhere fast. "You're impossible."

"Maybe so, but not as impossible as a Campbell and a Randall ever becoming friends."

☙

Robert watched as James and Eva drove away. His heart sank. What was James telling her? Would he try to poison her mind against him and his family?

The feud between the Campbells and the Randalls had begun so many years ago, Robert doubted any of the reasons he heard for its origins were completely accurate. Sure, there was probably a grain of truth in there somewhere, but information had a way of getting distorted over time. Both families had gone to the same church, even after the feud started, but once Robert's cousin, also a Campbell, became a pastor at the church when Robert and James were teenagers, everything changed. The Randalls' attendance came to an abrupt halt, and Robert never saw James in church again. Until today.

Robert could only imagine what James had heard about his family. None of it had been good, obviously.

Robert had heard plenty about the Randalls, too, but he knew it had nothing to do with James. In fact, Robert had heard some good things about James's business ethics.

"Hey, Pastor, wanna come over for a big ham dinner?" one of the men from the church called out. "Betty outdid herself this time. There's a table filled with sweet potatoes, coleslaw, lima beans, and some of Josh Goody's honey, straight from the bees."

"Sounds good, Andy, but I think I'll pass. I promised some friends I'd meet them at Granny Palmer's."

"Why don't you stop by later and pick up some leftovers, then? There's enough ham, you can take some home and have sandwiches all week."

Robert nodded and smiled. "I just might do that."

The people in the church were, for the most part, not well-to-do, but they were kind and took care of their own. No one would ever want for anything as long as they had each other. Robert felt warm inside at the thought of how close he felt to everyone there, even those he didn't know well, because of their openness and generosity.

After the last car had left the parking lot, Robert locked the church and took off toward town. Hopefully, his friends were still at Granny Palmer's waiting for him. He'd told them he'd be late, but many of the church members had lingered a little longer than usual because of the perfect weather. Robert wasn't about to run people off just so he could eat dinner.

The first car he noticed in Granny Palmer's small gravel parking lot was James Randall's. His heart sank. He didn't want to antagonize the guy, but he wasn't going to let anyone stop him from eating here, either.

He entered the small dining room, where long tables were filled with families and groups of singles, all sitting together as if one big, happy family. Industrial-sized bowls filled with generous amounts of butter beans and corn were being passed from one person to the next, until everyone's plates were filled. There were always seconds.

"Hey, Rob, over here," Jerome Townsend hollered. One of Jerome's great-great-uncles had pastored the church many years ago, so he came from a line of old family friends that went way back several generations.

All heads turned toward him. Robert felt heat on the back of his neck as he made his way to where Jerome and a few of their old high school buddies, all of them still single, were sitting.

"This is the best chicken I've ever eaten," Jerome said. "Better grab some before it's all gone."

Very quickly, everyone else in the dining room went back to their own business, and soon Robert was deeply involved in a discussion about upcoming church activities. Since he'd returned to Hickory Hollow, some of the younger members who'd fallen away had come back to church. Robert knew this was one of the reasons he'd been given the job.

As Robert chatted with his buddies, he glanced around the room, looking for Eva. He didn't want to admit, even to himself, that he cared where she was or that she was there, but it didn't work. He cared. And he felt his heart lift when he met her gaze the instant he spotted her. Her smile warmed him from the inside out. Those big, green eyes of hers were filled with life and laughter.

Eva held his gaze for a moment before turning to look at James. Robert followed her glance, and he found himself being glared at with pure hatred. The heat returned to his neck as he quickly looked back at his friends, who had apparently observed everything.

"Things haven't changed much, have they?" Jerome asked.

"Afraid not."

"Too bad James is stubborn and bullheaded."

Robert shrugged. "He's not so bad. A little misguided, that's all."

"Well, maybe," Jerome said cautiously. "But I, for one, have never trusted the guy. He's always up to something."

Robert hated gossip, so he quickly changed the subject. He knew how out-of-control this kind of discussion could get, and as tempting as it was to participate, he forced himself to return to church matters.

⁂

"Just stop it, James," Eva scolded.

"Stop what? That guy has some nerve following us here."

"What?" she shrieked before forcing herself to hold her

voice down. "You don't own this place."

"No, but there's not enough room here for a Randall and a Campbell."

Eva rolled her eyes. "You're impossible. Just eat so we can go."

James shoved a forkful of potato salad in his mouth. Eva felt his animosity spilling across the table, where they were surrounded by other people from the small town. She'd seen several of them out and about, but she didn't know any of them. Hopefully, that would change, but as long as she was with James, she suspected he'd try to prevent her from getting to know too many people. He was introverted and kept his circle of friends way too small to suit her. Eva's life had always been filled with friends and oodles of laughter. James's somberness would suffocate her if she hung around him for long.

Eva was stuck with James for awhile, and she saw that she had two choices. She could either meekly accept his dour attitude, or she could be herself. She chose to act in a way that was true to her nature: chatty.

"Wasn't that a great sermon?" she asked. "I can't wait to hear what he says next week."

"He won't be preaching next week," James said in a monotone. "The pastor will be back."

The smile quickly faded from Eva's lips. Okay, so he was determined to be miserable. She couldn't let him get to her.

"That's okay. I'm still looking forward to church next Sunday. The people all seem so nice and friendly."

"They're not the kind of people who can do anything for us. I've been thinking we need to go to a church in town where the mayor and some of the business owners go."

That did it. Eva wasn't about to sit back and let James act like such a jerk.

"Look, James, if you want to go to church with business owners, then go right ahead. I want to go to that little church by Hollow Creek."

"Your parents might have different ideas," he said as he placed his napkin on the table and stood. "Ready to go home now?"

Eva got up and followed him to the cash register. Her blood was boiling, although she knew it wouldn't do any good to get mad.

When they got to her family's house, James got out to come around to her side. They walked up to the house in silence.

"I need to talk to Ted," James said when she shot him a questioning look.

"Okay," she answered. "I have to put a few things away in my room, so I hope you don't mind if I excuse myself."

Maybe he was a good businessman with contacts, but that didn't give him the right to be such a sourpuss and make her life miserable. She knew her father wanted to keep James happy because of his connections. This town was getting ready for a humongous growth spurt, and Dad wanted to take advantage of it.

Eva made her bed since she hadn't had time before

church. Once that was done, she went out to see if her mother needed help in the kitchen. She stopped in her tracks as she overheard her father in the living room, telling James he had no desire to go back to that poor little church. He wanted to be with the movers and shakers of the community.

Now, Eva couldn't help herself. She strutted out there, shoved her hands on her hips, and looked her father in the eye.

"You might want to hang out with the movers and shakers, Dad, but I'm going back to that 'poor little church,' as you put it. Those people might not be rolling in the dough, but at least they're all nice."

Dad's eyebrows shot up, and James covered his mouth with his hand as he waited for something to happen. Eva continued to stare at the two men, almost as if daring one to defy her.

"Eva," her father said as he leaned forward, "sometimes you can't just do what you want. You have to understand how important this is for business."

She shrugged. "Okay, fine, Dad, you can go to any church you want. I'm going back."

Her father's gaze remained fully locked with hers. She knew her father hated being backed into a corner, particularly in front of people.

"We'll see," he finally said. Eva knew she hadn't heard the last of this. After James left, she'd have to deal with defending her decision—probably at the top of her lungs.

James obviously sensed the tension, so he tied everything up quickly, then left. Eva was in the kitchen with her mother when she heard the car door slam.

"Your father will be in here in a moment," her mother said. "Brace yourself."

When her dad came to the kitchen doorway, his eyes were shooting daggers. "Eva, come here right this minute. We have a few things to discuss."

"Okay, Dad," she said, "as soon as I wipe off the table."

"Now," he ordered, pointing his finger to the floor. "Right this minute."

"Better do what he says, Dear," her mother said as she took the rag from Eva. "I'll finish up in here."

Dad's voice came out in a low growl. "You will not embarrass me again in front of my business partner," he said slowly. "Understand?"

Eva nodded. She knew better than to argue when he was in such a dither.

"We'll go to whatever church I decide on, and we'll go as a family. Understand?"

She paused and glanced away.

"Understand?" he repeated, his voice a little louder this time.

Chapter 5

Robert couldn't believe his timing. He'd driven out to Paradise Acres to visit the Hargrove family and to thank them for attending church this morning. As he turned into the subdivision, he saw James leaving—again. Based on the look on James's face, he was unhappy about something.

Robert pulled to the curb and thought about turning back around, but that didn't make sense. The Hargroves had visited his church, and he always made a point to stop by and see how he could minister to families looking for a church home. With that purpose in mind, Robert drove the rest of the way to their house.

He was a little shaken up by Ted Hargrove's expression as he opened the door. There was a scowl on his face and a hardness in his glare that Robert hadn't noticed before.

"Is this a bad time?" he asked tentatively.

"No," Ted barked. "Come in."

Robert did as he was told. "Seriously, if you're busy, I

can come back another time."

Rather than answer Robert directly, Ted turned around and shouted, "Eva, we've got company!"

Seconds later, Eva appeared at the doorway, her face flushed and breathing hard, as if she'd been running. She smiled shyly at Robert, then looked at her dad, a streak of worry flitting across her face.

"Hi, Reverend," she said softly.

Eva glanced nervously at her father. Robert noticed the way they communicated without saying a word. To his surprise, Ted backed away and said, "I'll go get Eunice." On his way to the back of the house, he pointed to the sofa. "Sit down, Rev. I gotta go get the wife and boy. Don't go anywhere."

Once Robert was alone with Eva, he gave her a questioning glance. "What's going on here? Did I do something wrong?"

Eva snickered. "No, but I'm afraid you walked into a trap. My dad and James have decided they want to go to a different church. One in town," she added. "A bigger one."

"There are several churches," he said. "And I can certainly understand wanting to check all of them out firsthand. But I'm afraid there isn't a bigger one."

"There's not?"

"No, in fact, in case you haven't noticed, we're having to expand. There's a new wing going up on the western side of the church where we'll eventually put our offices. We need more classroom space." He paused. "We have the largest congregation in town."

"The sanctuary isn't very big," she said. "Don't you have to have more room for people on Sunday?"

Robert nodded. "Yes, but we've decided rather than expand the sanctuary at this time, we'll save money and offer another service. Once we have the additional wing completed, we'll start saving for another sanctuary and use the existing one for smaller chapel services and weddings."

Ted and Eunice appeared at that moment. Eva tilted her head toward her father and said, "Dad, did you know there isn't a bigger church in town?"

Ted squinted. "There's gotta be." He nodded at Robert. "I don't mean to sound disrespectful, Reverend, but we're used to a bigger church with a lot more going on."

"Oh, we have quite a bit going on," Robert told them.

Eunice smiled. "May I get you something to drink?"

"No thanks, Mrs. Hargrove," he said as he sat in the nearest chair. "I just stopped by to answer any questions you might have about the church and to let you know how happy we are that you visited us this morning."

Eunice glanced at her husband, then back at him. She obviously didn't want to speak out against her husband, but Eva didn't seem to mind.

"I, for one, want to go back to your church." All heads turned to Eva. She lifted her shoulders and raised her eyebrows. "Well, I do. I really liked the peaceful surroundings, and the sermon was fantastic."

Robert's face became hot. "Thank you."

"Really," she said. "No thanks necessary. I think everyone

should listen to what you were saying. We could all use a lesson on forgiveness." She paused, pursed her lips, and gave him a quizzical look. "One thing has me baffled, Reverend."

"What's that?" Robert asked.

"Something's obviously going on between you and James Randall. I asked him about it, and he said something about a rift between your families going way back. I want to know what it's all about and why he's still so upset about it."

"Eva," Eunice warned. "That's family business. Stay out of it."

"No, that's fine," Robert said. "I don't mind discussing it."

"Good," Eva said with a quick smile. "It's about time someone told me why James is acting so weird."

Robert steepled his fingers and hesitated, gathering his thoughts. The feud between the Campbells and the Randalls had so many twists and turns from generations of folklore, he had to be cautious.

"It all started back in the James Gang days," he began.

"Cool!" a voice said from the dark hallway. Robert's attention snapped over to the sound, and he saw a very interested boy sitting on the floor, until now unnoticed.

"Get in here, Jack," Eunice said. "What are you doing, hiding in the hall?"

"I wanted to hear what was going on," he whined as he stood.

Eva patted the spot beside her. "Then c'mon over here so the reverend can finish his story."

The four Hargroves sat in silence and listened to the

whole story about how one of his ancestors had taken a bad turn and put a dark mark on the family name. One of the Randalls had been in love with the same woman as his ancestor, and that was how the feud began. "Plus, there were some land disputes, but I'm not clear about the details." He stopped and gave them a chance to question him.

"You mean, after all this time, people are still mad about this stuff?" Eva asked.

"Afraid so," Robert replied.

"I don't know why James would hold this against you," she said before glancing at her father, who had the scowl back on his face.

"The story might have changed," Robert explained, "and I'm sure the Randalls have a slightly different version. But that's what my grandparents told me, and I don't know any other reason the Campbells and the Randalls would be so antagonistic toward each other."

"Sounds pretty stupid to me," Eva said.

Jack's eyes were wide with wonder. "I think it sounds neato."

Rolling her eyes at her little brother, Eva said, "You would." Then she turned her attention back to Robert. "What I don't understand is why you and James don't talk about it to each other. Seems like something you could even laugh about."

Robert wondered the same thing, but he didn't want to make James sound like the bad guy. Instead, he shrugged. "I guess some family feelings run pretty deep. Maybe one of these days, we can get past all that. In the meantime, I'd like to invite your family to join us next Sunday. We're having a special get-acquainted covered-dish lunch after the services, and we'd love for you to take part. All the families bring a dish to share."

"Sounds like a blast!" Jack said as he jumped up and down. "Can we go?"

"You only wanna go for the food," Eva said.

Eunice looked up at her husband with pleading eyes. Robert noticed how he'd put Ted on the spot with his family, so he decided to give him an out. "Tell you what, Mr. Hargrove. You and your family discuss it and come if you feel led in that direction."

"Okay, Rev, we'll do that." Ted stood and folded his arms, which Robert took as his cue to leave.

"Well, I guess I better get back on the road," he said as he stood up and headed toward the door. "I have a couple more families to see before I go home."

"Let me walk you to your car," Eva said. She was by his side in a flash.

Having Eva next to him made Robert feel warm inside. She was pretty, spirited, and playful, which drew him to her. If only her father didn't have such a stubborn streak, he might be able to get to know her better.

"What do people our age do for fun around here?" Eva asked once they got outside.

"Fun?" he said. "People our age?"

She laughed. "You make fun sound like it's bad. Back

home in Atlanta, groups of people used to go to drive-in movies and have a blast."

"We don't have a drive-in movie theater here."

"What do you have?" Her expression was challenging and flirtatious. He did a double-take. Was Eva flirting with him? He looked more closely and realized he'd been missing all the important signs.

Puffing out his chest, Robert replied, "Well, we have the church, of course, and we have the Dairy Dip."

"Oh, yeah, the Dairy Dip, where all the high school kids hang out."

"They have good ice cream," he said in defense of his favorite place to grab a quick bite to eat. "And their cheeseburgers are out of this world."

"Really?" she said as she batted her eyes at him. "I've never had one."

Okay, now he had to take a chance. Sure, it was a risk, but she was practically asking him out.

"Would you like to go there with me?" he asked. "For a cheeseburger and ice cream?"

"Yes," she replied. "That would be very nice. When?"

Robert licked his lips, which had suddenly become quite dry. "Uh, how about tomorrow night?"

"Swell. Pick me up at six?"

He nodded. "Maybe afterwards, we can go for a drive. I can show you some of the sights around here."

❧

Eva bounded back into her house, a smile on her lips and her heart fluttering. She was so giddy, she let the door slam shut.

"How many times do I have to tell you kids? Don't slam the door!" her father hollered.

"Sorry, Dad. Couldn't help it. Besides, I'm not a kid."

"You'll always be my kid," he told her as he caught her in a big bear hug. "What were you and the reverend talking about outside?"

"Oh, nothing," she said as she looked away.

"C'mon, Eva, I know you were talking."

"Yeah," Jack piped up. "And you had an ooey, gooey look on your face. If I didn't know better, I'd say you were in love with that preacher."

Dad's nostrils flared. Eva shot her brother a withering look. "No, Jack, that's not it. We're friends."

Jack made a mock smooching sound and ran away, leaving Eva in the living room to face her father. She dreaded the explosion she knew would hit any minute.

But it didn't. Her father motioned toward the chair across the room. "Sit, Eva."

She did as she was told. "Really, Dad, it's nothing. He did ask me if I wanted to go out tomorrow, but it's just to the Dairy Dip for a cheeseburger."

Her father sat silently for a moment, seeming to think the matter over. Eva held her breath until he finally nodded.

"I s'pose that would be all right. Sounds harmless enough. But if he goes getting any funny ideas about you, he has another thing coming."

"Oh, Dad, don't be silly. He's a man of the cloth. They

don't get funny ideas like that."

Later that night, after Eva was in bed, she stared up at the ceiling, thinking about how the day had gone. Did she really have a date with the preacher? That thought made her smile.

⁂

Robert couldn't remember a day ever dragging by so slowly as the day before he was to take out the prettiest girl he'd ever met. After watching the clock all afternoon, the time to leave work and change for his night out with Eva finally arrived. Light on his feet, he headed home.

Robert changed clothes, then knelt down beside his bed and prayed for guidance in his relationship with Eva as well as in knowing the right words and attitude when it came to discussing his relationship with James. Unfortunately, they'd grown up in the same town without saying more than a half-dozen words to each other their whole lives. James had moved away first and immediately gone into business, while Robert had gone to seminary. He never thought their paths would cross again. *Lord, You must have a purpose for this, or it wouldn't be happening,* he prayed. *Let me do Your work and do it well. Amen.*

With that, he was on his way.

When Robert arrived at the Hargrove residence, Ted answered the door. "Come on in, Rev. Eva will be right here." He tilted his head and from beneath hooded eyes said, "She's my little girl, so don't keep her out late."

"Yes, Sir," Robert replied, feeling like a teenager on his

first date. *Hopefully, she won't take long to get ready.* Robert shifted from one foot to the other, not knowing what to say to Eva's father.

When she appeared in the room, he felt his heart rate pick up a notch. Standing before him was a woman, not a girl, with the brightest eyes and smile he'd ever seen. Nothing had prepared him for the feeling of utter helplessness that came over him as he openly stared at her.

"G'night, Dad," she said as she lifted up on her tiptoes to kiss her father. "We'll be in early, right, Reverend?"

"Right." What else could he say with her father's protective eyes glaring at him?

Robert's hands shook as he held the door for Eva. He'd never imagined feeling this way, although he'd heard about it from other guys. This wasn't love, but it certainly was one big case of infatuation.

Now all he had to do was find out where she was spiritually. He knew he couldn't spend much time with a woman who didn't put the Lord first in her life.

Chapter 6

Once they were on their way, Robert turned to Eva and smiled. She felt warm inside. And safe.

"Windows down or up?" he asked.

She shrugged. "Doesn't matter much to me."

"Most girls don't want to mess up their hair," he said, "but I like fresh air."

"Then let's roll them down," she said. Eva always carried a scarf in her handbag for occasions such as this.

"I'm curious about something, Eva," Robert asked once they were on their way.

"What's that?"

"Do you and James have a relationship?" He cleared his throat. "I'm talking about personal."

Eva's lips twitched. "No, there's no relationship as far as I'm concerned. My dad would love for me to fall for James, but that isn't likely to happen. He and I are very different."

"Your father sure seems concerned about you." Robert cast a quick glance in her direction before turning his attention back to the road.

"Yes," she said very carefully. "My father wants to make sure I don't do anything to hurt business." It was hard to keep the sarcasm from her voice.

"Oh, I'm sure it's much more than that."

They drove along in silence for a few minutes until they arrived at the Dairy Dip. As he pulled into an open parking space, Eva felt a pang of pride. She knew Robert was well known in town, and from what she'd gathered already, he was quite respected and well liked. James drew a different reaction.

The amazing thing about both men was how the one who was more concerned about reputation was less respected than the one who seemed to be himself at all times. Eva watched as a group of teenagers grinned at Robert and waved.

"You have friends of all ages, don't you?" she asked.

He chuckled. "I love people of all ages. I guess you can call them friends, but you wouldn't have said that two months ago. I had to run that very group off the church property when I caught them vandalizing the new construction."

"They were vandalizing?" she asked. "What'd they do?"

With a shrug, he replied, "Nothing big. Just writing their names on some of the lumber and concrete blocks. I put the fear into them when I told them I knew their parents. Most of them didn't know who I was because I'd been gone so long. Once they knew I went to school with their older brothers and sisters, they realized I had a way to track them down."

"They seem to really like you," Eva reminded him. "I would have thought they'd be afraid."

"It took a little extra effort on my part, but I managed to stop by and visit each of their homes. You should have seen one boy's face when I pulled up in front of his house right after the incident."

Eva laughed out loud. "I can only imagine how scared he must have been. Did you tell their parents?"

"No, I didn't have to," he said. "I went specifically to invite their families to church and to let them know about all the new ministries we planned to start once the new wing is completed."

"Great psychology. I'll have to keep an eye on you."

Robert's eyes shot her a glance that seemed shocked at first but quickly softened as the skin around his eyes crinkled with his grin. "Yes, I'd like that," he said after several seconds of silence.

Eva allowed Robert to order dinner for her, then they had a scoop of ice cream. Afterwards, they drove around, and he pointed out a few spots of interest. Eva settled into her seat and relaxed, knowing she was completely safe with Robert.

As they came to a traffic light, he turned to face her. "I've had a blast, Eva. You're a really sweet girl, and I'd like to get to know you better. Do you think your father would mind if we went out again soon?"

Her insides melted. "Oh, I don't think he'd mind at all." That was what she hoped, anyway.

"Good. I guess I better get you home now. Maybe next time we can go somewhere and talk. I'd like to find out more about you and your dreams."

"That would be very nice," Eva told him. "And I'd like to hear about yours, too."

Robert pulled up in front of the Hargrove house, got out, and walked her to her door. As they approached the front stoop, the porch light came on. Eva smiled up at him.

"He doesn't miss much, does he?" Robert asked.

"Not much."

She held her breath, unsure of what to do next. Would he kiss her? Shake her hand? Or just say good night?

Gently taking her shoulders in his strong hands, he leaned down and planted a quick kiss on her forehead. "Thank you for the wonderful evening, Eva. I'll talk to you soon, okay?"

Eva swallowed hard and nodded. Her voice had left her the minute his hands had touched her shoulders.

She opened the door and stood to watch Robert pull away from the curb. Her father came up from behind, startling her.

"Well?" he asked as she jumped around.

"Robert Campbell is one of the nicest men I've ever met."

"Now don't get too carried away," he warned. "He might be a preacher, but he's still a man."

"I know," she replied with a sigh. "I'm tired. I think I'll go on to bed now."

"Your mother wants to talk to you."

Eva closed her eyes as she paused. "Can't she wait until morning?"

"No. She's in the kitchen waiting for you."

Rather than defy her father, Eva figured it would be best to get her mother-daughter talk over with first. This wasn't any different from any other first date she'd had with a guy.

"Hey, Mom." Eva crossed the kitchen, pulled a glass from the cabinet, and poured herself some water. "You didn't have to wait up."

"I know, Dear, but I thought you might want to tell me all about it."

Sitting down, Eva began right away, more than anything, to get it over with. "Okay, we went to the Dairy Dip first and had cheeseburgers and fries. They have the best French fries in the whole world. Then we got ice cream with hot fudge. Afterwards, we drove around and he showed me the area."

Her mother's eyes widened. "Where did you go?"

Eva leaned forward. "Around town, Mom. And don't worry. I'm a grown woman, and I know what I'm doing."

"You don't know this man very well."

Eva stood up and carried her glass to the sink before turning to face her mother again. "Robert is not only a man, he's a pastor. He treats me with the utmost respect. Wanna know what he said, first thing, when I got in his car?"

Her mother looked up at her from where she still sat at the kitchen table. She didn't say a word, but her eyes were questioning.

"He asked me if I wanted to roll the windows down or if I wanted to keep them closed. Isn't that nice? Most men would do whatever they wanted, regardless of how I felt." Eva was fully aware of the urgency in her voice. She was so frustrated over how her parents treated her, she couldn't help sounding defensive.

"Dear, I didn't mean—"

"I had a wonderful time, Mom," Eva interrupted. "And what's more, we're going out again, this time to talk. He said he wants to get to know me better. He wants to know more about me and hear my dreams."

"That's nice," her mother said.

"Yes, it's nice. More than nice. No guy has ever cared about my dreams before, Mom. Not even James."

"But James—"

"James is Dad's business partner, period. I don't like being forced on him."

"It won't hurt for you to be a little nicer to him, Eva. Your father was hoping. . .well, that you and James would hit it off."

"I know exactly what Dad was hoping." Eva moved toward the door. "I'm sorry if he's disappointed, but I don't like James in that way."

It took every ounce of self-restraint for Eva not to run to her room. She forced herself to take each step slowly and deliberately. Her dad had already gone to his room, so she didn't have to face him after her talk with her mother. However, she did know she'd have him to deal with in the morning.

෨

The next morning, Eva awoke to the aroma of bacon and coffee. Saturdays were always cheerful times around her house. Hopefully, today wouldn't be any different.

"G'mornin', Sunshine," her dad said as she joined him at the breakfast table.

"How was the date?" Jack asked.

Eva resisted the urge to make one of her typical remarks. Instead, she smiled and turned to her mother. "I'll get the orange juice."

"James came by," her dad said. "Last night, while you were out. I told him you'd get back with him first thing today."

"Did he say what he wanted?"

"I think he wants to take you out to dinner."

Jack made that annoying smooching sound. Eva shot him an angry glare.

"Tonight," her father continued, ignoring Jack. "I told him as far as I knew, you were free."

"Oh, Dad, I really don't want to go out tonight. We have church in the morning, and I have things to do to get ready."

"If you're not too tired to go out with your preacher, you can certainly go out with my business partner," he said, his tone firm and final.

Eva knew she'd been cornered. "Did he say where he wanted to go?" she asked.

"Someplace really nice," her mother offered.

Suddenly, Saturday morning seemed dark and gloomy, even though the sun was shining as brightly as ever. She dreaded spending an evening with James, but she didn't see where she had a choice.

"He'll stop by sometime this afternoon," her father said as he dug into the eggs her mother had put before him.

Eva's appetite had left the instant she heard plans had been made for her. She picked at her food and left the table as soon as she was able to without causing a scene. She knew better than to rock the boat too much because she couldn't win.

That night, James bought her a big steak dinner at the Palace Steak House. She would much rather have been with Robert at the Dairy Dip, but she had to pretend to enjoy the evening, listening to James go on and on about business and how he and her father would make millions off this deal they'd signed on the new dam.

"They're planning a huge recreational facility, and we can bid on other stuff, too," he said with a sparkle in his eye. As long as he was talking about business, James seemed excited.

"Have you decided where you're going to church tomorrow?" Eva asked.

Suddenly, the excitement faded from James's eyes. He slowly shook his head. "I was thinking we'd check out one of the other churches in town, but you seem determined to go back to the one by Hollow Creek."

"Yes, that's what I'd like to do," she agreed.

"Your father will do what I want. I haven't decided."

Her blood came to a quick boil. "James, you are so bull-headed. Why wouldn't you want to go there? Just because some people from your family, generations back, had a problem with someone from Robert's family? Why can't you and Robert talk this out and leave the past behind?"

He narrowed his eyes. "You don't understand these things, Eva. Don't try to fix something you know nothing about."

"I'm not trying to fix anything. All I want to do is have the freedom to worship at a church I want to attend."

James shrugged as he picked up the check to study it. "No one's stopping you."

Eva growled. "You know as well as I do, Dad won't go back there unless you agree to go with us."

"But you can still go back, even if your father doesn't go," he replied, challenging her with his glare.

Eva had heard enough. She stood and faced him off. "So you're saying you'd go so far as to divide my family like that, just for business?"

"No, Eva," he said as he reached out and tugged at her to pull her into her seat. "Sit back down. Let's talk about it."

"I have nothing left to say." She turned on her heel and stormed out of the dining area, leaving him behind. She needed to get away from James or she might say something she'd regret.

She was standing outside, starting to cool off a little, when James appeared at her side. "Would it make you happy if I agreed to go back to Campbell's church?" he asked softly.

"Yes," she replied. "But I don't expect you to do that."

"Oh, yes I will," he said. "I'll do that, Eva, if it'll make you happy."

She turned to face him, a smile quickly making its way to her lips. "You will?" She paused for a moment as he nodded.

"Yes, that makes me very happy," she said as she started walking toward his car.

James brooded all the way back to her house, but Eva was ecstatic. "I'll talk to your father," James said. "Go on and get ready for bed. See you in the morning at church. Save me a seat."

"Yes, of course," she said as she headed for the open door where her father stood, waiting. "Good night, James, and thanks."

He nodded but hung his head. Eva left her father with James as she went straight to the kitchen. To her surprise, her mother wasn't there to hear about her night. What a relief. Eva was exhausted after the emotional turmoil she'd been through all day.

❧

The next morning, Chuck Davis, the senior pastor, had returned, and he was standing at the door greeting people when she and her family arrived.

"It's so nice to see you," he told Eva's parents as he shook her father's hand. "I've heard some wonderful things about your family." He winked at Eva, which caused her cheeks to grow warm, then he quickly turned to Jack and said, "You look like an athlete, Boy. Did anyone tell you we're starting a softball team for kids your age?"

"No!" Jack said with excitement. "When?"

"Not too much longer," Reverend Davis replied. "We'll let you know. Make sure you read the church bulletin. There's all kinds of news in there. Sorry to be so abrupt, but I need to meet with Robert before the service starts. Find a seat and get comfortable." Then he was gone.

Eva settled in her seat in the back of the church. She watched families, couples, and individuals file in, all of them quiet and appearing to be at peace. She loved the ambiance of this church, although she knew there was much more to church than the way it made her feel. There were still some things that confused her, but she could ask Robert about them.

About a minute before the services were scheduled to begin, James slipped in beside her. He offered a weak smile and a nod, but he quickly turned his attention to the front. Robert was sitting in the first row, and Eva suspected James was looking for him.

Rev. Davis's message was on justification by faith, something that confused Eva. As he quoted Romans 5:1, she listened and tried to make sense of it. "Therefore being justified by faith, we have peace with God through our Lord Jesus Christ." *How about those who have never heard of Jesus?* she wondered.

As Eva heard more from the Word of God, she became more curious. She jotted things in the margins of the church bulletin, trying to ignore curious glances from both her mother and James. She had so many questions for Robert, she was certain she'd forget them if she didn't write them down.

Once the service was over, Eva waited in the pew for her family's turn to leave. Her dad was looking at his watch, so she knew he was eager to get home. She had no doubt that her mother's mind was on the pot roast she'd cooked early and left in the oven to keep warm. Jack was probably thinking about how he'd spend the rest of this beautiful Sunday afternoon. He'd met several neighborhood kids, and they spent most of their time outdoors.

Robert surprised her by suddenly appearing by her side. "What'd you think of Rev. Davis?"

"He's great!" Eva said. "I have so many questions for you, I'm not sure where to begin."

She saw Robert's eyes dart behind her, which reminded her that James was still there. Robert stuck his hand out and greeted James. "Nice to see you in church this morning, Randall," he said. James made a grunting sound and turned away from Robert's offer of a handshake. "I'll stop by sometime this week, and maybe we can go for a drive," Robert said as he turned to Eva. "Hopefully, I'll be able to answer most, or at least some, of your questions."

Eva smiled but with caution. She didn't want to upset James, and she had a feeling it wouldn't take much to set him off—at least not where Robert was concerned.

"Did you all remember the covered-dish lunch we're having today?" he asked.

"We have to get back to the house," Dad said firmly.

A flash of disappointment darted across Robert's face, but he quickly recovered. "Too bad. We have some mighty fine cooks in this church. They love to share."

Eva had forgotten all about the covered-dish meal. "I'd love to stick around. I wish I'd brought something."

Robert looked from Eva to her father and then to her mother, before he glanced back at Eva. "You're welcome to stick around. There's plenty of food."

"But I didn't bring anything," Eva reminded him.

"That's okay. I didn't, either. Next time, you can bring something." He turned to her father. "If you don't mind, I can bring Eva home after the meal is over."

Eva held her breath. She knew her father didn't like being put on the spot, but he also wasn't likely to do anything that would embarrass the family. He looked at James, who stood with an emotionless expression, not saying a word. Finally Eva couldn't stand it anymore.

Chapter 7

I'd love to stay, Robert." She forced herself to smile at James. "Why don't you stick around, too, James? I'm sure it'd be fun for you to get reacquainted with some of your old friends."

"Nah, that's okay," James said. "I have some things I have to do."

Eva turned back to her dad. "You don't mind, do you?"

"Your mother went to a lot of trouble to cook that roast," he said, a warning lacing his deep voice.

"Mom?" Eva said. "Do you mind? You know I love your roast, and I'll eat leftovers tomorrow."

Mom wasn't used to being put on the spot. She cleared her throat. "That'll be fine, Eva. If it's okay with your father."

"I guess it's okay," Dad said as he looked directly at James, then turned to Robert. "Just don't keep her out late. I want her home before dark."

"Don't worry," Robert told him. "I'll have her home long before dark."

Eva noticed the glance James shot Robert. He was smiling, but she could see the anger.

The minute Eva's family and James left, Robert let out a deep breath. "I wish I knew how to get through to him."

"I don't think you'll ever be able to," Eva admitted. "He's obviously one to hold a grudge."

Silence fell between them for several minutes before Robert turned to Eva. "Why don't we join the others? There are some people I'd like for you to meet."

The afternoon raced by as Eva met members of the church. These people were all eager to welcome a newcomer into their fold, and they deeply cared about the Lord.

As Robert drove her home, Eva said, "There's something I need to tell you, but I'm sort of embarrassed about it."

He smiled as he reached over and patted her hand. A bolt of pleasure shot up her arm from the point of contact. "You can tell me anything, Eva. I doubt anything you say will shock me."

"Oh, I don't think you'll be shocked. It's just that. . ." Her voice trailed off as she thought about how to let him know something she couldn't keep quiet much longer.

"Just come out and say it," he said, his voice firm.

"I've never actually read the Bible," she said, her body tensing as the words tumbled out. "In fact, I know very little about what the Bible says."

Robert's jaw tightened. He didn't look shocked, but then again, he definitely didn't look pleased about her admission.

❧

Robert had suspected as much. The one woman he had felt

an attraction to was one he needed to be very cautious around. He couldn't deny his attraction, but he couldn't get romantically involved with a nonbeliever.

"Do you have a desire to know more?" he asked cautiously.

She nodded. "Oh yes."

"How do you feel about group Bible studies?"

"I'll do whatever it takes to learn more about your God."

"He isn't just my God," Robert said softly. "He's our Creator, the only way to true eternal life."

"See?" she said as she began to fiddle with the folded church bulletin she still held tight. "I don't even know the right words to say when I ask about God. Maybe it's too late for me."

Robert thought for a moment, then made a quick decision. "Tell you what, Eva. There is a Bible study class in session, but they're pretty advanced. Why don't you let me tutor you on the basics, then you can join the group once you have a stronger foundation and feel more comfortable?" He knew this was risky to his heart due to how he felt about her already, but his first duty was to minister to those who needed to hear the Word.

"You'll do that?" she said. "How much do you charge for these private lessons?"

She sure did have a lot to learn. He smiled at her when they came to a light. "Nothing. It's part of my job."

Eva stopped twisting the bulletin as she thought about what he'd told her. Each time he glanced over at her, he noticed a new expression, going from acceptance to confusion, then seeming almost disappointed. He had no idea what she was thinking, but that didn't matter. He'd continue to pray about his relationship with Eva and the Bible study so he could focus on what was really important. Even preachers could get off-track if a very pretty, petite, green-eyed diversion crossed their paths.

෫

Eva studied his tight-jawed face for a moment before turning away to think. He was clearly hiding his feelings. As she pondered and tried to remember every word of their conversation a few minutes ago, she couldn't imagine what would have made him stiffen up as he had.

"When do you want to start the lessons?" she asked. "Since you're giving me something for free, I guess you get to call the shots."

"That's not how it is, Eva," he said. Now his voice was even more formal and stiff than before. "What I'm going to teach you is very basic. God loved us so much, He sent His Son to die for our sins. All I'll do is show you Scripture that backs up those concepts."

She nodded. "Yes, I've heard that before, but I never really understood why God would do that—especially after what people in this world do and the things they say about Him."

Robert visibly relaxed. "Let me give you an analogy, which might help you understand. When you do something that angers your father, do you think he stops loving you?"

"No, of course not," she said.

"What does he do?"

254

"Well, when I was a kid, he grounded me."

"Does he cut you off from food?"

Eva made a face. "No. A decent parent wouldn't do anything like that."

"Then think of God as being the ultimate parent. A perfect parent, in other words."

Nodding, Eva finally had a better idea of what he was talking about. "Okay, I think I get it."

"I have no doubt you'll get all of it once you hear more. Why don't you start reading the Scripture listed in the church bulletin? Rev. Davis generally puts several verses in there for people to study during the week."

He'd pulled up in front of her house. Eva glanced over at the picture window right as Jack peeked out. She chuckled.

"My little brother is driving me nuts."

Robert chuckled. "They'll do that if you let 'em."

"I can't help but love the little squirt, though."

Raising one eyebrow, Robert said, "He's not so little, Eva. He's at least a head taller than you."

"He'll always be my baby brother, no matter how big he gets."

"Just like you'll always be your father's little girl, even now that you're an adult."

"Uh, yeah, I guess so," Eva said. "Thanks for talking to me about all this," she said as she got out and held up the bulletin. "And thanks for taking me home. I had a great time."

"How would you like to start the first lesson on Tuesday?"

"Tuesday's fine. What time?"

They agreed on a time—after dinner on Tuesdays and Thursdays. "Maybe after a few weeks of working with you privately, you'll be ready for the advanced group. I just don't want you to feel lost," he said.

Eva was thankful for everything Robert was doing. "See ya Tuesday," she said before running into the house and catching Jack as he was running toward the bedroom. She laughed. Robert was right about her brother. He was bigger than she, and it wouldn't be much longer before he was out of his childish phase of spying on her.

When Eva told her parents about Robert's offer to give her private Bible lessons, her father wasn't pleased at all.

"We were thinking we'd attend several churches before making a decision," he informed her. "If you get too chummy with that preacher, you'll be obligated to go to his church."

"No, Dad, it's not like that at all. Robert just wants to help."

"Maybe so, but I don't like it."

For the first time Eva could remember, Mom spoke up in support of her. "I think it's an excellent idea for Eva to learn more about the Bible. One of the reasons I never went to Sunday school was because I was afraid I'd sound stupid."

Eva looked at her mother with a new understanding. "That's exactly how I feel, Mom. I'm glad to know I'm not the only one."

Her mother smiled. "Oh, I have a feeling there are plenty of people like that. Maybe you can teach me some of what that young man shares with you."

"I'll be glad to," Eva said.

❧

Robert had spent much more time with Eva Hargrove than he initially intended. Once they'd gotten into the Word, she was hungry for more. And to his delight, she understood all she heard and read, and she sincerely accepted the Lord into her life.

Sitting in his office reflecting on everything that had happened, Robert said a prayer of thanks. When he opened his eyes, he lifted a small framed photo of Eva she'd given him when he saw it in her picture album.

He was about to leave when someone rapped on the half-open door to his office. "Yes?" he said.

James suddenly appeared, his arms folded over his broad chest, his mouth set in an angry line, his eyes narrowed in fury. He saw the picture Robert was holding, and his anger intensified. "I want you to stop," he growled as he pointed to the picture. "No more poisoning her mind."

"What are you talking about, Randall?" Robert asked.

"You know exactly what I'm talking about. You've been filling Eva's head with all sorts of lies about my family."

"I haven't mentioned a word about you or your family, other than telling her about the silly feud that started back before our grandparents were even born." Robert felt an icy chill as James continued to glare at him. "Is there anything else I can do for you?"

"You can't do anything for me, Campbell. Just don't get in my way, or you'll be sorry."

Robert started to speak out about ending this feud once and for all, but James turned and stormed out of the office and church before he had a chance to complete his thought.

On his way to his car, Robert checked on the new wing that was near completion. They'd finished all the outside work, and now the construction workers had to do the inside walls and trim. It looked very nice. In fact, if things continued at this rate, the new offices would be ready for them to move into within a month. That brought a smile to his face. He and Rev. Davis had worked long and hard for this, and they were very close to seeing a dream realized.

All the way into town, Robert imagined what things would be like soon. With all that additional space, they'd be able to add classes for adults and teenagers, something that was long overdue. Since he'd been added to the church staff, the attendance numbers had nearly doubled, and they really needed the space.

He stopped off at the hardware store first to chat with the owner about ordering the paint. The painters had told him if he ordered it, they'd pick it up when they were ready.

Next, he grabbed a quick bite at the Dairy Dip. As he sat at the window table, he saw James driving by, probably going to check on the project he and Ted Hargrove were working on. James wasn't such a bad guy, he thought. He was just a little too intense and territorial. Maybe once they became friends, they could laugh about today, but right now, Robert had to admit feeling anger in response to the accusations James had hurled his way.

Robert's last stop was the bank. He made the church's deposit first, then did a little personal banking. Just as he'd thanked the teller and turned to leave, someone rushed into the lobby and in an excited tone, shouted, "The church is on fire!"

"The church?" Robert said. "What church?"

"Your church, Reverend. There's a fire crew on the way to put it out."

Robert ran to his car and, throwing caution to the wind, sped out of town, down the narrow road, all the way to the church. His heart sank as he first smelled the smoke, then saw the entire new wing aflame.

All that hard work was gone in a matter of minutes. The firemen had put out the fire, but there was nothing left save a concrete slab and a few stones. All the offices and new classrooms no longer existed. Fortunately, the old part of the church had been spared, with one wall of the stone blackened but otherwise intact. The new wing had been made of wood.

"I saw him leave, Reverend," one of the young construction workers called out.

"Who?" Robert asked.

"James Randall. He didn't look happy, either. And I couldn't help but overhear him saying you'd be sorry as he left."

Of course. James. Robert let out a shaky breath as he remembered James's last words to him. *"Just don't get in my way, or you'll be sorry."* The words reverberated through Robert's mind. *No, Lord, please don't let this be the work of*

James Randall, he prayed.

"Don't jump to any conclusions," Robert advised the man. "This needs to be investigated just like any other fire."

"But I know what I heard."

"Yes, I'm sure you do."

Sadness overwhelmed Robert as he turned and drove back into town to let Rev. Davis know what had happened. Rev. Davis had left for the afternoon to visit some of the church members who lived in the nursing home. Robert hated being the one to break the bad news to him, but it would be better to hear it from him rather than someone else, he figured.

No matter how hard he tried, Robert couldn't banish the image of the smoking ruins from his mind. A lump formed in his throat as the dreams he and so many people had for the future had burned to the ground. How could this have happened?

Did James do it? He certainly was angry. But Robert didn't think James had the criminal tendency to carry out something as evil as setting the church on fire. He'd known James since they were children, and the worst thing James had ever done was call him names. They'd been in situations where James could have done much worse, but he was never physically violent.

By the time Robert found Rev. Davis, the news had spread. "Yes, Robert, I know about the fire. Did you hear who started it?"

"I don't think anyone knows yet," Robert replied. "In fact, we're not even sure the cause was arson."

Rev. Davis gently placed a hand on Robert's shoulder and looked him in the eye. "Son, you're a very kind and understanding young man, but when someone storms out of your office as I heard James Randall did this afternoon, the evidence is incriminating."

"I've known him all his life, and I don't think he'd do something like that."

Rev. Davis offered a sympathetic smile. "You were always one to give a person the benefit of the doubt, even when the writing was on the wall."

Robert could see that his doubt of James's guilt wasn't making any difference to the senior pastor, so he excused himself. "I need to go see a few people before I go back to the church," he said.

"I'll see you there in a little while."

The first place Robert went was to the place where James was staying. He wanted to let James know he wasn't one of his accusers, but it was too late. "He left with the police about an hour ago," his neighbor informed him. "I heard he set fire to the church out by Hollow Creek."

"Thanks," Robert said as he took a couple steps back. Then he stopped. "We don't know how the fire started, Ma'am. Please don't assume James did it until we have more of the facts."

Robert's next stop was Paradise Acres. Hopefully, he'd be able to explain the situation to the Hargroves before they heard from someone else. Eva answered the door, her face tight with worry.

"Is your father in?" he asked quickly.

She shook her head. "Dad went down to the police station. They have James in custody, and it doesn't look good. Dad's worried about business if James is guilty."

A sense of dread flooded Robert. "We don't know if James is guilty," he told her. "I really don't think he had anything to do with that fire."

Eva shook her head in disbelief. "I can't believe you're sticking up for him after the way he acted toward you. Besides, I heard about what he told you when he left your office this afternoon."

"Those were just words, Eva," Robert said. "People say things when they're upset or angry."

"So you're saying it's just a coincidence that the church burned down, even though he threatened you?"

Robert raked his fingers through his hair as he took a step back and stared down at the ground. "I don't know what I'm saying. I just don't want to start placing blame on someone until we know for sure how the fire started."

"You have to admit, Robert, it doesn't look good for James. He's not exactly a likable guy."

"I've known him practically all my life, and he's never been a criminal."

"As far as you know, he hasn't," she reminded him. "Maybe this is the first time he ever got caught."

Robert wanted to yell at the top of his lungs. If anyone had a reason to lay a finger of blame on James Randall, he certainly did. The fact remained, James had threatened him, but he hadn't exactly been specific. It was more of an empty threat to stay away from the Hargrove family.

"Did you want to come inside?" Eva finally asked.

"No, I don't think so, considering the circumstances," Robert replied. He hated seeing Eva this frustrated. Part of her world had been shattered because the stability her father had tried to create for her had become shaky. He wished he'd gone more into Scripture that dealt with how nothing was solid in this world, except for the love of the Lord. Family, friendship, business, and anything else created by people could fail—no matter how stable they seemed. "I think I'll go on down to the police station and see if I can help James out."

"I'm not so sure that's a good idea," she told him. "Dad's furious with you. He says you provoked James, and that's why he torched the church."

Robert decided not to argue with her. Instead, he told her he hoped to see her later, after they got to the bottom of this tragedy. He loved Eva, but the timing was all wrong to discuss that or any of his other feelings.

He arrived at the police station just as Ted Hargrove and the police chief were leaving. Ted glowered at him, and the police chief nodded.

"Got a minute, Campbell?" Chief Collins asked.

"Sure." Robert stopped and tried to focus on the chief rather than on Ted's anger. "What can I do for you?"

"We need to know the exact words Randall used when he threatened you. Can you remember?"

Robert slowly nodded. "Yes, I can remember, but I have to explain the whole scenario so you'll understand."

The chief paused, then looked over to Ted. "I need this information. You can either wait out here, or you can join us inside."

"I'll wait here," Ted snapped.

Robert followed the chief inside and told him the entire situation. "But I don't think he'd resort to burning down the church."

"You haven't been around him for several years," Chief Collins said. "Is this correct?"

"Yes, Sir, it is."

"He's mighty angry."

"Did he say he was guilty?" Robert asked.

"Well, no, not exactly. But he did come in here hotter'n a hornet, saying all kinds of things not fit for the ears of a godly man."

"He's always been a talker," Robert admitted. "In fact, he's all talk. I've never seen him take so much as a swing in a playground fight back when we were kids—not even at me."

"Things change with people. His anger and animosity toward you may have grown so intense, he took action this time. Maybe your relationship with his partner's daughter was what it took to make him snap."

"Maybe," Robert agreed. "But I still don't think he did it. Where is he? Is there any way I can see him?"

Chief Collins pulled back and studied him. "You're a glutton for punishment, young man. I realize you're a man of the cloth, but that doesn't protect you from an angry man's wrath."

"I realize that, but I wanted to let him know I don't think he's guilty."

"If that would make you happy, tell the officer on duty in the back to let you in. We're holding him in one of the cells here until his hearing."

"You've already scheduled a hearing?" Robert asked in disbelief.

The chief shrugged. "Since not much happens around here, that pretty much took priority right away."

Robert said good-bye to the chief before heading back to the small jail area. He said he wanted to see James Randall.

When James spotted him, he began to run his mouth again, shouting obscenities and accusations that shocked even Robert. "James, I'm not here to argue with you. I just wanted to let you know I don't think you did it."

"Oh, that's right," James said with sarcasm in his voice and flames in his eyes. "You're the do-gooder preacherman who wants to save me from my soul. Well, it's too late, according to everyone in this town. That little church of yours burned down, and now everyone thinks I did it. They might as well hang me on the town square."

"No one's going to hang you, James. As soon as we get to the heart of what happened, everyone will know it wasn't you."

"Oh, save your breath, Rev. Don't waste your do-gooder act on me."

"I can see I'm not getting through to you, Randall," Robert said. "Too bad. I wanted to let you know I'm on your side."

James snorted. "I just bet you are, now that your precious picture of Eva is nothing but ashes."

Robert frowned as a thought flickered through his mind. "Did you know that they put the fire out fast enough to save most of the church?"

"Yeah, so I heard. But the offices burned to the ground."

Taking a step toward the bars, Robert looked at James. "The new offices burned, not the old. The wing where you stopped by this afternoon was left unharmed."

James shook his head and scowled. "Too bad."

"No, it's not too bad. You didn't even know what part of the church had burned. How could you have done it?"

"Get outa here, Rev. You're making me sick."

This time, Robert left. He drove straight out to the church, where a large crowd had gathered. He tried to talk to the police chief, but everyone was so busy, he wasn't able to until an hour later.

"Look, Campbell," Chief Collins said when he was finally free, "the fire inspector will be out here first thing in the morning. Save what you have to say for him. I'm sure he'll be interested in whatever it is."

Ted was standing on the church lawn, staring at it, deep in thought. Robert joined him. They stood in silence for several seconds before Robert spoke.

"I don't know whether you think James is guilty or innocent, but I know he didn't do it," Robert told him.

Chapter 8

"You baffle me, young man," Ted said. "This is your big chance to play the hero with my daughter. Why would you defend someone who hates you as much as James does?"

"He doesn't hate me," Robert said. "And I don't want to play the hero with your daughter. I admit, I love her, but I refuse to pursue her under these conditions."

Ted shook his head and walked away, leaving Robert alone. He hated that James would have to spend the night in jail, but he didn't see how he could change that. The entire town was convinced James had made good on his threat and gotten back at Robert by burning down the church.

Although Robert loved Hickory Hollow with all his heart, he knew how quickly gossip traveled. He also knew that once people made up their minds to believe something, they needed solid proof to change their minds. It went against the judicial principle of "innocent until proven guilty."

Bright and early the next morning, Robert was at the

church, waiting for the fire inspector. Shortly after nine, the fire inspector showed up. "This won't take long," he said. "We look for very clear signs of arson when it's suspected."

"What if it wasn't arson?" Robert asked.

"Then it'll be even easier." He reached out and patted Robert on the shoulder, something that seemed to be happening quite a bit lately. Robert wasn't used to people comforting him, and he wasn't so sure he liked it. He wanted to be the one providing the kind words of comfort.

"Calm down, Rev. Campbell. We'll find out exactly what happened, and you'll be able to get back to the Lord's work."

A lump formed in Robert's throat. "Okay, thanks. Mind if I stick around until you're finished?"

"Be my guest. Just don't follow me around."

Robert decided to walk down to the creek where he could think. He'd done this on occasions when his soul had felt restless, and now he felt like jumping out of his own skin. He'd only been at the creek for about an hour when he heard the fire inspector calling for him. He quickly turned and ran back to the church yard, where the inspector was waiting for him.

"You were right, Reverend," the inspector told him. "The fire was definitely not started by an arsonist. I found some grease rags in a storage room, probably left behind by one of the construction workers."

Robert's heart flitted with joy. "Are you certain? You mean James Randall for sure didn't start the fire?"

"Nope. It wasn't intentional arson. This was more of a

case of negligence and lack of knowledge."

Robert could hardly wait to let people know. He drove to town, following close behind the fire inspector's car. First thing he did when he arrived at the police station was run inside and ask to see James.

"What're you doing here again, Campbell?" James asked. His eyes were bloodshot, and he had a scruffy growth of facial hair.

"I wanted to be the one to tell you, it wasn't arson. The inspector found some grease rags left behind by the construction workers. You're off the hook."

A quick flicker of relief flashed across James's face before it was replaced by another angry glare. "It's all your fault I was left here to rot. I'll never forgive you for this."

Robert took a step back as he realized he might never change the mind of this man who wouldn't drop a grudge that had nothing to do with either of them. "You may never forgive me, but I forgive you, James. I'll continue to pray for you."

As Robert left the holding area, he heard James mutter, "Don't bother."

Next on Robert's list was the Hargroves' house. He wanted to see Eva and her father, to explain what had happened. Robert knew Ted Hargrove was an honorable man, and he cared about integrity in business.

Eva wasn't home, but Ted was. "She took off with the car, Reverend. C'mon inside and wait."

Good. That gave him time to talk to Ted about James.

When Robert first started to explain, Ted tensed. But

after he heard what had caused the fire, Robert noticed the man's muscles relax.

"I never thought he was guilty," Ted said. He pursed his lips, then slapped his thigh. "Oh, what am I talkin' about? I did think he was guilty. I didn't believe him when he said he had nothing to do with starting that fire." He looked Robert in the eye and with a strained, shaky voice, pleaded, "Will you forgive me, Reverend?"

Robert nodded. "Yes, of course. I can certainly understand why you thought he was guilty because of his deep anger toward my family."

"But you knew he was innocent all along. Most men would've let everyone go on believin' it."

Robert didn't want to agree or disagree with Ted, so he didn't say anything.

Eunice came into the living room. "You men want something to drink while you're waiting?"

They accepted iced tea. Robert figured they'd discussed James enough, so he changed the subject and began to tell how he'd left Hickory Hollow and come back when the church began to expand. To his delight, Ted listened to every word and actually seemed interested.

"I'm pretty handy with a hammer," Ted finally said. "If you need someone to help rebuild that wing, I'll be glad to lend a hand."

Robert knew this was Ted Hargrove's way of showing appreciation and even apologizing. He extended his right hand. "Thanks, Ted. I'm sure we can use you soon."

That single handshake solidified their friendship.

Eva arrived minutes later. "I saw your car out front," she said to Robert. "What're you doing here?"

Ted shook his head. "Don't talk to my guest that way, Eva. It's rude."

She burst into laughter. "Okay, Dad." Robert studied her face as she turned to him and said, "Can we talk?"

Robert nodded and glanced at Ted, who'd already started backing toward the hallway leading to the bedrooms. "I'll leave you two alone."

As soon as Ted was gone, Robert turned to Eva. "What's on your mind?"

She held out her hands and shook her head. "I'm very confused about everything. I don't know what to think about anything anymore."

"That's certainly understandable," Robert said. "We've all been through quite a bit lately. Take all the time you need."

Eva cleared her throat and paused for a moment before she said, "Thanks, Robert."

As he left the Hargroves' house, Robert had an overwhelming urge to jump for joy. Ted had committed his time and energy to the church, which meant more than anything else to Robert—besides Eva, of course. He knew, deep in his heart, that he cared for her more than he'd ever cared for another woman. Her strength and vulnerability overlapped in so many areas of her life, he'd been thrown off-kilter, but he knew he loved her, flaws and all. Hopefully, she'd eventually feel the same toward him.

When he arrived back at the church, Rev. Davis was waiting for him. "We need to talk, Son."

Robert followed the senior pastor into the main office and sat down after Rev. Davis shut the door. The room was filled with reference books, Bibles, and concordances. Both men had the same work ethic, and they took their responsibilities as spiritual leaders very seriously.

"What's up?" Robert asked after a long silence filled the room.

Rev. Davis leaned forward. "I was hoping you'd tell me."

"I don't understand."

The senior pastor grinned. "You've been acting like a teenager in love ever since you met that Hargrove girl."

"I have?"

"Not only that, you've actually started taking a little personal time, which I've been trying to get you to do since you started your job."

Robert nodded. "I just hope I'm not taking too much time away from my work."

"Trust me, Son, you're not." Rev. Davis leaned back in his chair and folded his hands behind his head. "There is one matter we need to deal with, though, before you can continue with this young lady. Someone needs to have a long talk with James Randall, or you'll never have any peace."

"I've tried," Robert said. "But my very presence seems to irritate him."

"That's putting it mildly. You're not the one to do the

job, Robert. Let me handle James. He's more likely to listen to me."

"Yes, you're right," Robert agreed with a sigh. He hated the fact that there was anything he couldn't do, but this was obviously a time to let go. His biggest flaw had always been unrealistic personal expectations of himself.

"Once I speak to him, you can pull out all the stops in courting Miss Hargrove."

Robert smiled. "You have such an interesting way of putting it."

"When you want something, you can't hold back, I'm afraid. Especially in matters of the heart."

When Robert felt that Rev. Davis had said all he'd intended to say, he stood. "Thanks. I'll let you know what happens."

Rev. Davis belted out a hearty laugh. "Oh, I think it'll be obvious. When it comes to true love, most people are pretty transparent."

Obviously. Robert had never mentioned his feelings to his mentor, but still, his heart had shown through.

≈

Eva's heart belonged to Robert. As much as she tried to deny it, she knew she couldn't any longer.

"Dad, what did Robert say before I got home?" she asked, trying to hide her feelings.

He snickered. "Sweet on the boy, are you?"

"A little." She might as well admit it, she figured. It was too hard to disguise.

"I've suspected that for a long time," he told her. "And I give you my blessing."

"Blessing?" she asked. "For what? I have no idea how he feels about me."

"You're the only one who doesn't know. It's obvious to everyone else you two only have eyes for each other."

Eva gulped. "Even James? Do you think he noticed?"

"He'd have to be a blind man not to notice how you and the reverend look at each other."

"Dad, how do you feel about me loving a preacher?"

Her father rubbed his neck and paused long enough to make her squirm. "I'm just fine with it, Eva. As long as he's good to my little girl, I can't complain. I already told you you've got my blessing."

"Yes," she said, "you sure did. Now all I have to do is let Robert know without making a fool of myself."

"It's okay for people in love to act like fools. In fact, I think it's required."

Eva couldn't remember her father ever sounding so light-hearted and philosophical, but she liked it. "Thanks, Dad."

He glanced at his watch. "Your mother invited the reverend over for dinner tonight. Go clean up."

"Really?" she squealed. She ran over and kissed her dad on the cheek. "Thanks!" Her heart raced as she headed back to her room to get ready.

Eva had just finished applying her lipstick when she heard the door knocker. Her heart leapt, and her face grew warm. Merely the thought of seeing him increased her pulse rate.

As she entered the living room, Eva felt as though time stood still. All heads turned in her direction. Robert gazed at her appreciatively.

"You look lovely, Eva," he said softly.

"Why don't the two of you go on out to the porch while Eunice and I put the finishing touches on dinner?" Ted asked. "Jack, c'mon. You can give us a hand."

"But—" Jack started to object but stopped when he got the look from their dad. "Aw, okay."

Robert and Eva walked outside and stood looking out over the field across from the Hargrove house. "The sun's getting ready to set," Robert told her. "This is a very pretty view."

"Yes, my mom picked this lot because they're not building any houses across the street."

Robert turned to her and gently lifted her hand from where it dangled by her side. She didn't resist as he lifted it to his lips.

"Eva," he said, turning his attention completely away from the view and focusing on her, "I've been trying very hard to deny my heart, but according to Rev. Davis, I'm not doing a very good job."

Eva turned her head to one side. She felt her pulse in her throat.

When he stopped talking, she tilted her head toward him. "Continue."

He lifted her other hand. "Eva, you're a very special woman. Warm, kind, fun, understanding, strong. . ."

"Flattery is a wonderful thing, Robert. I'm enjoying every second of it."

With a chuckle, Robert tugged at her arms until she was close enough to pull her to his chest. He leaned down and lightly kissed her forehead, the tip of her nose, and then brushed her lips with his. She knew he must have been able to feel her heart hammering against his.

"I love you, Eva," he whispered into her hair.

She sighed. "I thought you'd never say that."

"Really?" he asked.

"Really. I love you, too."

"This is even better than what I'd imagined," he said. "Now I have to take a chance and ask a question."

Her heart still pounding out of control, Eva looked up into his eyes. "Go ahead. Ask away."

"Would you consider. . .um, well. . .I was wondering."

"Come on, Robert, it can't be that hard to ask a simple question."

"You're right, Eva." He drew in a deep breath, tucked his finger beneath her chin, and held her gaze to his. "How would you like to be the wife of a country preacher? I can't promise worldly riches or fancy jewelry, but I can promise to love you for the rest of my life."

"I'd feel like the richest woman in the world if that country preacher was you, Robert."

This time, when Robert bent over to kiss her, she knew she was sealing her future. They loved each other, and nothing would come between them.

"I s'pose we'd better go inside. Dinner is probably on the table by now, knowing my mother," Eva finally said, although she hated breaking up the closeness she felt at the moment.

"Yes, we'd better. I don't want to get off on the wrong foot with my future in-laws."

Eva felt positively giddy as she walked back into her house, hand in hand with her intended. Jack whistled when they walked into the dining room, and her mom giggled. Her dad slapped Robert on the back and said, "It's about time you two got together."

Chapter 9

"How do I look, Mom?" Eva asked as she stood in the tiny classroom doubling as a dressing room for the bride.

"Fabulous, Dear. I've already told you, you're a beautiful bride."

Eva turned to her mother. "Thank you so much for being there for me all my life."

"That's my job. I'm your mother."

"And thanks for making me come here instead of letting me stay back in Atlanta."

"You really weren't ready to be out on your own. I think you realized it, too." She paused and offered Eva a warm smile. "But you're ready now, Dear."

"Yes," Eva agreed. "You're right." She turned and checked her image in the mirror once more before turning back to her mom. "Ready to face the crowd?"

"Yes." Mom brushed a stray strand of hair from Eva's cheek before she left her alone in the room. Eva peeked through a crack in the door and watched an usher escort her mother to the seat in the front row of the church.

She only had a few seconds before her father knocked on the door. "Ready or not, Eva, time to make your last walk as a single woman."

Eva took her father's arm, and together they went up the aisle toward the front of the church, where Robert stood waiting, her brother Jack by his side and James off to one side, looking very uncomfortable. Although the two men still weren't close, Robert had asked and somehow convinced James to fill in for his brother, who wasn't able to make it to the wedding. They needed him to be one of the ushers to balance the number of bridesmaids Eva had invited from Atlanta.

As Eva and Robert said their vows, her heart flowed with love and happiness. She knew that her husband would be a strong spiritual leader and he'd give her room to be herself. No other man she'd known had his combination of strength and understanding, so she had no doubt she'd made the right decision to be his wife.

Rev. Davis instructed Robert to kiss his bride. Her heart raced, and her cheeks flamed as he lifted the veil, leaned over, and dropped a featherlight kiss on her lips. Before straightening back up, he whispered, "The Lord will bless this marriage, Eva."

She knew he was right. This wonderful man had not only won her heart, he'd taught her the most valuable lessons in the world. As long as the Lord was first in their lives, they could face anything.

DEBBY MAYNE

Debby has been a freelance writer for as long as she can remember, starting with short slice-of-life stories in small newspapers, then moving on to parenting articles for regional publications and fiction stories for women and girls. She has been involved in all aspects of publishing from the creative side, to editing a national health publication, to free-lance proofreading for several book publishers. Her belief that all blessings come from the Lord has given her great comfort during trying times and gratitude for when she is rewarded for her efforts. She lives on the west coast of Florida with her husband and two daughters.

Cornerstone

by Paige Winship Dooly

Dedication

To my husband, Troy.
Thank you for being my soul mate and best friend.
I love you!

*As ye have therefore received Christ Jesus the Lord,
so walk ye in him: Rooted and built up in him,
and stablished in the faith, as ye have been taught,
abounding therein with thanksgiving.*
COLOSSIANS 2:6–7

Chapter 1

Hickory Hollow, Missouri, Present Day

April Russell paced the length of the covered front porch, mentally willing Matt Campbell to hurry up and arrive. Reaching the far end, she leaned on the vine-covered porch rail, cradling a mug of hot tea in her hands.

There was no sign of the man. The entrance to Russell's Wildwood Resort stood empty and quiet, save for the echoes of bobwhites singing back and forth from their perch on the white boards that hugged the gravel road and identified the resort with a rustic placard that hung over the entrance.

April sighed and sank down onto the soft floral cushions of the porch swing, idly moving it with her toe. Patience wasn't her forte, but she knew it was time to put it into practice.

The thing was, so many important events depended on Matt's arrival. Her small town of Hickory Hollow was falling apart around her, and she seemed to be the only one who cared to see it restored, starting with the church her family helped found back in the mid-1800s.

April looked up the street toward the ancient structure as her musings took her to the building. She could barely see it through the trees, but she knew the stones were loose, the roof in total disrepair, and the landscaping overgrown. April chose to see the beauty of what it could once more become—focusing on the history that surrounded the quaint building—instead of looking at the decrepit building as it was now.

Others in town seemed to view it only as an eyesore and would rather see a new super-church built closer to the highway. April was fighting a losing battle at this point with the town council and hoped that Matt would ride in and save the day. After all, his great-great-grandfather had helped found the church, too.

The sound of tires crunching over gravel had April on her feet and hurrying to the rail. A sleek, black car had entered the gate and was pulling up in front of the resort's office.

April hesitated for a moment, glancing over at the cabin that awaited its first tenant, having just been refurbished. She hoped all was in order to woo the man—sparkling cider chilling on ice, fruit tray in the fridge, anything he could need amenity-wise to welcome him back to town.

The resort was April's life. It always welcomed her home and had been a wonderful distraction when her life dreams fell apart. Though small in modern terms—twenty-two units circling a large pool and set beside a quiet lake—the resort provided well for April and would soon do even better since now she didn't have to put every penny back into refurbishing the cabins and outbuildings. Only one unit remained to be remodeled. The main lodge was complete, as were the four large duplexes set up for family reunions and youth retreats. April couldn't imagine a better place to live and relax. Her whole motto was for Russell's Wildwood Resort to be a place where people could step back in time and forget about the problems of the fast-paced world they lived in.

Taking a deep breath, April hurried over toward the office to greet her childhood friend. Suddenly nervous, she muttered under her breath as she walked, "Okay, Lord, this is it. Please let Matt help save the church. He's my last hope."

⁓

Matt looked around the rustic office space with a grimace. Though obviously remodeled in recent months, the resort was a far cry from the elegant hotels he usually stayed in—and designed. He'd stay long enough to get his business dealt with and then scurry on out of this tiny, suffocating town, returning to the life he enjoyed elsewhere.

Matt hadn't been back to Hickory Hollow since his grandmother had passed away, and he didn't regret the fact. Though he'd had fun there as a child, he preferred the excitement of the city any day to a forgotten place like this.

The screen door squeaked open and slammed shut, causing Matt to jump and diverting his thoughts to the pretty female who entered the office. She tripped on the threshold, and he automatically reached out to right her. He smiled, his charm always at the ready for a time like this.

The woman, with shoulder-length blond hair in a stylish cut and unique green eyes, was vaguely familiar. She turned a slight shade of pink, hesitated, and then slowly returned the smile. Pulling away, she put distance between them, making

Matt feel oddly adrift. She'd felt right in his arms for that tiny moment. He'd felt a zap of recognition but couldn't place why. The only person he expected to remember was his friend April, and she'd been a gawky teen last he'd seen her. This woman had curves in all the right places and shapely legs that didn't escape his notice. It couldn't be April. Besides, April had been off to explore the world same as him last he knew. She'd be far away from here by now. Maybe this woman was a distant relative of April's.

*

"Matt?" April asked, the man before her so changed in looks and attitude that she had a hard time pegging him as the boy she'd played with during summers as a child. "Is that you?"

The man frowned, and it was obvious he didn't remember April at all—or he wasn't who she thought he was. The eyes were familiar, but lots of men had blue eyes. Her Matt had been fun loving and fancy-free, black hair always falling over his forehead. This man was stuffy, every hair in place, and looked to be all business from the way his fitted suit hugged his fit body and expensive Italian loafers adorned his feet.

"You are Matt Campbell, aren't you?" April struggled to place him in her memory. She didn't have any other guests due to check in today, and this man didn't appear to be the type to walk into a place without a reservation. Not this type of resort anyway. She didn't have any more units open even if that were the case. She was full up for the week, save the last old unit that hadn't been remodeled and wasn't really fit for occupancy, especially by a man with apparent rich tastes such as his.

A smile finally reached the man's features, working its way across his face like water crossing a parched desert. It was obvious he hadn't smiled in awhile. It was also obvious that she was facing a grown-up Matt. Distant or not, the crooked smile was all Matt. April's heart skipped a beat.

"April Russell?" he asked. "Is that really you?"

He stared at her a moment, the slight smile still on his face. "I didn't recognize you without the long blond ponytail and gangly legs. Though your appearance at the doorway should have clued me in. You did always have a way of making a grand entrance." He chuckled.

April was relieved that he remembered her, but was confused that he seemed so surprised after all their correspondence of late. She wanted to hug him, but his distance kept her at arm's length.

She laughed, the sound hollow. "Well of course it's me. Who do you think you've been writing to all these months? Why do you think you're here?"

Matt frowned. "I'm here to see to the church and finish up a deal. My secretary handles all correspondence, so I didn't have any hands-on with that part. Sorry if you thought otherwise."

April flushed. All this time she'd been sending the letters to Matt, thinking he was personally answering her, only to find out she'd been yammering away at some distant secretary who had no clue who she was. How humiliating that the unknown woman hadn't explained the fact instead of acting like Matt himself was writing to her.

"Oh, I see," April forced out, though she didn't see at all.

How could a person go through life in such an impersonal manner? How could her buddy Matt have changed so much? She hadn't seen him since they were fourteen, but she hadn't expected him to change any more than she had in the past fifteen years. Matt, the fun-loving dreamer, had turned into a no-nonsense executive.

"Well, we better get down to business, then. Would you like me to show you to your cabin first? I've prepared the best we have for your stay. It was recently improved from top to bottom, and you're the first to stay there. I've added some extra-special touches to welcome you back to Hickory Hollow."

She paused, and when he didn't comment, she continued her spiel. "I've remodeled each unit one at a time. I only have one to go, but we'll get to it soon enough. I'm sorry! I'm rambling. So, do we go to the cabin or the church first?"

Matt wrinkled his nose. "I'd actually rather see the church and land. I want to wrap this up as quick as possible, and I don't plan to linger around, so the room can wait."

Again disappointment filled April, but she should be happy he wanted to see the church right away, shouldn't she? That was what this visit was about after all. It was just that she'd expected him to be as excited to see the resort and what she'd done with it as she had been. As teens they'd hung out here and had talked about what they'd do differently if they ran it. Now that time was here, and April had used a lot of Matt's dreams to make the resort what it was today. Matt apparently had forgotten all about those dreams.

April led the way out the door and up the path toward the church. Her resort was located at the edge of town, with the first block of old buildings beginning opposite the entrance. The church was located to the west, and a trail led from the resort to the rustic stone building. April loved the small hike through the woods, over the winding creek, and up a rocky incline. The church rose majestically before them as they stepped out of the trees.

She always felt such a sense of peace well up inside her as she approached the humble building. So many of her important life decisions had been made there. Whenever life got to be too much, she sat in the sanctuary or out back in the gardens, feeling closer to God as she prayed and relaxed in His presence. Today, for the first time in ages, she felt unsettled.

"Wow, the old place is really run-down." Matt's first comment didn't encourage April.

"It isn't as bad as it looks," April defended. "A little TLC would fix it right up."

"A little TLC and a whole lot of money," Matt retorted, confusing April. His blue eyes were the same under the sturdy wall of mousse that formed his black hair into a solid mass, but that was the only resemblance she found to her old friend. Matt had always been so optimistic. What had changed him?

"But isn't that why you're here?" she asked, her bewilderment getting the better of her.

"To put a lot of good money into an old church?" Matt quipped. "If you want to look at it that way. I'd prefer to think of it as buying a prime piece of land and improving it by building the new resort. It doesn't sound as foolish that way."

April's heart filled with dread. "New resort?" she parroted, feeling like a fool. "I don't know anything about that. I was under the impression you were coming to rebuild the church, nothing more."

Matt turned to look at her. "I am rebuilding the church, but not here. I'm donating a huge piece of land near the highway in trade for this lot, plus some of the old buildings across the street there. You'll have the mega-church you've all been wanting."

April felt sick to her stomach. "I don't want another church! I was under the impression you were coming to fix this one up! How could you tear down what our ancestors fought so hard for?"

"It's all in the name of progress, April. This is prime land for a resort, and the church will be better off toward the new side of town."

"I know it's prime land for a resort. . .that's why I run one! Do you realize what another resort will do to Wildwood?"

"I plan to buy you out, too. Haven't you read the correspondence at all?" Matt stared at April like she had no sense. "We suggested you have an attorney read over it with you if you couldn't understand the offer."

April was affronted that he assumed she was too stupid to read a document for herself. "Maybe if you did your own correspondence, you'd know what was going on in your company. I'm totally capable of reading a document, and the only thing I've received has centered on, and I quote, 'Bringing the church back to its original splendor.' There has been no mention of my selling Wildwood."

Matt muttered under his breath as he stalked away. "Well,

this is just great! I come all the way out here to find out the done deal isn't even started. I have permission to tear down the church, part of the old town, and now I have your resort stuck right smack in the middle between the lake and my resort!"

He paced back and forth as he ranted. "What happened to you, April? I thought you were going to get out of here, too, and make something of yourself. Why would you want to be stuck in a town like this with all that is out there in the bigger world?"

He swept his arm in an arc, gesturing to his bigger world, but all April could see were the beautiful rolling hills around them, the lack of pollution in the fresh mountain air, and the quiet, sleepy town she loved. Matt's words were beyond disappointing.

April had never felt so angry in all her life. "I did get out, and I didn't like what I found. I'd prefer this life and place any day to the dog-eat-dog world I lived in before. I won't sell the resort, so you can plan to build yours somewhere else. What a pathetic disappointment you've turned out to be, Matt Campbell."

With that last cutting comment, April turned and stalked back into the woods, wanting to get away before Matt saw the tears of heartbreak that burned behind her eyes. Even here in her little corner of paradise, money and greed—masked in the name of progress—waited to stalk and devour.

❧

Matt watched her go, then turned back to the decrepit building before him. How could she care about such an old place when he'd offered a brand-new building with everything her heart could desire? Why would she want to bury herself in this forgotten little corner of the world?

His frustration boiled over, and he turned back toward the resort, anxious to make the call to his secretary that would explain how she'd botched this assignment up so badly. He was now starting from square one, and before it was all over, he'd probably end up in a lawsuit with the first girl he'd ever loved and kissed.

Matt stomped down the hill, ruing the mud that coated his expensive but inappropriate shoes. As he stepped onto the small bridge to cross the creek, he slipped on the first plank of wood, teetering before falling face first into the cool, clear water. He let out a roar of anger, not caring that the air was at least semi-warm on this beautiful spring day. He shouldn't have come. He should have sent one of his lesser employees to handle this job. Then again, delegating had been what put him in this mess in the first place. This whole situation just reaffirmed what Matt already knew: He couldn't count on anyone but himself in this world. If he wanted something done, he had to do it himself, lean only on his own abilities.

He sloshed his way back to the resort office and retrieved a cabin key from a glaring teenager who was soon unsuccessfully fighting back her laughter as she took in the sight of his sopping wet appearance. Obviously she was loyal to April, who had disappeared, and knew what had just transpired at the church with her boss. He could imagine she would happily give April an earful as soon as the screen door slammed shut with its irritating shotgun sound behind him.

Not wanting to ruin the interior of his car, Matt pulled his suitcase from the trunk and found the way to his cabin, which of course had to be the one farthest from the office.

Ankles and heels blistered from his now-ruined shoes, knees scraped from the rocks in the stream, and his entire body chafed from his wet clothes, Matt finally found his building at the end of the line of units. Wanting only a hot shower and dry clothes, he looked forward to the amenities April had dangled before him, not an hour earlier.

He wasn't impressed as the key stuck in the rusty lock. Someone needed to inform April that first impressions were everything and an old door on a new unit wasn't very inspiring.

He immediately realized why when he finally disengaged the key and entered the small, musty-smelling foyer. He had to smile at April's ingenuity and attitude. Instead of his refurbished and amenity-filled cabin, April had stuck him in the one last old unfinished unit. From the looks of it, the rooms hadn't been touched since their great-great-grandfathers were alive—and that was pretty bad since the resort hadn't even been built back then.

Matt smirked. He had to hand it to her. The April he'd known might be all grown up, but she was still as spunky as ever in that pretty little body. She'd always put up a good fight in their day, and he might actually look forward to going to war with the petite, feisty lady. At least life wouldn't be as dull as he'd thought over the next few weeks.

He sighed, and his enthusiasm fell as he glanced around and saw what awaited him in the dismal room. The weeks ahead would be challenging indeed.

Chapter 2

April walked into the office, screen door slamming behind her with its comforting sound, and saw Cammie sitting at the front desk, a huge pink bubble hiding half her face. April poked the bubble as she walked by, the bubble popping on Cammie's carefully applied makeup.

"A–a–a–pril!" she blustered, jumping to her feet and heading for the rest room.

April shrugged and reminded the girl, "No bubbles on the job, Kid."

Cammie scuffed around the corner to fix her face, and April slid into the chair, pulling bills and ledgers in front of her. She could hear the teen muttering from the bathroom and smiled. Cammie was a great employee, but she had some rough edges to work out.

April loved training her and a few other young girls from town, though it could be challenging at times. She found the girls hanging out at various places, their boredom apparent and just ready to get them into trouble, and built friendships with them. They now had a small Bible study going, and April offered them jobs at the resort if they wanted on-the-job training and if they were willing to work hard and pull their weight. So far it had been a great deal, and April had watched several girls thrive.

The resort was laid-back enough that if one of the teen moms had to bring along a toddler, it could be arranged. Most of the girls came from pretty rough homes. If the teen's parent had been drinking or was in a mood to kick the girl out for a few days—which happened way too often and for all the wrong reasons—they'd come and crash in April's guest room until they could go back home.

April sighed as she thought about Matt's plan to buy her out. That would once again leave these girls on the street with nowhere to go. Right now she was in their neck of the woods and was there the moment they needed her. What good would she or the resort do them if she were clear across town? It was ludicrous for Matt to just waltz in and think he could rearrange all their lives in a way that suited his wallet, without considering what the repercussions would be for the local people. She'd have to be the one to explain those repercussions to Matt—no doubt he'd done this to plenty of others in his career path.

Cammie returned from the rest room, bubble free, and plopped into a chair. Her face lit up with mischief as she told April of Matt's condition upon his return from the church. "What did you do to him, Miss April? It was great. He was wet from head to toe, and I could almost see the steam rising off him, he was so angry."

April's heart sank. This wasn't the lesson she wanted her girls to learn, though in all honesty she'd have given anything in her earlier mood to witness his return. She'd been so flustered, she'd immediately changed his room from the resort's nicest to the roughest, just to make her point. She'd felt so smug when she told Cammie to give him the old key, but she hadn't thought ahead to how it would look to the teen. Corralling those thoughts, she hurried to clear herself.

"I didn't do anything. He was dry and intact when I left him, so I'm not sure what happened after that. Maybe he slipped into the creek. Did he appear to be hurt?"

Cammie shook her head. "Only his pride. He was limping a bit, but that looked more like from blisters than a twisted ankle or anything. He wasn't very friendly, so it serves him right if you ask me."

"No, Cam. That's the wrong attitude. It was wrong of me to lose my temper with him, too, and to assign him to the rugged room. I'll have to make that up to him. He does have a way of irritating a person, though, and we'll have to work around that. Look at it as another challenge."

Cammie grimaced. "Oh. The turn the other cheek thing, huh?"

April laughed. "Yeah, that thing. It isn't as bad as you make it sound, you know. If you do it right, you'll feel so good inside, it won't matter how the other person reacts. Concentrate on that."

She tweaked the teen's ponytail and turned back to her books. The bills were routine, and her mind wandered as she worked. Even with her pep talk to Cammie, she wasn't ready to admit her mistake and move Matt to the nice cabin. Maybe it would be good for him to hang out and see how the little people lived for awhile, to remember his roots. His grandmother had lived in a tiny, old stone house on the hill, and they'd had the time of their lives there. How could he forget that and now want to demolish the area?

"I know. I'll invite Matt to a special dinner, prepared by me, and welcome him back properly. Maybe he just needs to be reminded of how down-home Hickory Hollow is in order to put his feet back on the ground so he can appreciate and relax again in our country ways. His roots have been transplanted, and he needs time to reacclimate and dig them deep again."

April was sure of it. There was no way he'd changed that much. The meal could serve the dual purpose of showing him she was sorry for losing her temper, too.

Cammie looked skeptical. "Are you sure you want to cook for him? Maybe you ought to let Cookie prepare your meal."

"Very funny. I'll be over at the kitchen." April put Cammie back in charge and headed out to plan the meal. "Cookie," the chef, was deep cleaning and not in much of a mood to be bothered. He was another of April's street conquests and one of her best, if she had to say so herself. Cookie was an ex-military chef, down and out when she met him, and he'd thrived in his position as kitchen manager.

Though gruff, he had a heart of gold and could outcook anyone around him. April couldn't cook to save her life, so when she inherited the resort, Cookie moved into the room behind the kitchen, and they were all happy with the situation.

"You're going to do what for who?" Cookie now bellowed

from the walk-in refrigerator.

"I just want to make a simple, down-home dinner for an old friend. To welcome him back." April explained. "Nothing difficult, but surely even I can barbecue a steak and make a salad for the guy without causing too much damage."

Cookie's snort could be heard from the cooler. His tattooed arm waved toward the counter, where he had various items laid out. "Help yourself to whatever you want over there. It's all extra inventory that I was planning to sort for the next few days' meals. I won't miss anything."

April perused the food and picked two steaks from the far end of the table, and a bag of salad greens. Plucking up a few veggies to top the salad, she added two potatoes and called out her thank-you to Cookie.

Sticking her head in the office door, she told Cammie to go inform Matt he was expected for dinner at April's place at 5:00 P.M. She decided a direct approach would be better than an invite so he wouldn't be as likely to turn it down. She doubted he had food with him anyway, and it was late for a trip to the store. Cookie always had Friday night off to prepare for the weekend's new arrivals and to sort out the kitchen, so Matt would most likely show.

Besides, he had a deal to make, and April was sure he'd take every opportunity to work it out.

✦

Matt didn't know what to make of his invitation to April's for dinner, but he didn't intend to waste time analyzing it, either. He was famished after the long drive and his walk in the woods. He needed to get on April's good side so she'd sign the papers, and he hoped she'd see the benefit of selling out and leaving this awful place.

He'd left his cabin a bit early so he took the roundabout way to April's. As he walked by the pool, he had to smile at the daring children who were already braving the cold water with squeals of laughter and discomfort. A small boy about five years old declared through bluish lips and chattering teeth that he wasn't cold at all. His mother bundled him up and carried the howling child off toward their cabin.

Okay, so maybe the old place wasn't so awful after all, but after seeing the condition of his cabin, he was a bit biased.

Matt's mouth began to water as he smelled the aroma of barbecue drifting from behind the various cabins he passed. Children called to each other from the playground/park set at this end of the pool. Matt had to admit the layout of the resort was nice. The cabins encircled all the amenities, so while each had privacy out back, they all faced the main play areas that catered to the children. He noticed that it wasn't only the children who enjoyed the space, as several men were playing horseshoes in the pits set up for that purpose while their wives laughed and cheered them on.

There was a communal shelter house where a large family—probably one of April's family reunion groups—prepared dinner. Matt felt like he'd just stepped into a Norman Rockwell painting as he took in the scene before him. Time had stopped in this corner of Hickory Hollow, and while it felt nice for now, he couldn't imagine living this way day after day. Shaking his head, he hurried on to April's.

He could hear a ruckus out back and walked around the corner of the house to see a gangly yellow mutt running off with a huge steak hanging from its mouth. April was standing on her porch looking defeated as she called threatening words to the animal, the tongs she held accentuating every word she yelled.

Matt's chortle cut off April's words, and she wheeled to see her guest had arrived at the most inopportune time.

"Welcome." She knew her face was flushed, but she couldn't help it. Between the barbecue grill's heat and her frustration that Goldie had just stolen half their dinner, she deserved to be a bit flustered. The grill had taken way too long to light, and she'd had to trek all the way to the kitchen to find out how to best cook the meat. All had combined to knock her off schedule, allowing Matt to walk in on pure chaos.

She motioned Matt to her comfortable patio table. "Have a seat. The rest of the meal that didn't just get carted off will be ready in a few minutes."

Before going inside for the salads, she glared once more in the direction of the mutt, who now sat down by the lake devouring its treasure. She already had salad dressing and the potato toppings placed on the table, so it only took a moment for the meal to be pulled together.

"You take the steak," Matt insisted as she tried to place it before him.

She sat down across from him. "To be honest, I'd really rather eat only the potato and salad. I'm not much of a meat eater anyway."

Matt didn't argue the issue. "The steak smells wonderful, and you seem genuine in your words, so I intend to enjoy every bite. Thank you."

April felt him watching as she bowed her head in a silent prayer over her meal. He'd apparently forgotten that little trait of her family's, but he quickly laid his knife down and joined her in silence until she was finished.

"I appreciate your inviting me," Matt stated as he carved at his steak.

April frowned. It appeared to be a little on the tough side. Matt was good, though, and didn't comment. She saw him rub his thumb along the edge of the steak knife, testing it for sharpness. A small bead of blood confirmed the knife was indeed sharp.

April dabbled with her salad. "It's my pleasure. We didn't get off to such a great start, and I wanted to apologize."

"No apology necessary," Matt was quick to insert, speaking around the piece of meat in his mouth. The way he chewed on it reminded April of Cammie and her gum. Why hadn't she grabbed the chicken instead? At least if it had been tough, the poor guy still could have managed to swallow it!

He finally gave up and drank it down with a swig of tea.

"Wonderful," he grimaced, his attempted smile looking pained as he peered with trepidation at the massive piece of meat on his plate. "Are you sure you don't want at least part of this? I'm sure I can share and be completely satisfied."

"No, really, I don't want any. But if it's too much or too tough, please don't feel you have to eat it all. I'm a bit short on cooking skills. You won't offend me."

Matt's eyebrows rose as if that was the understatement of the year, but he didn't comment other than to say it was wonderful and he'd eat it just fine. April noticed he cut smaller pieces and continued to wash them down with tea.

The meal was strained, and April searched for a topic to discuss.

Matt saved her, laying his knife down and pushing back his plate. He'd managed to make quite a nice dent in the slab of meat and had polished off his potato and salad. Leaning back in his chair, he said, "I'm the one who needs to apologize. I've talked to my secretary and know where the communication mishap came from. She's new and came in during the middle of this land deal and apparently didn't want to admit her lack of experience so just did what she felt best, which had nothing at all to do with the papers I'd written up for you to look at. She's faxing them down—that is, if you have a fax machine around here—or she can overnight them if not."

"Of course we have a fax machine," April huffed in exasperation. "We aren't that primitive around here. But I still don't intend to sign. I don't care what you promise or what you offer. I love my resort and the history as much as I love the church. I'll fight you on tearing either one down for a superstructure."

She jumped to her feet and began to pace. She hadn't wanted their dinner to end this way. "Can't we call a truce? Figure out some other way?"

Matt was starting to look a bit ill, but whether from the tough steak or the topic at hand, she couldn't be sure. "There is no compromise. I need this land, and I'm offering you a fair deal to go rebuild a top-of-the-line resort elsewhere. You can even recreate this place if you're so inclined."

His expression showed he didn't think that would be a good idea, but at least he didn't give voice to the thought.

"Then why can't you go build somewhere else and leave us alone?" April had had enough of his self-centeredness and put-downs. "Build your super-resort somewhere else."

"I need the lake setting, and like I said, I've already acquired the couple blocks of downtown that stand to the north of you. I need all of it for the size I'm creating. It won't work across town because I need the lake, too."

"Well, I don't want to give it up! I need the lake."

They were at a stalemate, and April couldn't imagine how the dinner could have gone more wrong. She should have prohibited conversation about the deal. Nothing could top off the way this dinner was ending.

As if to correct her, Goldie chose that time to waddle up from the lake and heave her steak all over Matt's second pair of Italian loafers.

"No–o," April bellowed, waving the dog away. "You dumb mutt, that's what you get for overeating that huge steak you stole. Get, get! Go on."

The dog slunk down with her tail between her legs and curled up by the corner of the house.

April grabbed the roll of paper towels from the table and quickly wiped at Matt's shoes. He hadn't said a word, and she looked up at him to see him turning a unique shade of green. She pointed the way to the bathroom just as her cordless phone rang.

Grabbing it up from the barbecue grill where she'd placed it earlier, wondering what crisis demanded her time now, she snapped, "April here."

"Miss April," Cookie's voice floated over the line, "please tell me you didn't take the steaks from the far end of the table this afternoon."

April's heart sank. "Um, yes, why? Is there a problem?"

"They were outdated, Miss April! Didn't you see the date on the label?"

"Well, no. You said to take anything there. Why would I feel the need to check the date? I trusted they were all good!" April suddenly thought back to Matt's expression a moment earlier. "Cookie, I just fed the steak to my dinner guest. The dog stole mine, bless her heart."

April could hear Cookie mutter a prayer under his breath. "From the dates that were on the label when I pulled them out to throw away, I'd say you better get your dog to the vet and your guest to the emergency room as soon as possible. Bye, Miss April."

April wanted to cry. Goldie looked fine after throwing up her share, but Matt was a different story. April grabbed her keys and ran to retrieve Matt from the bathroom. According to the sounds coming from the other side of the door, the steak had indeed been bad. As they headed out the door, April grabbed a small waste can for good measure.

Chapter 3

M att was certain there were worse things in life than food poisoning, but at the moment he sure couldn't think of any. He'd never been so sick.

April got him to the emergency room in record time, apologizing all the way for the bad meat. "I had no idea I picked the wrong steak up. It was an honest mistake—Cookie forgot he laid it there and only thought of it later, after he'd finished cleaning up and remembered his mental note to throw it out after inventory was done."

Matt didn't answer, instead picturing the mutt running off with the steak in her mouth. Was it really a coincidence that she stole it, or had April staged that part in order to get even with him for messing up her church rebuilding plans?

Matt knew he had to be sick to even consider that April would do something so underhanded. She was just a small-town girl. She wouldn't do something like that. Matt had spent too much time with big-city women who manipulated, connived, and tried to control the men around them. He was hallucinating from the sickness wracking his body. His sweet, laid-back April just wouldn't do such a thing.

"Dr. Russell! What a pleasant surprise to see you here. Did you decide to accept our offer to join the staff after all?"

Matt was brought out of his musings with a jolt as his ill mind tried to grasp the words he'd just heard. Surely he was delirious. It sounded as if someone had called April "Dr. Russell."

April stopped the wheelchair carrying Matt at the counter. He was too ill to even make it inside on his own.

"No, I'm afraid not. Instead of coming here to heal patients, I'm bringing in a friend I just gave food poisoning. Show us where you want us to go."

Matt tried to follow the words. Instead he gave up, too sick to concentrate. He closed his eyes and sank into darkness.

*

"Matt, wake up. Come on, you need to focus on what we're telling you." April knew from Matt's groan exactly when her words pulled him from his rest and back to the pain in his stomach.

"We have to pump your stomach, and then you'll feel much better. They want to keep you here overnight for observation, but you're in good hands. I'll return for you tomorrow."

With that, April backed out of the cubicle, glad to escape the scene before her. She felt so helpless at first having caused this and then having abandoned Matt. There was no reason she could think of to stay. She was glad Matt was sick enough he wouldn't have caught the earlier reference to her being a doctor. That was one area of her life she didn't like to talk about. Matt would never understand why she'd walked away from her career to take over the ailing resort, and she didn't intend to try to explain it.

☙

Sunday afternoon Matt was almost feeling human and decided to walk across the street to take a look at the old buildings that would soon be demolished.

Even he had to admit his appreciation for the architecture and beauty of the historic structures. He felt a pang at the thought of his company being responsible for tearing out the history just to build new structures on the basis of money. But that was how things went, and if he didn't do it, someone else would.

He glanced across at the old church. He might as well scope it out, too, while he was there.

The building was beautiful. Surrounded by trees, it was peaceful and serene: two characteristics Matt didn't come across much anymore. The stones that made up the building actually were quite sturdy, and though the wood trim around the windows was rotting out, it would be easy to replace.

Matt stepped up to the door, surprised to find it unlocked. He entered, and a flood of memories assailed him. Memories of his grandmother taking him here after his parents were killed in a car wreck. Memories of April sitting with her parents and passing notes to him during prayer. Walking up to the small balcony that had been added in later years, he even found the small heart he'd carved in the pew with their initials centered inside. Boy, had he caught flack for that! He ran his fingers over the letters and wondered how he and April had lost touch through the years.

As soon as possible, he'd gotten out of this town that had felt suffocating after his parents' deaths, and he'd never looked back. April must have felt abandoned by him.

Matt walked outside and found an old ladder. He pulled it around to the rear of the building and climbed up to check out the roof. He was a bit unsteady after his ordeal with the steak, but he took his time and was cautious. Again he was impressed at how sturdy the roof was and how easy it would be to repair.

Shaking his head, not knowing why he was thinking such ridiculous thoughts, he eased down, needing to focus on how to demolish the building before the crew arrived, not on how to salvage it for April's sake.

"What are you doing on a ladder after just being released from the hospital!" April's voice was shrill and caused Matt to lose his footing. Fortunately he was only a few steps from the bottom, but he still wrenched his ankle as he landed.

*

April couldn't believe Matt was up and about, let alone climbing around on the church roof. She hurried over to where he sat in pain, massaging his ankle as he glared at her.

"Do you have a death wish for me or something?" he ground out around his pain.

"I'm not the one up on a shaky roof after just getting out of the hospital. What were you thinking?" She removed his shoe and began to poke and squeeze his ankle, while he tried to slap her hands away.

"Stop it, and let me see what you've done," April said in

exasperation. "Don't be such a baby."

"I'm NOT a baby. I'm just scared to have you anywhere near me, let alone touching my body. You cause unnecessary pain when you're near, not quite what I thought doctors were all about."

April gasped, affronted. She'd really hoped he wouldn't remember that part of his hospital visit. "Well. How rude."

She tossed her hair over her shoulder with what she hoped was a gesture of disdain. Instead her fingers caught in a tangle, and she had to dismantle them before finishing her theatrics.

"I was quite a good doctor, thank you very much, before I realized how poorly the system worked. As to your pain, the food poisoning was totally accidental, and your falling off the ladder was your own foolish choice."

"Only after you shrieked at me and scared me to death," Matt quickly intervened.

"I don't shriek. I was surprised and scared to see you up there." She looked at his ankle, already twice its normal size and bruising rapidly. "For good reason I might add."

Matt sighed. "Okay, I've decided not to try to reason with you. It won't work anyway. I accept defeat. Now how am I going to get home?"

April bit her lip, a habit Matt remembered well from their childhood. "I can go get my car, or we can take the crutches from the sanctuary that we leave for a couple of the members."

Matt sighed. "I'll try the crutches. From the looks of my ankle, I'm going to need them for a few days anyway."

"Well, I can tell you nothing is broken, but we ought to get an X-ray just to be on the safe side."

Matt argued, but in the end April went for her car and dragged him to the ER for the second time in three days.

As she said, it was only a sprain, but Matt was ordered to stay off his ankle as much as possible and to avoid work of any kind.

※

April ran through the pounding rain to Matt's cabin that evening, determined to make life easier for him while he was housebound. She knocked and called out that he wasn't to get up but that she'd come to make dinner.

Matt didn't answer for a moment and then called out that while her offer was appreciated, it was unnecessary and that she could go on home.

April opened the front door and headed in. Matt was sitting on the old couch, his sore foot propped up on a pillow, perusing a stack of blueprints that lay scattered across his lap, on the coffee table, and even on the floor.

He jumped as she entered, feigning fear—or at least April hoped he feigned it—and pulled the paperwork defensively across his chest.

"What now? You've really done enough," he stated, his blue eyes darting around as if looking for help where there was none.

April laughed. "Very funny. I'm just coming to take care of you."

She heard him mutter something under his breath that had to do with, "That's what I'm afraid of. . .you're here to take care of me permanently. As in if you get rid of me, you get rid of your problems at the church. You're out to do me in."

"Matt! That's not true, and you know it. I realize it's been sort of fluky around here lately, but it isn't intentional. I came to make you a grilled-cheese sandwich and some chicken noodle soup—from a can. Even I can't mess that up."

Matt didn't look so sure.

April frowned as she took in the noise around her. For the first time, she noticed the cacophony of sound in the room. Looking for the cause, she saw Matt had most every pan from the kitchen set about catching drips from the ceiling. She blushed.

"I'm so sorry. I did try to get you back into your original room, but Cammie had already booked it for the weekend with a walk-in. I'll make sure you get moved tomorrow or the day after."

Matt just nodded, still clutching his paperwork as if she were about to snatch the plans away from him.

"Okay, you get back to work, and I'll get to your dinner." April picked up the grocery bag she'd brought along and headed into the small, dark room. Flipping on lights, she was pleased to see the kitchen was at least clean. Finding the one lone pan for soup, she started opening drawers, looking for a can opener.

"Matt?" April called through the open doorway. "Do you have a can opener in here somewhere?"

"In the drawer to the left of the stove," he called back, papers rattling as he sorted through them.

"I'm not finding it. Would you have put it somewhere else?"

April hated to bother him when she was there to help, but without the can opener, she could hardly make soup.

"I put it there this morning, I'm sure it's there."

"I'm not seeing it." April stood and peered at the various ancient gadgets in the drawer, but none looked like a can opener to her.

She was chagrined to see Matt appear at the doorway, leaning heavily on the crutches. "Oh. I didn't want you up. That was the whole purpose of my coming here!"

"Well, if you couldn't find the can opener, I had to get up, didn't I?" Matt reached around April to pull the object from the drawer. It was right at the front, and April was embarrassed that she'd missed it.

She motioned him out of the kitchen and back to the couch and returned to her duties. After buttering two pieces of bread, noting there were only four pieces total, she placed them in a pan, dismayed to see that the stove was gas. She'd never worked a gas stove before but figured it wouldn't be hard to figure out.

Turning the burner on to high, she pulled a match from the holder to her right, lit it, and placed it over the burner. With a huge *whoosh*, it lit, causing her to scream as the flame almost reached the ceiling.

"Crying in a bucket! What on earth have you done now?" Matt bellowed as he flew into the kitchen, crutches splaying in all directions from his haste.

April had had the presence of mind to turn the burner off, so was standing with her hand to her chest, breathing hard, as the smoke detector shrieked through the room.

Matt used his crutch to knock the battery out of the detector as April opened a window over the sink.

"I lit the burner," she meekly explained.

Matt peered at the dark spot on the ceiling. "How?"

It was such a simple question, but somehow April knew he wasn't going to like her answer. She told him, and he turned slightly pale.

"You could have blown the cabin up! Watch."

April watched as Matt hobbled to the stove, turned the burner, and it self-lit.

"Wow. Isn't that interesting?" April was surprised that such an old cabin had such a modern stove.

Matt hobbled his way back to the couch, shaking his head and talking to himself.

April placed the bread in the pan and turned back to the soup. The can opener wouldn't cooperate. At home she had an automatic, but this was ridiculous. The last thing she wanted to do was bother Matt again. She finally gave up her pride and carried it into the living room.

Matt sighed, laid his papers down, and held out his hand. With expert precision, he opened the can and handed it back without a word.

April smiled and returned to the kitchen. Smoke rose from the pan with the bread in it. April grabbed the two pieces of toast, now blackened on the bottom, and looked around for a place to dispose of them. She hurried to the window and flung them outside, whispering a prayer for the safety of any creature that attempted to eat the blackened bread. She was pretty sure Goldie would be safe as lately she'd kept to her dog food and steered away from anything April offered.

April heard a chuckle behind her and turned to see Matt leaning against the doorway. "It's fine. Really. I could have scraped off the black part."

April didn't argue. She tossed the last two pieces of bread into the pan and placed slices of cheese on top. Walking to the sink, she stopped as she saw a large, black spider in the window.

"Matt!" April hated spiders with a passion. Matt had just sat down, springs creaking on the sofa. "I hate to bother you, but there's a huge spider, and I need to get to the sink. You'll have to kill it."

"Work around it." Matt called back. "You're bigger than him, I'm sure."

"Matt, you remember how much I hate the horrid creatures! You have to get it out!" April couldn't look at the spider, let alone do it in.

"Squash him!" Matt said, exasperated, his tone making April feel like an idiot.

"I can't."

Matt must have heard that she was near tears, so he hobbled back in yet again. April moved to the table at the far end of the kitchen and sat down, looking away as Matt reached up into the window to remove the creepy intruder.

A moment later he was hopping around, swatting at his arm and side. "Stupid thing jumped on me!"

April had to laugh. "Not so tough now, are you? Kill it, you say. You didn't tell me you are as scared as I am of the creepy things! All these years!"

"Just get him off me!" Matt yelled, turning back and forth while still swatting.

"I don't see him. You must have scared him away."

Matt left the room, heading for the bathroom, where he could look in the mirror and be sure the hairy thing wasn't hitching a ride.

April poured water into the soup and placed it on high, making a mental note not to let it burn. She wanted to speed this process up and get this ordeal over with. Here she'd felt it her Christian duty to take care of Matt, but she didn't think the point was getting across very well.

She only needed to ice down the glass for Matt and fill it with cold water, and she could be on her way home. April had no appetite after all this. She'd feed Matt and be out of here in a few minutes.

She stared at the refrigerator and realized there was no freezer.

"Matt, why don't you have a freezer?" she called out.

"I thought you owned this place," he retorted.

"I do, but this was old Mrs. Henson's cabin, and I was never in here. I told you it was the last to be refurbished."

"You have to open the fridge to get to the freezer."

"Interesting." April opened the door and saw that he was indeed right. She tugged at the freezer door, but it didn't budge. She tugged harder. Still nothing. She gave it a huge yank, and the entire freezer came out of the refrigerator and crashed onto the floor.

Horrified, she doubled over with laughter as Matt skidded around the corner, his eyes huge. He didn't even try to ask her to explain.

Instead he skirted the mess as well as he could on crutches, turned the burners off from under the scorched soup and burned grilled cheese sandwich, picked up the phone, and called in an order for pizza. Turning back to her, his mouth quirked as he fought his smile.

Tears ran down April's cheeks. Never had she been so mortified.

"It wouldn't open," she stated inanely. "I pulled and pulled. . ."

She reached down and showed him, shrugging when it still wouldn't budge.

Matt reached down and gently pulled the metal piece on the other end, the door opening from its upside-down perch, showing the jumbled food inside. "Maybe that's because you were pulling on the hinge, not the handle."

April bit her lip and nodded, still laughing as Matt struggled to lift the small freezer back into place, his eyes meeting hers with humor at the jaunty angle in which the appliance now rested.

"April?" Matt gave her a measured glance.

"Yes?" April wanted to sink into the floor.

"Promise me you'll never try to make this up to me."

April nodded and went to the living room for her purse. The least she could do now would be to pay for the pizza. If she ever felt the need to feed Matt again, she'd do it over take-out.

Chapter 4

Matt carried his coffee out to the back patio and sank onto a rusty iron chair. Fog floated over the lake, obscuring the view of the bluffs on the other side. He was up early, and the eerie quiet made him feel as if he were the only person on earth. After the hustle and bustle of the city, waking to horns honking even at this early hour and people yelling outside his condo, the quiet was welcome, yet unsettling.

Matt wondered what April was up to, smirking as he thought of the fiasco of the previous weekend. He'd never seen her so flustered. She appealed to him in a way no other woman had, but then she'd always had that effect on him. Again he wondered why he'd lost touch with her so completely.

He knew it was partly due to his running from his past. When his parents died and he went to live with his grandmother, he'd felt he had a second chance at love. When Gram had died, he felt adrift and suffocated in the town that had brought him so much grief. He'd buried himself in school and his career. He'd wanted to return a few times but until now hadn't had the courage.

This opportunity had dropped in his lap, and Matt couldn't pass up the enticing prospect it offered. He hadn't even realized where the town was located when he first started negotiating the deal. Then, when he had realized it was Hickory Hollow, he relished the chance to change the place that had caused him such joy as a child, then such grief as a teen. Maybe it would heal the old wounds to tear it apart and rebuild it his way.

Of course, that was before he'd seen April and watched the disappointment and pain cross her face when she realized he'd come not to rebuild her dream, but to tear it down. He felt like a heel, but it was the way the world went. If April didn't know that by now, it was time she learned.

Again he thought of the previous Sunday evening and wondered how a doctor could be so inept in the kitchen. Of course cooking skills were a far cry from medical skills, but he just couldn't picture the woman who demolished his kitchen saving lives in a calm, efficient manner.

He knew one thing, inept or not, she was more beautiful than ever, and he wanted to make his friend smile again. She'd been frowning since she'd first realized what he was up to, and he was sure that wasn't her nature. He'd taken her smile away, and he'd do his best to put it back again.

Matt pushed himself up out of the chair and leaned against his crutch, wanting to explore more of April's world. He hobbled to the water's edge, saw a small dock, and worked his way over. Memories assailed him of spending summer days lying out in the sun with April on that very dock, which was now rebuilt, and swimming in the cool water with their friends. They'd race across to the bluffs on the far side, and it was there that Matt had kissed April for the first time.

April's grandmother would bring out lemonade for all the gang, and they spent most of their time there, together. It would soon be hot enough for the new batch of teens to hang out at the water's edge, and Matt hoped they made as many good memories as he and April had.

Frowning, Matt wondered why he'd forgotten the memories until now if they were that wonderful. When he tore down the resort, no other group would ever have a chance to live those same dreams. He made a mental note to incorporate a swim dock of some type into the new place. Modern kids could learn to have fun there, too.

Turning back to head up to his cabin, Matt watched as the sleepy resort awakened. A tiny girl still in her pajamas lounged on a patio chair, her little legs swinging as she watched her father cook breakfast over a grill. Again, that wouldn't happen at his resort because barbecue grills wouldn't be safe on a high-rise balcony. The new resort could only be economical if Matt stacked the condos upon each other, packing in as many guests as possible. But the new amenities would be worth it. A barbecue pit could be built, and though not as convenient as cooking out on a private patio, the die-hard barbecue fans would make it work.

Matt didn't like the niggling doubt he was feeling. He'd never before questioned his plans, but now everywhere he looked were memories of the past or memories being made that he'd prevent from ever happening again if he had his way. He felt like a money-chasing creep and didn't like it.

The best way to avoid more thoughts like that would be to get to work and bury them, his favorite way to evade situations he didn't want to think about. Returning to the cabin, he changed from his sweats into work clothes and headed into town to resume the evaluation he'd started before spraining his ankle. Since it was Saturday, just a week after his arrival, he hoped the town would be quiet, and he could look around unhindered. He had yet to scope out the lay of the land or explore to see what all had changed. From what he saw so far, there probably wasn't much new at all.

Matt decided to avoid the church. It reminded him of things he didn't want to think about, things beside April and her hurt. It reminded him of how long it had been since he'd darkened the doorstep of a church for a reason other than a wedding of a friend or a funeral. He couldn't remember the last time he'd talked to God or even thought of Him.

It wasn't that he didn't believe, he just hadn't had time or taken the time to give it a thought. He traveled so much, it wasn't convenient. But Matt had a feeling God didn't buy those excuses. And now he was about to tear down his childhood church. The church his ancestors supposedly built, according to family legend. He shook off the guilty thought. Rebuilding a new super-church would surely counteract that small detail, right? The old church was falling apart, so it should actually buy him some brownie points. That thought made Matt cringe. He knew brownie points with God didn't happen that way. How far had he gone from his basic beliefs that he had allowed thoughts like that to sneak in?

Rather than face the thoughts that were assailing him, Matt limped to his car, stowed his crutches in the back, and drove toward the exit of the resort. He slowed as he passed April's cabin and was surprised to see her step out onto her porch, juggling several containers in her arms. Rolling down his automatic window, he called out to her.

"Hey, Buddy! Want to head over to the Dairy Dip and grab a chocolate dipped cone?" His words surprised him.

April whipped her head around and grinned—the first original smile he'd seen since he arrived. "It's a little early, isn't it? Besides, how do you know it's even still around? Have you been checking out the town?"

Realization seemed to dawn, and she rested her armload of boxes on the rail of her porch. "Or is that another conquest you're tearing down to rebuild into something bigger and better?"

Matt winced. "No, I'm not touching the Dairy Dip. Some places just can't be replaced."

"But my resort and the church can be?"

Matt wasn't scoring points here, either. He turned off the engine. "Can we use your idea and call a truce? I don't want to fight. Let me drive you wherever you're headed, and I promise I won't talk about buildings or anything else. I just want to spend some time with my old friend. Please?"

April bit her lip and considered his offer, looking torn.

"Okay. I'd like that. I'm heading to church for our annual fund-raiser and bazaar."

Matt hid his frustration. The one place he hadn't wanted to go, and here he'd volunteered to spend his day with her. God apparently did have a sense of humor and was intent on aiming it Matt's way for the day.

❧

April was thrilled to have Matt join her for the church event. Maybe he'd get a feel for the special place and remember how much he'd loved it in the past. April would get to introduce Matt to the newcomers who'd moved here just to get away from "progress" and wanted a simpler way of life.

He'd also meet old friends and remember faces from his youth, people who would be displaced as much as she if he continued with his plans. April had spent a lot of the previous night praying that God would open a door for her to show Matt what they had here and how wrong he was to try to change it. Maybe this was the answer to her prayer.

The trunk popped open by remote as she approached, and she stowed her supplies before walking to the passenger side and opening the door. She joined Matt in the car and buckled her seatbelt. Noticing Matt's sideways glances, she grinned for the second time.

"What?"

"I just wondered if you needed to get right over to the church or if you had some time to spare."

"What did you have in mind?"

"I just thought we could drive around a bit. I'd like to see the place, and this is the first chance I've had."

April blushed. "You mean since you've been sick with food poisoning or flat on your back with a bum foot for the duration of your visit?"

"Something like that." Matt smirked, glancing at her, his familiar quirk pulling his smile up to the left.

"I have a bit of time to spare. I was planning to walk so I was leaving early."

Matt looked toward the trunk, where she'd deposited her box.

"It looks more awkward than it is. I love my hike through the woods, and besides, parking will be at a premium around the church. I didn't want to take up an extra spot."

"Maybe I should just drop you off when we finish our tour and head back here. I don't want to take up space, either."

April laughed. "Nice try, but you're stuck with me for the day. Now head on for the grand tour. Though I doubt you'll find anything new since you left."

Matt drove to the Dairy Dip, looking oddly pleased to see that it was exactly as he'd left it. "It's too early for a cone, but I promise we'll get one before the day is out."

He drove on, following the road to the high school, slowing as they passed. "It's like being in a time warp. I've been gone for over a decade, and I feel like we just walked out those doors. It's weird."

"It isn't weird," April said defensively. "Not everything has to change in this world. Some things are set in stone and need to always stay the same—like deep friendships. Family. God."

"I don't mean anything by that," Matt said quickly, trying to smooth her ruffled feathers. "It just feels strange."

April didn't want her feathers smoothed. She wanted Matt to stop forcing change on everything and to see how good some things were if they stayed the same. Their teen relationship was a good example. April had to admit she wished they could pick up where they'd left off. She thought she'd gotten over Matt long ago when he'd left without looking back, but apparently those feelings were still right there, lurking under the surface.

She figured he'd sail back out of her life just as easily as he had before, after his deals were done, but she'd fight tooth and nail, if she had to, so he wouldn't take her resort with him.

"Do your parents still live over in Paradise Acres?" Matt broke into her thoughts, turning into the subdivision and heading toward her old house.

"No, they live in Florida. Daddy retired two years ago when I came home. He was thrilled when I wanted to take over the resort so they could play. His words, not mine."

Matt slowed as he passed the house where she'd grown up. He'd spent a lot of hours there, too. "I can see that time has changed this neighborhood."

"A lot of the houses are rentals now."

April wanted to move on. She didn't like seeing how the neighborhood had changed. It wasn't bad, but the homes were all fifty-some-odd years old, and most were showing it. A few young families had started moving back in, though, and they'd already banded together to refurbish the pool.

They'd built a new clubhouse and were pushing home ownership to the renters, trying to make the place what it had been previously. The changes were happening slowly, but April could see them and was excited about the potential.

Matt turned his car back toward town and headed for the bazaar. They pulled into a full parking lot, bustling with townspeople, and found a place to park in the grass. April grabbed her box, promising Matt it had nothing to do with food, just odds and ends for the rummage sale. They walked over to dispose of it on a table, and April motioned for Matt to follow her across the expanse of lawn to the church itself.

An elderly man propped the front door open and was working on the latch. "Matt, you remember Robert Campbell, don't you? He's been with the church for as long as I can remember."

Robert turned around. "I've been with the church since way before you were born, Miss Russell. And I remember this whippersnapper."

Matt grinned. "I remember you, too. You're Grandpa's older brother who he said tormented him through all his teen years and then some. How are you? I didn't realize you were still around here."

"Still around here? Or still around period?" Robert asked, peering at Matt through his bifocals. Matt looked relieved when Robert chuckled at his own attempt at humor.

"Still around here, Sir. I thought you'd moved away years ago."

"Oh, some well-meaning relatives tried to ship us off to

a retirement home a few years back, if that's what you mean, but I fought them tooth and nail and made it clear this is where I grew up, and it's where I'll die. I don't need some fancy schmancy old-folks home. My wife, Eva—she's around here somewhere—and I have a small place behind the church, and I can putter there to my heart's content. What would we do in a retirement home?"

Matt laughed. "Still a workaholic I see."

"That's me, and the day I can't get off my chair and work is the day they can take me to see my Maker." He laid down his tools and gave Matt a bear hug. "It sure is good to see you, Boy. Don't be a stranger now, you hear?"

Matt nodded. "I'll drop by to visit in the next few days."

April wondered if Matt realized what he'd do to Robert and Eva when he tore down the church. The church had been Robert's life for decades. Without the church, he'd have no reason to get up and face another day. The thought made her sad. Matt suddenly looked serious as they walked off, as if he, too, had just realized what his plans were going to do to the actual people of the church.

Good, let him stew a bit. This was just what April had hoped for. Better even.

She purposely led him over to John and Joan next. "Matt, you remember the Taylors, don't you? John's family owned the pharmacy, and now he and his wife run it. Best candy in town!"

Again Matt grinned as the memory of Taylor's Pharmacy came to mind. "I remember. How are you doing, John?"

John took the time to introduce Matt to his wife, Joan, but April noticed John wasn't his usual friendly self. "So, you're the one who bought out the buildings and are going to tear them down for a mega-structure? I knew the name, but as common as Campbell is, I'd hoped it was a stranger coming in to wipe out our heritage. I'm surprised, Matt."

April was sorry she'd brought this on, but maybe it was for the best, too. She hadn't thought about the fact that Taylor's would be affected by the buyout. John had worked hard to keep his father's dream going and had even added handmade candy, salt-water taffy, and homemade ice cream to the business. Their success was bringing new life into the downtown area.

April led Matt to a quiet table under the trees, where they sat down. Matt looked strained. "I really liked him in high school. I didn't expect him to react like that."

April looked across at the couple. "Their livelihood is in one of the storefronts that you're about to tear down. They've worked hard. I hadn't even thought of the fact that they'll be out of work after this."

"I'm paying good money for the storefronts. They'll be fine."

"They don't own the store, Matt! Most everyone there has a long-term lease, but with the sale, those aren't worth anything. Taylor's Pharmacy is famous for its nostalgia as much as for its great candy. The store won't make it in another location. John has worked so hard, and now he's about to lose it all."

April placed her hand on Matt's. "I know to you this is just business. But for us it's a way of life. I don't want to put a damper on your day, but think about it, Matt. Look at the people around you. You might have left the town, but the town still went on. You can't just make it disappear. I'll be back in a bit."

With that parting comment, April stood and walked off toward the rummage sale, leaving Matt alone to deal with his thoughts. She didn't want to abandon him, but she needed some time alone to deal with her feelings. She was confused. She cared deeply for Matt and enjoyed his company but was only now realizing how many people were going to be hurt by his destruction of the town and church.

Chapter 5

April stayed busy, helping first with the cakewalk, then the bazaar, leaving Matt plenty of time to think. He watched storm clouds gather on the horizon, and they matched the storm that was gathering in his heart.

Suddenly the things that he loved most, things that had always made him happy, weren't making him happy anymore.

His life was always rushed, his stress level huge, yet as he watched things here, the people seemed to be happy to live a simpler life. Even with Matt there to tear down their dreams, they were friendly. He didn't blame the Taylors for their words; he'd feel the same way. He was surprised at himself, too, now that he looked at things through their eyes.

April's grandparents, the Randalls, would be so disappointed in him. They'd be proud of what he'd achieved but disappointed to find that he'd used that achievement to tear down the town they'd held dear.

Matt looked at the clouds again and set out to find April.

"Hey. Looks like the festivities are going to be cut short. That's a pretty serious storm coming up."

April looked at the clouds and agreed. "I better go talk to the powers that be and see if they want to shut down. The bake sale just sold the last cake, and we've sold pretty much everything at the bazaar anyway. I'll just drop the other items off at the local charity on our way home. That is, if you don't mind."

"No problem. I'll start loading up."

Matt kept his eye on the clouds as he loaded the odds and ends in his car. He was thankful his foot had finally stopped throbbing.

As he put in the last box, movement on the church's rooftop caught his attention. The first raindrops fell as he started around the building to see what was up on the roof, and a huge bolt of lightning hit nearby, causing everyone to scramble for their vehicles. Small children cried, while a few others screamed at the nearness of the huge clap of thunder.

Matt's heart sank as he realized the smallest Taylor boy was at the top of the ladder, the same ladder Matt had fallen from days earlier. The little boy was clinging to it for dear life, his terror obvious.

Forgetting about his tender ankle, thinking only of what a great lightning rod the kid made, Matt tore off running. He climbed the ladder, and just as he reached the little boy, the tyke turned and flung himself into Matt's arms.

Off balance, Matt could only cling to the child as they both fell backward with the ladder. He braced the boy against himself and prayed he'd land on his good foot, protecting the weak one. He connected with the ground, hard, and felt his ankle give, but as his weak foot landed, the sensation of cutting pain flooded his senses.

Matt crumpled to the ground, secure in the thought that the small boy was safe, and gave in to the welcome darkness that wiped the pain away.

❧

Rain pelted down as April supervised Matt being loaded into the ambulance. She climbed in with him, and the vehicle slowly took off in the direction of the hospital.

April kept pressure on Matt's bleeding ankle as the attendants took his vital signs. "He seems stable for now, Ma'am, but it's going to be a hard trip to the hospital. Tornadoes are touching down not far from here, and the storm winds are doing some major damage to the trees and roadways."

April peered through the front window as the ambulance stopped for a downed tree that blocked its path. Exasperation and panic filled her. This type of injury was exactly why she'd pulled out of medicine. The last time she'd dealt with it, she'd not been able to repair the damage, and the man would never be able to use his foot fully again.

She'd done her best as a surgeon, but she couldn't do miracles. The foot had been too damaged to repair completely. The man's family had sued, not wanting to accept the other expert opinions that she'd done everything she could. April had settled out of court and had left the field of medicine, happy to return home to run the resort.

She didn't miss the rat race and hadn't looked back with regret or nostalgia since.

Giving herself a shake, she said to the ambulance crew, "We have to get him to the hospital, pronto! He's bleeding too much. I can't do anything for him in these conditions."

And I don't intend to do anything for him anyway, other than find him the best surgeon in the area, she thought.

As April spoke to the attendants, she noticed a large pickup truck pull ahead of the stranded ambulance. Several men jumped out, attached chains to the fallen tree, and heaved it out of the way.

Another truck pulled ahead of the ambulance, a seeming caravan at the ready to clear their path. April glanced behind them and saw more trucks at the ready. She smiled through her tears and wished Matt were awake to see the town pull together so that he could get to the hospital, regardless of the threat the weather was to them.

Blood was seeping out through the towel April had applied to the wound, and she grabbed another, praying for a speedy trip. The driver was trying in vain to reach the small medical center by radio. This concerned April, too. If they couldn't get through, the on-call surgeon wouldn't arrive in time.

Watching the wicked weather, April knew it would be impossible for the doctor to get out anyway. The wind howled, and trees touched the ground, whipping back up or snapping down across houses and cars. Two had already landed on the ambulance, fortunately hitting with glancing blows. Between the weather and the condition of Matt's foot, April's nerves were shot.

The usual five-minute drive took thirty, but they finally arrived, thanks to the crews that helped clear the roads. The truck drivers dropped out of the way so the ambulance could get to the door, pulling to the side of the road with their headlights shining, making a corridor for the ambulance to pass through. The wind blew so hard, the paramedics had to fight to keep upright while wheeling Matt into the emergency entrance. April chased along at their heels.

"Is Dr. Brandon here?" she called out to the secretary as they passed.

"No." The woman looked concerned as she took in the blood-stained towels covering Matt's ankle. "I doubt he'd be able to get through in this weather even if the phones were working. But since they aren't, we can't call anyone."

"We'll just have to stabilize him and wait it out," the paramedic called over his shoulder, heading toward one of the emergency room cubicles.

"That won't be necessary," a deep voice boomed out from down the passageway. "April, you'll have to do the surgery. You're qualified, and from the bleeding I see, I don't think that this can or should wait."

April was already shaking her head and backing away. "No, you know what happened last time. I can't go through that again, especially with Matt. We can stabilize him. He'll be fine."

The paramedics were watching with curiosity, and Dr.

Hunter pulled April around the corner, away from their probing eyes.

"April, you can do this. You did a great job on the other case. I've reviewed the report. We aren't miracle workers, and you need to accept that, but I know you'll do your best, and you are a superior surgeon."

"I was sued! I did my best, and it wasn't enough. I can't live through that again. I can't face Matt if I can't save his foot."

"Can you live with the fact that you might have saved it if he loses it anyway due to your waiting out this storm for a different surgeon? What if you lose him? He's bleeding heavily. He might get infected if you wait, or worse. Can you live with the fact that you had a chance to try and save his foot and instead chose not to and he died? Can you?"

April shook her head, her tears overwhelming her. She was ashamed of her behavior. She was a trained doctor and should be completely objective, but she wasn't in this case. This was Matt, and he thrived on his career. How would he work if his foot had to be amputated? How could she ever look at him again?

The other things she'd done to him the past week or so paled in comparison. But Dr. Hunter was right. She didn't really have a choice.

"We're sure Dr. Brandon isn't available?" April tried one last time, terror threatening to overtake her.

"We're sure. He might show anyway if he comes in due to the weather, but he might not be able to get through. If he gets here, we'll send him in immediately. I'll be there, and I'll help."

Realizing she had no other choice that she could live with, April sighed. "All right," she said, "I'll do it."

April was relieved to have Dr. Hunter by her side. She took a moment to pray for steady hands and for God to direct her every move and felt peace come over her. She and Dr. Hunter scrubbed, side by side, and entered the surgical suite that Matt had been taken to. He was already prepped and ready, the anesthesiologist waiting at his shoulder.

April felt her confidence return at the familiar sights and smells. Though she'd not performed surgery here, she was familiar with the setup. Praise music piped through the speaker system, soothing April with quiet words of encouragement.

April felt as if God had taken her by the hand and was leading her step-by-step. She gowned up and put on her gloves, finally removing the towels from Matt's ankle. She winced at the sight of the damage caused by his landing on a misplaced hoe.

Clearing her mind of the fact that this was Matt and moving into surgeon mode, she tapped into her surgical skills and began to repair the damage.

Matt felt woozy and couldn't figure out why he was having such a hard time opening his eyes. He heard voices from far away and then placed April's voice speaking quietly from beside him. Why was she sitting next to his bed as he slept?

"He's starting to stir," April whispered. "Have that pain med handy in case he needs it. I'm not sure how numb he is at this point, and I don't want Matt to feel any pain."

Pain? Matt struggled to awaken, finally opening his eyes enough to squint at his surroundings. Flowers covered every surface, balloons bobbing above over half the arrangements.

"Did I pass out in a flower shop, or is this some type of crazy birthday party?" Matt croaked out in a hoarse voice.

April laughed and sobbed at the same time. "You're in a hospital room. These are from people who love you. I think everyone in town has shown up with something, showing you how grateful they are that you saved Perry Taylor from a bad fall or worse."

She caressed Matt's hair, and he hoped she'd continue to stay close. Her hands felt good. He strained his memory. The fall from the ladder was starting to come back to him, but everything after that was blank.

"How do you feel? I have pain meds for you if you need them."

Matt waved that notion away. "No meds. Not for now anyway. So the little guy is okay?"

"He's great. Well, he's grounded for life according to his father, but he's unhurt. You took the brunt of the fall and landed on a hoe."

Matt's mouth quirked up in a half smile. "And you were nowhere around when it happened! I did this one all on my own."

Matt felt April's hand gently swat at his arm. "I was

around and saw the whole thing. It was horrible. You really need to stay off ladders from now on."

She told Matt the whole story, and Matt was touched at the way the town had come to his aid, even though he'd been so self-centered in his single-minded plan to demolish what they all loved.

"Who did my surgery?" Matt asked. He knew the storm had been bad and the town was small, but he was confident April would have made sure he had the best care possible.

"I did." April looked apprehensive, her fingers lying quietly on his head. "No one else could get here."

Matt knew that must have taken a toll on April. She'd been adamant that she'd not return to medicine.

"It went fine. You'll have full use of your foot."

"I wouldn't expect anything else with you at the helm," Matt said gently. "I have complete faith in you."

April looked shocked. "Even after all that I've put you through? You still have faith in me?"

Matt grinned. "Yeah. Strange, huh?"

April swatted at him again. "Thank you, Matt. That means a lot to me."

She stood and picked up her purse. "Now I need to be on my way. You'll be in good hands here, and I'll be back later. I have to check out the damage at the resort and see if everyone's okay there."

Matt noticed the circles under April's eyes and that she still wore scrubs. She must not have gone home since his surgery, and from the daylight pouring through the window, at least a day had passed since the storm and accident.

"What day is it?"

April turned. "Sunday. You've been out since yesterday afternoon."

Matt closed his eyes.

"Matt?"

He looked over at her. She stood in the doorway. "I'm glad you're okay. I'll be back."

Matt smiled and nodded. "And I'm glad you're okay after the surgery. Thank you. I know it wasn't easy."

"It was good. Not easy, but good. I had a lot of time to think while sitting here, and I actually miss medicine. God gave me the talent to heal people with my hands, and I need to use that skill. This hospital is different from the one where I used to work, and I've committed to be on call and will also be helping out one day a week. I have you to thank for that." She waved her fingers at him. "Now get some rest."

With that she disappeared out the door.

Matt leaned back and fell into another deep sleep.

❧

April headed for the hospital a couple days later with mixed feelings. She was bringing Matt home and had the nice cabin ready for him this time. She was anxious to get him back to the resort, but also apprehensive as to how everything was going to work out.

The townspeople had really rallied for Matt, which didn't surprise April. But how he'd thank them concerned her. Would he still tear down all they held dear? Would the fact that he got hurt make him more determined to tear down the old church?

She had so many feelings that were all mixed up. She was still angry with Matt for wanting to change things. She also had to admit she'd fallen in love with him, despite the changes. That made her even more mixed up and angry.

"Hey." Matt's welcoming grin caused her heart to skip a beat as she entered his room. It made her melt, and she forgot her mixed-up feelings.

"Hey back. How are you feeling today?"

"I'm going home. I feel great. I can't wait for you to break me out of here. The doctor is ruthless, and I think she enjoys watching or causing the pain of others."

April gasped. "I do not! I just wanted you to take it easy."

"It isn't taking it easy when you poke and prod at me all the time. And you make me go sit in that chair over there with my ankle throbbing in pain at the very thought of my taking a misstep? Cruel and unusual punishment is what I'd call it."

"You're still whining about that? You did fine, didn't you? And you couldn't go home until you showed you could get around on your own. Now you're ready."

"And the good doc gets to take me home so she can continue the torture."

April smiled. Home. She wished she were taking him home with her forever. Instead she was just taking him back to the resort until he recuperated. Well, she'd take what time she could get with him, and when it was time for him to move on, she'd deal with it. And if she had to move on, she'd deal with that, too.

"Let's go, big guy."

❧

Matt groaned as April forced him to his feet. His foot was better, but still tender. He wanted to leave on crutches, but April insisted he leave in a wheelchair. Hospital rules.

They arrived home with only one minor glitch. As she eased him into the passenger seat, he kicked his foot into the door of the car. Other than that, the ride was painless.

He was thrilled to see he had new home quarters, but he'd miss that older unit for its charming memories. Each time he got something out of the tilted freezer he thought of April. He knew he was falling in love.

He also knew he had some tough decisions to make. April was wonderful to him, but he could tell there was a distance between them due to his job, his plans, and her resistance to those plans.

He saw that the flower shop from his hospital room had been moved to his cabin—the place reeked of flowers. Baked goods covered his table and countertops, and when he hobbled to the refrigerator, sure enough, it was full to bursting with casseroles and fruits and vegetables.

April snickered from behind him. "Like I said, the townspeople are eternally grateful to you for saving Perry. Every single woman in town—and I mean single as in "What a catch Matt would make"—has brought a dish, and most of the married women sent something over, too."

And I only have eyes for the noncooking woman who saved my foot and reminded me of my roots. Matt's thought surprised him, and for a moment he feared he'd muttered it out loud. April was looking at him funny. She backed out of the kitchen, giving him space to maneuver into the living room and over to the couch. She placed a pillow under his ankle and backed up. "At least you won't have to suffer through another of my meals. Well, if that's all for now, I'll leave you to rest. You need to sleep a bit. I'll be back in awhile."

She looked sad as she glanced back at Matt, then headed out the door. She was so wonderful but didn't seem to realize just how much she'd grown to mean to him. He realized she'd never stopped being wonderful to him. He'd just buried her in his heart as he had God, his family, and anyone else he cared for and was afraid to lose. It was time to remedy that. He just needed to figure out how.

Chapter 6

Matt limped toward the old church building, hoping to find April. She was weeding and pruning the decrepit, overgrown garden at the front left corner. He watched as she tugged on a particularly difficult plant, and then he saw her wipe a tear from her eyes.

Not wanting to intrude on her emotions, but not able to stand watching her cry, he was in limbo.

"Probably my fault she's upset because I want to tear this place down," he muttered, looking around for inspiration on how to go about diverting her and announcing his approach.

Instead, he went down to the bridge and stared into the creek. Even with all the mishaps he'd gone through the past couple weeks, Matt had grown to like this place again. He was starting to wonder if tearing it down to rebuild was as important as the people he'd tear down with it.

When he thought of the issue that way, there was no contest. He couldn't hurt the people who had been so kind, open, and caring just to put more money in his pocket. He had more money than he could ever spend as it was.

He could keep stockpiling material things, or he could invest in improving people's lives, like April did with Cookie and Cammie. This would be a great town to revitalize, a great place for him to set up programs to help others and give a little back.

Matt felt as if a load had been lifted from his shoulders. Maybe this was why he'd gone through so much here, both in the past and in the present. He hadn't taken time to relax in ages, and he'd become a robot in business dealings. He'd shut off his emotions so they didn't hurt as bad after all the losses he'd suffered, but he had also shut off his entire self in the process.

Then, too, he'd shut out God, and if the food poisoning, sprained ankle, and surgery were what it took to get his attention, Matt was glad they had all happened.

Those experiences had also given him new insight into April and what made her tick. She'd turned out so different from what he was! She had the ability to make a fortune as a surgeon, but she never placed a desire to gain material things above the importance of relating to the people around her. She introduced them to her Lord and Savior, bringing healing to their souls as well as their bodies.

Matt knew he could learn a lot from April, and he intended to do exactly that. Sinking down onto his knees with the bubbling water as his background, he poured his heart out to God. "Lord, You gave me such talent, and I chose to abuse it and grow away from You and all the people I love. Please forgive me and help me to show April that I've changed. Help me to grow to be more like her. I want to be open and giving and reach out to help the people around me. I feel I'm on the right track, but if You could also show me a sign that this is where You want me, I'd really appreciate it. I can't imagine returning to my life in the city after being here, but if that's where You want me to work for You, I'll be obedient. I know a lot of people need You there, too. But to be honest, I'd rather be working here in the quiet beauty and by April's side. Help me to learn, Lord."

Matt stood, intending to go talk to April. He didn't care any longer that he'd be intruding. He wanted to tell her how he felt.

"Hey," Matt said softly as he approached. "Looks like you can use some help."

❧

April tugged at the offending bush, chopping angrily at it with her pruning shears. "Not really. I'm doing just fine."

With another angry tug, she fell onto her backside. What she really wanted was for Matt to go away, far away, back to the big city and fast life he wanted to recreate in her home. Ever since she'd left him in the cabin, after she brought him back from the hospital, she'd realized that her dream—to always have him beside her—was beyond her reach. His dreams were not her dreams, after all.

"Everything you touch here seems to cause you pain," she snapped at Matt. "Obviously even in the past Hickory

Hollow only caused you pain. Maybe you should leave while you still can."

And he inflicted pain, too—to her heart. He'd broken it ten years ago when he'd disappeared without a backward glance, and he was going to do it again, this time taking the town down with him.

April didn't know how she could even like the guy, let alone be in love with him, but she was. She'd realized it the minute he returned to town and even more so when she thought she'd lose him if she botched the surgery.

Matt grabbed her wrist, stopping her from mutilating the plant. "Maybe I don't want to leave. Maybe I have other plans."

"Oh, yeah, like tearing down all that I love and hold dear. Then you can prance away with a pocket full of money, not caring who you trample in the process."

Matt winced at her harsh words.

She pulled free of his grasp. "If you're going to continue to stand there, why don't you make yourself useful and get this bush out of my way."

Matt took the pruning shears and began to cut the bush. Making no progress, he looked at the tools April had assembled in her garden cart. "Hand me that saw."

April did so, making sure she didn't touch him in the process. She didn't want to feel that jolt of emotion that came from contact with him.

Matt began to saw the stubborn branches one by one until only a thick stub and the roots were left. No matter how hard he tugged, the roots wouldn't pull free. "I think these are here for good, no matter how we try to pull them out. I can saw this stub off at the ground, but if you want the roots totally removed, we'll have to get bigger equipment to dig them up."

April bit her tongue instead of blurting out what she was thinking—that he seemed to be good at that, digging at the roots until all remnants of them were gone. She suddenly decided the roots would stay.

"Matt, I want them to. . ." April's words trailed off as she took in Matt's pale appearance. "Matt! What is it? Did you hurt yourself again? I should have never let you. . ."

Matt waved her off, pointing toward part of the building that had been hidden by the overgrown bush. "It's my sign."

He suddenly grinned, his whole face transforming. "It's my sign, April! God wants me to stay. I get to use my talents here for Him!"

April was lost. "By tearing down the town? I don't see how God just showed you that. I'm missing something."

"No you aren't, Honey. You have it all. I was the one missing something, and you've given it back to me. You've shown me what is important—people, compassion, family, roots. Look here at the wall."

April leaned around him and saw engraving on the ancient cornerstone of the church. "What is it? What's it say?"

Matt was up and limping over for the hose. He returned to spray the cornerstone, then took a brush from April's cart and gently rubbed away over a century of dirt.

As the wall dried, the words became clearer. He read it again, out loud:

> *Despite all manner of hardship that rose against us, we, the people of Hickory Hollow, through the Lord's divine favor, have prevailed. From this day hence, may future generations who look upon this spot remember not the adversity that threatened to tear us apart; but rather let them recall the unity that bound us together, as one body, in building this House of God. On this eighth day of November, in the eighteen hundred and sixty-ninth year of our Lord, this church is hereby dedicated to God's glory, consecrated for His service, for all generations to come. So be it.*

A list of names followed, showing the founders of the church.

"Wow." April was speechless. "Zeke Randall. That would be my mom's great-grandpa. Grandpa Randall. She'd told me our family helped found the church, but I've never seen proof, just heard the rumor. So he would be my great-great-grandpa."

"And look." Matt pointed to another name. There his name was, clear as day. "Matthew Campbell."

"So that would have been your great-great-grandpa! Our grandfathers worked together to build this church. Matt! That's so cool! I'd heard there was a feud, but I wasn't sure I believed it. They obviously bonded together in the end."

"Maybe, or maybe not, but I have a way to remedy that

now, even if they never did end the feud. You and I are going to restore this church together."

April forgot her animosity and threw her arms around Matt. Matt was quiet, and she quickly realized what she'd done and pulled away.

Matt stopped her. "Please don't. You feel right in my arms. I've wanted you here for a long time, and I don't intend to let you go now."

April held her breath as she gazed into his beautiful blue eyes.

"I want the life you have, April. I want to leave our roots deep in this community, just like the plant here. I was talking to God on my way over and asked Him for a sign if He wanted me to stay. Otherwise I'd go willingly and do His work elsewhere. I feel this is my sign. Our roots not only run deep, but they're entwined."

April reminded herself to breathe, then nodded her encouragement, her short ponytail bobbing.

"We'll restore this town to its original splendor, and then we'll have a wedding—that is, if you'll have me—like this church has never seen before. I don't want to be apart from you ever again. Marry me, April."

April felt happy tears forming in her eyes. Again she could only nod. She didn't know how everything suddenly righted in her world, but it did. She had Matt back, she had her church back, and their roots were going to grow deep— together.

"Let's seal this deal right now," she grinned. "Where's the

paperwork for me to sign?"

Matt pulled her close and kissed her gently on the lips. "The deal is done, sealed by this kiss, and other than that, the cornerstone says it all."

April sighed with contentment, settling back in Matt's arms to gaze at the cornerstone. She'd make sure from now on that no bush of any type hid this wonderful piece of history. "Let's place a spotlight here and a bench so people can see where it all began."

Matt flashed his crooked little grin. "And I want a plaque by the bench to commemorate our marriage. I'll donate it as part of the restoration. I want everyone to know that the Randalls and the Campbells have come full circle, and this cornerstone will attest to the day the Randalls and Campbells united in marriage to become one."

"May our roots grow deep," April whispered. "Our plaque can go on top of the roots we couldn't pull up. Right at the base of the cornerstone."

"I like that," Matt agreed, sealing the vow with another kiss. No more feuds would cloud the future of the Randalls and Campbells.

PAIGE WINSHIP DOOLY

Paige enjoys living in the warm panhandle of Florida with her family, after having grown up in the sometimes extremely cold Midwest. She is happily married to her high school sweetheart, Troy, and they have six, homeschooled children. Their oldest son Josh now lives in Colorado, while the newest blessing, Jetty, rounds out the family in a wonderful way. The whole family is active in Village Baptist Church.

Paige has always loved to write, first trying poetry in grade school—*not* for her, though she was published in the school paper!—and then writing short stories all through her youth. She feels her love of writing is a blessing from God, and she hopes that readers will walk away with a spiritual impact on their life and a smile on their face.

A Letter to Our Readers

Dear Readers:

In order that we might better contribute to your reading enjoyment, we would appreciate your taking a few minutes to respond to the following questions. When completed, please return to the following: Fiction Editor, Barbour Publishing, Inc., P.O. Box 719, Uhrichsville, OH 44683.

1. Did you enjoy reading *Church in the Wildwood?*
   ❑ Very much—I would like to see more books like this.
   ❑ Moderately—I would have enjoyed it more if _____
   _____
   _____

2. What influenced your decision to purchase this book?
   (Check those that apply.)
   ❑ Cover   ❑ Back cover copy   ❑ Title   ❑ Price
   ❑ Friends   ❑ Publicity   ❑ Other

3. Which story was your favorite?
   ❑ *Leap of Faith*   ❑ *Only a Name*
   ❑ *Shirley, Goodness, and Mercy*   ❑ *Cornerstone*

4. Please check your age range:
   ❑ Under 18   ❑ 18–24   ❑ 25–34
   ❑ 35–45   ❑ 46–55   ❑ Over 55

5. How many hours per week do you read? _____

Name _____

Occupation _____

Address _____

City _____ State _____ Zip _____

E-mail _____

HEARTSONG ♥ PRESENTS

Love Stories
Are Rated G!

That's for godly, gratifying, and of course, great! If you love a thrilling love story but don't appreciate the sordidness of some popular paperback romances, **Heartsong Presents** is for you. In fact, **Heartsong Presents** is the premiere inspirational romance book club featuring love stories where Christian faith is the primary ingredient in a marriage relationship.

Sign up today to receive your first set of four, never-before-published Christian romances. Send no money now; you will receive a bill with the first shipment. You may cancel at any time without obligation, and if you aren't completely satisfied with any selection, you may return the books for an immediate refund!

Imagine. . .four new romances every four weeks—two historical, two contemporary—with men and women like you who long to meet the one God has chosen as the love of their lives. . .all for the low price of $10.99 postpaid.

To join, simply complete the coupon below and mail to the address provided. **Heartsong Presents** romances are rated G for another reason: They'll arrive Godspeed!

YES! Sign me up for Hearts♥ng!

NEW MEMBERSHIPS WILL BE SHIPPED IMMEDIATELY!
Send no money now. We'll bill you only $10.99 postpaid with your first shipment of four books. Or for faster action, call toll free 1-800-847-8270.

NAME _____

ADDRESS _____

CITY _____ STATE_____ ZIP_____

MAIL TO: HEARTSONG PRESENTS, P.O. Box 721, Uhrichsville, Ohio 44683
or visit www.heartsongpresents.com